Days
on the Beach

HERB,
THIS IS WRITTEN TONGUE-IN-CHEEK,
BUT I PUT MY HEART INTO IT!

John

Days
on the **Beach**

A NOVEL BY

JOHN TAYLOR

Oak Tree Press   Taylorville, IL

Oak Tree Press books may be purchased for educational, business or sales promotional purposes. Contact Publisher for quantity discounts

First Edition, October 2009

Cover by MickADesign.com

Author Photograph permission from Sherman Lee and Lawson Lew,
The Public Safety Writers Association Conference, 2009

ISBN 978-1-892343-60-4

LCCN 2009937612

In memory of OPD Officer John Grubensky
for his heroic actions in the Oakland Hill Fire of 1991,
during which he made the ultimate sacrifice
for the citizens of Oakland.

Acknowledgments

First, I would like to thank retired OPD Officer Marvin Jackson for prodding me to persevere in my modest literary efforts, as well as convincing me to finally abandon my faithful but archaic word processor and take the quantum leap into the PC community's Brave New World. Likewise, I extend gratitude to my daughter, Taina Libbey, for guiding her technologically challenged father through computer-land's arcane matrix.

Retired OPD Officer's Everette Gremminger and Ben Denson deserve kudos for introducing me to the gritty underworld narcotics investigators navigate at their extreme peril. Thanks also go to Billie Johnson, my intrepid publisher, for having the courage to publish my quirky tale. And finally, I acknowledge the contributions of all OPD members, past, present, and future, especially those who spent their share of days on the beach.

"Days on the beach"

Oakland police slang
for time spent on suspension for disciplinary actions

LATE JULY, 1991

He survived the fall, but not for long. The man rocked back and forth on his hands and knees, his forehead resting on the blistering hot street. The late afternoon sun scorched the surreal scene, sending shimmering heat waves dancing across the pavement. A small crowd of wary onlookers gathered in twos and threes, keeping their distance from the grotesque figure. With mouths gaped wide in horror, they watched the rocking man in his final death throes, like voyeurs unable to look away from witnessing an obscene, indecent act. Vehicle traffic stopped and drivers gawked at the grisly sight uncertain what to do.

The rocking man resembled a broken, twisted, flesh and blood sculpture. The force of impact corkscrewed his legs into a contorted pose that defied reality and snapped his back at a sharp, severe angle. Both of his shoes lay in the street like bits of detritus, and his heel bones protruded through the bottoms of his feet, jagged stumps that glistened like ivory in the sun's bright glare. A few splatters and tiny rivulets of blood stained the asphalt around him. But not the gory mess expected from a nine story fall to the street. And he continued to kneel forward, rocking back and forth, like a condemned man praying for absolution.

A black and white police cruiser pulled to a stop a few yards away from the rocking man. Oakland Police Officer Bull Brewster took one look at the scene and exhaled a weary sigh. A 911 caller reported a man jumped from the top of the Murdock Professional Building, and Bull hoped it would be a crank call. He glanced at his wristwatch, made a quick calculation, and concluded that he would *again* have to work overtime for the third time this week. His shift ended in an hour, but a suicide investigation would take a minimum of two hours to complete. Bull scowled and cursed the jumper for not having the *courtesy* to wait another hour before taking his swan dive to eternity. Now, Bull would miss at least the first two innings of the A's/Yankees game at the Coliseum.

Bull notified the radio dispatcher that he required an ambulance, the fire department, and an evidence technician at his location. Then he stepped out of his car and launched his beefy body toward where the expiring man rocked his life away. At 5-10, 255 pounds, with a blond crew-cut that stood as straight and taunt as a bristle brush, Bull Brewster was a formidable force to reckon with on Oakland's mean streets. He didn't walk so much as lumber, and his heavily muscled arms flexed and rippled rhythmically as he swung them back and forth to keep symmetry with each stride. A devoted gym rat, Bull's daily workouts gave his torso the look of an NFL linebacker. His nickname was a perfect fit.

Bull stood over the rocking man with his hands on his hips and a look of fatigued resignation on his fleshy forty-three year old face. Twenty-two years of this shit, he thought to himself. Twenty-two years watching people die. He watched more people die in Oakland than he did during a tour of duty in Vietnam. As he used a yellow marking crayon to outline the rocking man's body, Bull wondered why *this* one decided to say, "Goodbye cruel world!" and end it all.

Over the years he investigated his fair share of suicides, and each one had a different reason. Like the gay guy whose lover decided to end their relationship, prompting him to jam a shotgun into his mouth and blow his brains all over his motel room ceiling. He left a long, tearful letter to his ex, declaring his never-ending love and his inability to live without him. Charlie Barker, an evidence technician and an aspiring country and western singer, read the letter and spied a guitar propped forlornly in a corner of the room. In a moment of artistic inspiration, Charlie strummed that guitar and composed a spur of the moment eulogy, using the suicide victim's own mournful words as the lyrics. Bull considered it a fitting memorial that might have been a Top Forty hit if Charlie had recorded it under different circumstances.

And now, he had to deal with this impending corpse.

"All right folks, please stand back," Bull implored the crowd. "The ambulance will be here shortly. Come on, just move to the sidewalk."

A young woman wearing a bright blue dress stepped forward and raised her hand to attract Bull's attention. "Excuse me, Officer," she called out. "I saw the man jump." She pointed to the top of the Murdock Building. "He jumped from the roof of that building."

Bull looked up and saw several heads peering down over the ledge of the top floor. "OK, lady," he answered. "Would you wait over by my patrol car until I have time to take a statement from you?"

The woman took a few hesitant steps toward Bull's car and then turned back. "Aren't you going to do something to help the poor man?"

Bull rolled his eyes with undisguised disdain. "Lady, the guy fell nine stories. The best doctors in the world couldn't do a thing for him. Nearly every bone in his body is broken. All his internal organs are a big gob of mush. It'd be like putting Humpty Dumpty back together. Right now, he's only a heartbeat away from checkin' into Hotel Heaven or Hotel Hell!"

The woman stared at Bull with open-mouthed disbelief and then whirled around and stomped away in a rage. Bull watched her disappear in the growing crowd and shook his head in exasperation. He couldn't do a thing for this jumper but watch him die. Naïve do-gooders irritated him. Sometimes blunt language was the only way to get through to them. Like the woman who tearfully called for police assistance to rescue her pet cat, who used his climbing prowess to enjoy the view from the top limb of a tall tree. Bull took one look at the meowing feline, shook his head in contempt, and asked the distraught woman a crass but honest question.

"Lady, you ever see a cat's skeleton in a tree?"

When the confused woman murmured no, Bull delivered the classic punch line. "That's because cats don't die in trees. Your cat will come down when it is damn good and ready."

Sometimes blunt actions revealed how petty citizen's problems could be. He once intervened between two families quarreling over a plastic garbage bag that mysteriously found its way to the middle of their shared front lawn. Both claimed that the other party dumped the bag there. For ten minutes their argument raged on, and Bull never said a word. When he finally heard enough, he raised his hands to signal that he'd reached a verdict. Then, with a great deal of theatrical show, he solemnly picked up the bag, ceremoniously plopped it in the trunk of his car, and drove off into the sunset like a reincarnation of the Lone Ranger, who once again used common sense to solve another ludicrous human problem. When he glanced in his mirror, the two families still stood there with bewildered, sheepish looks. And Bull could not resist. He waved his hat out the window and sang out the familiar refrain, "Hi-O-Silver and away!" as he disappeared in traffic.

The ambulance finally arrived in a flurry of lights and carted the rocking man away to the hospital, where he finally stopped rocking and the emergency room staff pronounced him DOA. Bull's investigation revealed that he just left an appointment with his lawyer before leaping to his death. Bull surmised the guy took one look at the attorney's bill and the monetary shock caused him to avoid payment by taking a plunge to the one place where a collection agency could not hunt him down.

When Bull concluded his investigation, he returned to his car and saw Sergeant Eric Stout, his supervisor, waiting for him. Bull regarded the sergeant's arrival with some trepidation and tried to read his body language. He wore a frown, had his arms folded across his chest, and stood with his legs spread wide apart. Bull recognized his stance and associated it with numerous ass-chewings the sergeant administered in the past. He made eye contact with Sergeant Stout and confirmed trouble lay ahead. The sergeant got right to the point.

"Bull, did you have contact with a woman named Mary Block during the investigation?"

Bull put on a thoughtful look. "No, I don't recall a woman by that name."

Sergeant Stout raised his eyebrows in response. "Well, let me refresh your memory. Do you remember a woman in a blue dress asking if you were going to give emergency medical treatment to the suicide victim?"

Bull concentrated on trying to remember what he already knew. "Oh, yeah, the lady who said she saw the guy jump. I asked her to wait by my car until I had time to take her statement, but the next thing I knew she was gone."

Sergeant Stout nodded. "Do you recall what you told her about his condition?"

"Well, I just told her his condition was kind of hopeless."

"Wasn't what you said a little more *graphic*?"

Bull's facial expression personified a childlike innocence.

Sergeant Stout shook his head and threw up his hands in disgust. "Bull, haven't we had this discussion before? Many times? About what constitutes rude behavior? About how the department's Manual of Rules *defines* rude behavior? And you told this woman that the suicide victim was only a heartbeat away from checking into Hotel Heaven or Hotel Hell?!"

Bull's mock innocence dissolved into open defiance. "Well, Goddamn it, Sarge, what the hell was I supposed to say? Here this jumper was, all broken up with his insides all torn apart, and this do-gooder bitch wants me to be Dr. Miracle and raise his ass from the dead! So, I told her just how things were. I don't believe in candy-coating. I tell it like it is."

"Yeah, well, telling it like it is may end up costing you some days on the beach. Now, I told her I'd talk to you about your rude behavior. But if she decides to file a personnel complaint with Internal Affairs, then whatever happens will be *shame on you*. Now, I'm tellin' you this as your immediate supervisor. Knock this shit off! Are you hearing me?"

Bull took a deep breath and dropped his eyes to the ground. "Yeah, I hear you."

"All right," Sergeant Stout said. "And run me off a copy of your report when you're through and put it in my folder."

Bull leaned against his patrol car and watched the sergeant drive away. His anger still smoldered, but he conceded that Stout wasn't a bad supervisor. He was only doing his job. But it irked him that most citizens did not see the world in the same way as cops. The *real* world. And suicide coexisted with the real world.

Tragically, some people did not grasp the concept that in most cases suicide was a permanent solution to a temporary problem. But *they* made that decision. No one made it for them. So, Bull had no sympathy for people who took their own lives. He reserved his sympathy for those placed in harm's way through no fault of their own.

Bull shook these somber thoughts form his mind and turned his attention to the ballgame ahead. In less than an hour, he would be chowing down on a hotlink and chugging an ice-cold brew, while he cheered on the A's to some serious Yankee ass-kicking. He put his patrol car in gear and raced through the heavy freeway commute traffic, using his lights and siren to clear cars out of the way. Bull knew using unauthorized emergency equipment would result in severe discipline if a supervisor caught him, but he cast caution aside and rocketed past the long line of drivers, who obediently pulled over to allow him to pass. He knew these drivers thought he was on his way to an emergency call. But to Bull, getting to the ballpark and missing as little of the game as possible certified as more of a crisis than spending two hours investigating why a man needlessly threw his life away by jumping from a nine story building.

2

The sweltering hot July day turned into sultry, muggy night. A blue Cadillac El Dorado coasted down a driveway into a dimly lit condominium underground parking garage, and the automatic security gate rattled down into place behind it. The Cadillac's three female occupants' animated conversation erupted in laughter as the driver turned into a parking stall. The tires made a screeching sound as the vehicle turned sharply on the slick pavement. The hardtop's two doors swung open and the three women clambered out still laughing at the shared joke. The driver locked the doors and then led the two younger women toward the elevator.

"Well, I don't care what Evelyn thinks," the driver said. "She should know better than to allow her son to grow pot in her house. The next thing you know the police will be knocking on her door."

"Mom," her youngest daughter interjected. "You should have seen your face when Damon told you it was a marijuana plant. Your mouth fell open. . ."

"Well, I didn't know what kind of plant it was, so I asked."

Two men stepped out of the shadows and blocked the women's path to the elevator. They both wore ski masks, gloves, and pointed pistols tilted sideways at them. The mother and her two daughters let out involuntary gasps and came to an abrupt halt.

"Brake yourself, bitches!" one of the men said.

For a few moments, the three women stood motionless, unable to speak. Then the youngest daughter broke the silence. "We'll do whatever you say. Just don't hurt us. What do you want?"

"All you got," the second man replied.

The mother placed her purse behind her back and stood her ground. "I work too hard for my money to allow hoodlums to take it from me."

The first man riveted her with his eyes, incredulous at her brazen retort. "What the fuck did you say?"

"Mom, just give them the money," the youngest daughter said.

"Please, Mom. . ." the other daughter echoed her sister's plea.

"Better listen to them old lady," the first man said. "Now, just hand over them purses like good little bitches."

The mother continued her determined stance, holding herself firmly erect, challenging the two men with a defiant glare. The daughters gave the second man their handbags and then frantically urged their mother to do likewise.

"It's only money, Mom, please. . ."

Their mother pursed her lips and shook her head.

The second man appeared confused about what to do. His initial cocky attitude wavered and his demand for the purse became a plea. "Come on, old lady, just give us the purse."

When the mother's silent refusal continued, the first man's eyes blazed through the mask's small holes, and he dropped his voice to a near whisper that he laced with menace. "Old lady, you give us your purse, or I'm gonna lay you in your fuckin' grave." He let those words register and then added a final caveat. "Your choice."

The mother shook her head. "I'm adamant. . ."

The gunshot reverberated in the cavernous garage, and the mother slumped heavily to the concrete floor with a bullet hole to her forehead. Her two daughters watched her fall, too shocked to move or scream, and then the gunman turned and calmly shot each of them in the head. They crumpled and assumed contorted poses where they fell. Three crimson puddles spread, merged, and followed the contours of the floor, forming odd patterns like Rorschach inkblots.

The gunman didn't move. He stood absolutely still as if in a trance and watched the blood flow, hypnotized as he stared at the liquid life force draining from its source until the gushing stream slowed to a trickle. Then the spell broke and his eyes lost their fire, as if extinguished in a cathartic release. The second man looked back and forth from the bodies to the gunman in rapid succession, his body language a combination of panic and despair. He walked in circles, holding his head with both hands, his pistol pointing at the garage ceiling, the two purses dangling by their straps from one arm, chanting to himself.

"Oh fuck, oh fuck, oh fuck," the second man moaned.

The gunman casually proceeded with the next task. "Guess I'll see why the old lady seemed so willin' to die for her fuckin' purse."

The second man continued his profane dirge. "Fuck, oh . . ."

The gunman turned his anger on the second man. "Nigga, stop trippin'! Someone might have heard the shots, so stop that moanin' shit and get the money out of them purses! Do it!"

The gunman picked up the older woman's purse. Blood soaked into its leather surface. He opened the purse's clasp, taking care not to stain his gloves. "Hmmm, a few Benjamins here. Looks like about a thousand. So, that's what the old bitch valued her life at. A thousand. Well, it was her choice. Come on, let's get back to the ride."

A man walking his dog in the shadows past the condominium complex saw two male blacks enter a new dark green Toyota Camry parked in an adjacent alley. He wondered why they seemed to be looking in all directions as they drove away, but he didn't think it suspicious enough to contact the police at the time. He made a mental note of his observation in event he later learned something happened. He would tell the police about the Camry then.

3

The day after the rocking man's suicide, Sergeant Duke Washington sat at his desk in OPD's Homicide Division. He glanced at his watch. Six A.M. The rest of the homicide investigators would not arrive for another two hours. During regular business hours, the office clamored with multiple conversations and the shrill sound of phones ringing, and he gave silent thanks for this brief respite from the normal chaotic conditions. It was his turn to staff one half of the week-long homicide call-out team, and a triple murder investigation kept him up all night.

The vicious crime concerned him. The suspect or suspects robbed and then shot and killed a mother and her two adult daughters in the underground parking garage of the mother's condominium complex. The case's unusual circumstances disturbed him most. The crime scene revealed no evidence that the three women did anything to provoke their murders. There were no signs of a struggle and nothing to suggest that they tried to flee. What happened in that garage? What caused the suspects to up the ante to murder? Thrill killings? A hate crime? A deliberate execution to eliminate witnesses? Did the suspects panic? Whatever the reason, Duke knew there was cause for alarm because criminals tended to repeat their actions in future crimes. It became their modus operandi, or MO. The concept reflected a simple, twisted kind of logic. If a crime plan worked once, then the suspects assumed it would work again. And again. And since the suspects committed multiple murders, the death penalty or life without possibility of parole would be their fate if captured. They would have no reluctance to commit further murders. They rolled the dice this time. Would they roll the dice again?

Duke pushed the crime report to the side and wondered why there were such evil people in this world. He focused on the photo of his wife, son, and daughter prominently displayed on his desk and shuddered at the thought that they could be the victims of a similar crime. They lived in the Oakland hills, where violent crime was not the norm as it was in the flatlands. Yet even the hills did not provide total security. No sanctuaries existed in Oakland.

Duke looked at his reflection in the photo's glass cover and noted the crow's feet starting to develop at the corners of his eyes. His wife, Brenda, called them stress wrinkles. Duke conceded that undue pressure came with the territory of working homicide. Overall, the years granted him considerable mercy. His forty-three years belied his youthful appearance, and his short natural hair style contributed to a clean-cut image that his teenage son mocked as old-fashioned. A light brown, unblemished complexion, coupled with a thin mustache gave him a suave, debonair touch that caused others, especially women, to replace his given name of Henry with the aristocratic title he bore now. So, he became Duke. And he carried himself with a sophistication the name implied. Just over six feet tall, with a slim, athletic build, Duke used his quick wit and ability to relate to people at every stratum of society to get the job done. He looked on his approach to law enforcement as *Old School* policing.

A phone call broke his reverie. "Homicide, Sergeant Washington speaking."

"Hey, Duke, Eric Stout here. Sorry to bother you, but I heard you were working a triple, and I wanted to reach you before you left the office."

Following a momentary pause, Duke wearily recited the line as if it he had it taped for instant recall. "What's he done this time, Eric?"

"Same old shit," Eric replied. "Just Bull being Bull." He

briefed Duke on the suicide and then concluded with his far too familiar plea. "Duke, you and Bull go back a long way. Will you talk to him? He'll listen to you. It's just that he's getting worse every day. Last week, some asshole demanded that he write down his name and badge number and give it to him. So what does Bull do? The guy was handcuffed at the time, so Bull writes his name and badge number on the guy's leather jacket, and now Bull is lookin' at a few days off on the beach. I'm telling you, Duke, I've had it up to here with him."

Duke's resignation showed in his tone of voice. "All right, Eric, I'll talk to him, but I don't know if it will do any good." Duke paused, then added an afterthought. "And Eric, will you tell Captain Ernie I'll be down to brief Day Watch on the triple?"

"Thanks, Duke, and yeah I'll tell the Captain you'll be down."

Duke sat back in his swivel chair and clasped his hands behind his head. He shook his head and grinned. Same old Bull. They knew each other almost twenty-five years. From the jungles of Vietnam as paratroopers with the 101st Airborne Division to OPD, Bull always marched to the beat of a different drummer. Duke classified him as *different*. A maverick, a rebel, a hell-raiser. Duke laughed when he thought about all the crazy shit they did through the years. That time at Phan Rang in The 'Nam, when they raided the ammo bunker and shot off a bunch of berry flares over the Officer's Club on New Year's Eve and then watched those sorry bastards scatter from the club, thinking that the base was under attack. And then here at the department, when they donned gas masks to hide their faces and "streaked" naked through the crowded Third Watch line-up room.

Bull was the instigator in these and other pranks, but he didn't have to work very hard to convince Duke to go along with him on his harebrained schemes. One problem existed, though. While Duke gradually withdrew from these adolescent high-jinks, Bull resisted making the transition to maturity. He still topped the list as the first to come up with some insane caper, on-duty or off, to prove that he ranked *numero uno* as a street cop's street cop. He just had to show the world he was the most balls-to-the-wall, kick-ass cop to ever pin on a badge. Duke recalled the pet store burglary, where the arrested suspect felt compelled to showcase his *in-custody courage* by hurling the one threat police officers hear over and over again: "Just take off these fuckin' cuffs and let me out of this po-lice car and I'll kick your motherfuckin' asses!" Bull found a baby alligator inside the store that the storeowner illegally possessed, and he put it in his patrol car's rear seat with the suspect and closed the door. The alligator bared its teeth, started hissing, and the suspect's screams could be heard a block away. That creative bit of genius cost Bull a week on the beach.

Duke knew Bull needed to tone down his act. But he also realized that the department would lose something intangible, a nebulous spirit that gave OPD its defining character. Bull Brewster exemplified part of a dying breed that would not be replaced. Although Duke realized the inevitability of change, he still felt a melancholic nostalgia for the old artifacts being cast aside. And Bull Brewster was one of them.

Duke glanced at his watch. Day Watch line-up—other police departments called it roll call—started in five minutes. Duke gathered his paperwork and left for the briefing. He would have his *talk* with Bull there.

~ ~ ~ ~

Duke stopped off at the OPD cafeteria, picked up a cup of coffee, and then entered the line-up room and took a seat on the dais, where the command officers and sergeants sat facing the rank and file officers. Duke looked around the room and realized how much he missed working in patrol. He transferred to homicide four years ago, and although he regarded investigative work as challenging and fulfilling, the *action* took place in patrol. Every officer craved the adrenaline rush responding to hot calls generated. It produced a high that transcended any drug sold on the streets. And patrol also worked the landscape where officers met the truly bizarre that made policing such a spellbinding experience. The streets served as the testing grounds for maniacal human conduct, and patrol officers inevitably arrived first on the scene to witness and document these incredible incidents.

Duke watched the blue suits amble into the line-up room, laughing and making small talk as they prepared for another day on the street. Because the department staffed the three watches according to seniority, Day Watch—the most preferred by older officers—filled its ranks with salty veterans and a few youngsters sprinkled among them. Day Watch also had a small contingent of females interspersed in its roster. When Duke and Bull started with OPD, the department had no female officers. It was an all-male fraternity. But in 1975, women made their debut, and Duke recalled male officers' initial reaction as a combination of shock and disbelief that women would be considered capable to do the job. And Duke shared his guilt with other male officers harboring this attitude.

Over the years this negative outlook gradually changed. With some exceptions, the majority of males now generally accepted their sister officers as equals. This female incursion also had historical antecedents, for Duke and other blacks recalled a time when white officers regarded blacks as intellectually inferior and not fit to be police officers. Now, all the traditional barriers crumbled around them. A minority or female Chief of Police stood next in line in OPD's future.

"Hey, Duke!" a female officer shouted.

Duke scanned the room to identify the caller and centered on a stout woman with curly blond hair, a fifteen year vet highly thought of by her peers and a close friend of Duke's for years. Duke smiled warmly and shifted his vernacular gears to street talk for comic effect.

"Wat up, Rita?"

"What's the count and amount?" Officer Rita Sims asked.

Duke assumed a mock frown and his voice feigned a reprimand. "The homicide total is *not* something to be taken lightly, Officer Sims."

His exaggerated verbal rebuke and sever mien caused Rita and several other officers to break up in a chorus of guffaws.

"Yeah, yeah, Duke," Rita said. "You can get off your high horse and stop preaching to the choir. But I still want to know what's the count and amount."

Duke's frown instantly dissolved, a wide grin replaced it, and his pontificating voice shifted to a pleasant, casual tone. "As of twenty minutes ago, it's 109."

All the officers tuned into the repartee clapped and whistled at the high number. One officer chanted, "We're number one, we're number one!" and several more took up the refrain until after a few seconds it lost momentum and died out. Police officers traditionally regarded a high homicide rate with perverse pride, for it reflected the harsh, dangerous conditions they worked under and represented what they called "real" police work.

Rita pressed on. "What did you draw in the pool, Duke?"

The Gilbert and Sullivan routine continued, when Duke affected a blank, bewildered look. "What pool, Rita? I'm afraid I don't know what you're talking about."

The line-up room burst out laughing at Duke's straight-faced reply, for it was common knowledge that although the departmental brass covertly discouraged the practice for obvious public relations reasons, homicide investigators took part in a secret yearly pool to determine which one of them would come closest to predicting the final homicide total. The losers then presented the winner with an annual Sherlock Holmes Award for being the best prognosticator in Homicide Division, and unsubstantiated rumors alleged that the award also had a lucrative stipend attached to it.

"Come on, Duke," Rita said. "We won't snitch you off to the brass."

Duke took sham furtive glances around the room and lowered his voice. "Well, it all depends on the Holiday Season. If Thanksgiving, Christmas, and New Years take their usual high toll, then we might reach 175."

More clapping, whistling, and chanting ensued until other topics took the forefront. Duke thought about the Holidays and the popular, iconic image they connoted to most people. But police officers knew a darker side that brought out the worst in some citizens. Bring family members together who may harbor long-standing animosities toward each other, mix in large amounts of alcohol or illicit drugs, add a gun or a knife, stir in an insult or two, and you have a recipe for violence.

Bull entered the line-up room and spotted Duke sipping his coffee. He crossed his massive arms over his chest and launched the first insult.

"Well, look what the cat done drug in! Now, why would one of homicide's finest leave that castle on the second floor to join we patrol peasants in the dungeon?"

Duke winced at Bull's grammatical carnage as if he'd scraped his fingernails down a blackboard. "Bull, why do you butcher the English language the way you do? You *did* get beyond the fifth grade, didn't you?"

"Yo' mama was my teacher," Bull shot back.

Tradition called for Duke to follow the script, so he rose from his chair and took a combative stance, with his fists balled up. "All right, now, don't be talkin' 'bout *my* mama!"

A tall, gangly Mexican officer from Texas, with the apt sobriquet of Tex-Mex Garcia, interrupted Bull and Duke's wit competition, also called "doing the dozens."

"Hey, *ese*," Tex-Mex said. "What brings you down to the tomb, Duke?"

"Just slummin', Tex-Mex. When are you gonna take the sergeant's exam and get out of this hellhole?"

"Can't take the pay cut, Duke," Tex-Mex replied. "With all the OT patrol's been gettin', if I got promoted I wouldn't be able to make my alimony payments."

A deep, gravelly voice, unctuous with contrived politeness and cordiality, oozed from the podium. "Ahem, excuse me Officer Brewster and Officer Garcia, but would you mind too terribly much taking your seats, so I may conduct my line-up? Or would that impose on your cerebral, learned, cogent discussion with the illustrious homicide sergeant?"

Bull and Tex-Mex turned toward the podium into the fake Cheshire-Cat grin of Captain Ernie Stanton. A stocky, gray-haired man of fifty, his troops affectionately called him Captain Ernie. He felt fiercely protective of his officers and known to tolerate minor departmental rule and procedure transgressions as long as his officers gave him a fair day's work for a fair day's wage. His line-ups always ended with the parting salvo, "Now, get out there and lock up the bastards!"

Bull adopted a hurt look. "But Captain Ernie, Officer Garcia and I were only talking about promotional opportunities with Sergeant Washington."

Captain Ernie's toothy grin dissolved into shocked incredulity. "You two? Promoted? The day that takes place this department will collapse like the Roman Empire. Now, *please* take your seats."

Bull, Duke, and Tex-Mex laughed in response and the two scamps headed for their seats as the room quieted down. Duke glanced at the rear wall behind the last row of seats. Six officers stood in silent dread holding newly purchased briefcases. These officers were among the latest batch of recruits to graduate from the academy and assigned to Day Watch patrol to begin their fifteen weeks in the field training program. This was their first day and their faces reflected visible apprehension.

Duke recalled his academy days and marveled that he survived to graduate. He and other vets called it Rookie School, and when he went through the harsh training, they faced twelve weeks of intense pressure that drained their energy and vitality. Now, the academy lasted twenty-six weeks, an eternity of hardship. But after the academy, the field training program became the real crucible where they would be tested, for now they had to put to actual use all of the instruction they learned. Duke knew how they felt. He went through this gut-wrenching first day eons ago. They all did. And the reason the six rookies still stood while the veterans took seats stemmed from a warning issued to them by the academy's recruit training officers or RTO's: under no circumstances should they sit down until all the veterans did so, lest they commit the egregious sin of sitting in a veteran's chair. If they committed that sin, the veterans would subject them to a slew of vile insults. Every rookie had to endure this hazing, and woe unto the lowly rookie who violated this taboo.

Captain Ernie leaned over the lectern and studied the line-up detail sheets. "Attention to line-up. Today is July 25th. . ." Captain Ernie began, but a voice from the back of the room stopped him.

"Captain Ernie?" Tex-Mex called out.

"What?" the captain's gruff tone betrayed his annoyance at being interrupted.

"Captain, the rookies are still standing."

Captain Ernie peered over the top of his glasses at the back of the room and frowned. "Why the hell are you all still standing? Find a seat and sit down."

"Ah, Captain, sir," a petite, blond female rookie stammered. "Our RTO told us not to take a seat until all the veterans were seated."

Captain Ernie let out a long sigh that came out loud and clear over the microphone. He removed his glasses, rubbed his eyes, and ran a hand through his thinning hair. Then he returned the glasses to the bridge of his nose, sighed a second time, and scanned the line-up detail pages for a few seconds.

"Let's see now," he said, slowly and methodically. "The detail has me listed as the Watch Commander. So, I guess that means I'm in charge here. And since I'm in charge, that means when I tell someone to sit down, it means sit down! Now do what I say and stop wasting my time!"

The entire line-up room erupted in laughter as rookies scurried around the room like mice in a maze to find empty seats. Their efforts resembled a game of musical chairs. The diminutive blond started for a chair, found it occupied by another rookie, and then reversed course for a second chair only to see this one taken too. She finally found an empty seat in the front row and attempted to hide her blushing cheeks by burying her face in the Department Daily Bulletin she pretended to read. The veterans howled with delight as this slapstick comedy played out.

Captain Ernie waited for the commotion to die down and then began again. "Attention to line-up. This is the. . ." but he stopped a second time, when a tardy officer jogged into the room.

"Sorry, Captain," Officer Lester Michaels muttered. "But the traffic was real bad and. . ."

Captain Ernie threw the detail sheets into the air and let them flutter to the floor. "Jesus Christ! Am I ever gonna be able to get through this line-up?" Then he left the podium, leaned through the door into the hallway, and let loose a furious tirade. "Is there anyone else out there delayed by traffic? Or caught in a blizzard? Or abducted by aliens?"

Now, the line-up room deteriorated into bedlam. Laughter cascaded off the walls and ceiling and shouts of encouragement punctuated the furor.

"Don't take no shit, Captain Ernie!"

"Kick some ass, Captain!"

But the chaos continued. The tardy officer, a black ten year vet, stopped his 6-5, 240 pound frame a scant two feet in front of the chair in which the hapless blond rookie planted herself and glared down at her. The rookie remained too absorbed in concealing her bright red face to notice this incredulous veteran looming over her, silently demanding to know why this midget of a rookie sat in his chair. For a moment the drama continued until she looked up, up, up, and met the demented gaze of a man not to be trifled with. Without a word, she abandoned her hard fought for prize and fled to the nearest wall, where she anchored herself and made no attempt to secure another chair. Yet again a gale of laughter swept over the room, and even Captain Ernie could not suppress a grin.

Line-up finally proceeded without any further delays, and after Captain Ernie finished, Duke gave his presentation concerning the triple homicide. The only lead in the investigation had limited value. A witness saw a new, dark green, four-door Toyota Camry, with two male black occupants, drive out of an alley next to the condominium complex where the murders occurred and thought their behavior suspicious. The witness did not get the Camry's license number but stated that the vehicle resembled a rental car. Duke apologized for the scant description and admitted no firm link existed between the Toyota and the crime. But he asked that officers forward field contact reports, or FC's, to homicide if they stopped similar vehicles. Then Captain Ernie dismissed line-up with his patented ending remark.

"Now, get out there and lock up the bastards!"

Duke caught up with Bull in the hallway. "What's this I hear about you bein' in the shit again?"

Bull's face reflected surprise. "Damn, Duke, you heard about that already? This place is a regular gossip factory. A soap opera. As OPD turns."

"Eric called me. Wants me to *talk* to you."

"All right, so I went off on that bitch a little. Asking if I was going to help that jumper. Shit, he wanted to die. Well, he got what he wanted. End of story."

"Bull, I do believe that police work has desensitized you to life's tragedies. What say we meet over at the Hit 'N Run after work and discuss the foibles of mankind over a libation or two?"

Bull responded instantly. "You buyin'?"

"Yeah, I'll dip into my life savings to cover your bar tab."

"Done deal. Meet you there at 1700 hours after I pump a little iron in the gym."

Duke sighed. "You still tryin' to become Mr. America?"

Bull grinned. "Better than bein' the skinny *before* dude in the bodybuilding advertisements at the beach always gettin' sand kicked in his face like you."

"See you at 1700, Bull," Duke said. "But don't forget to bring your ears and brains along with your muscles."

4

After leaving Duke, Bull drove out to the Days Inn Café for coffee with Tex-Mex. Bull arrived first and occupied their usual booth. A few minutes later, Tex-Mex pushed his way through the door.

At 6-5, 190 pounds, the thirty-eight year old Texan was slender bordering on skinny, and his lack of body weight only accentuated his height. He kept his medium length black hair swept back, and he sported a thick, bushy mustache that gave him a striking resemblance to the Mexican revolutionary, Pancho Villa. His off-duty wardrobe remained incomplete without a black ten gallon Stetson hat that he wore *everywhere.* Above all, Tex-Mex fancied himself a *ladies' man* always on the prowl for his next ex-girlfriend, since his abiding romance credo hinged on his ability to accumulate as many ex's as he could until his libido reached its peak.

Tex-Mex slid his lanky frame into the booth and accepted a cup of coffee from their server. "Thanks, Lisa."

While Tex-Mex began his ritual courtship overture with Lisa, Bull stared out the window and monitored the radio calls being dispatched. They were the usual assortment of early morning assignments. A homeowner discovered his vehicle stolen. A

Mom and Pop grocery store owner arrived at his business and found it burglarized. Two officers responded to an injury collision at a major intersection. The minutes ticked by and then the dispatcher called Bull's radio designator.

"2L31?"

"2L31," Bull answered over his portable radio transceiver.

The dispatcher's bored, nasally twang droned on. "2L31, respond to 821 Acalanes Drive on a report of vehicles racing in neighborhood. Your complainant is Mr. Upton, and your incident number is 1251."

"2L31 copy," Bull acknowledged and then turned to Tex-Mex. "Duty calls, Tex. By the way, I'm meeting up with Duke at the Hit 'N Run after work. If you're not too busy chasing skirt, why don't you drop by?"

"Is this gonna be a *march*, or just a couple of quick ones to let the commute traffic die down?"

Bull shrugged as he stood up from the table and placed his transceiver back in its carrying case. He recalled the many nights they spent marching from bar to bar until a bartender announced, "Last call for alcohol," that forced them out into the early morning hours to fend for themselves.

"How the hell should I know?" Bull said. "Just show up and we'll take it from there. Whatever happens, happens."

~~~~

When Bull arrived at the Acalanes address, Mr. Upton stood in front watering his lawn. Bull recognized him as an elderly black man he often waved to as he patrolled the neighborhood.

"Mornin', Officer. Hope I didn't drag you away from something important."

Bull reached out to shake Mr. Upton's hand. "No, sir, this is my first call of the day. What can I do for you?"

Mr. Upton paused, searching for the right words. "Well, I don't rightly know how to explain what I saw. It was just *unusual*."

Bull nodded and waited for the man to continue. He always made it a point to give senior citizens the respect they deserved. He reasoned that a person didn't grow old by acting a fool.

"About fifteen minutes ago," Mr. Upton said. "I was out here waterin' my lawn like I'm doing now, when a bunch of cars drove past like they were racin'. There was like six or seven of them, and I mean they were really movin'."

"Go on, sir."

"Anyway, after they went by they turned the corner on Bergedo and were gone. But I could still hear them racin'. Heard tires screechin', motors all revved up, had their radios on full blast playin' that damn rap music they all listen to these days. Wait a minute, Officer. Listen. Do you hear that?"

Bull swiveled his head and cocked it to one side to concentrate. At first he didn't hear anything, but then he caught the faint sound of tires burning rubber and rap lyrics growing louder.

"There! Officer, do you hear them now?"

Bull didn't reply because the dispatcher called him.

"2L31, we received a call from Save-A-Lot Rentals that several of their vehicles are missing from their lot, and the office was burglarized and the keys are gone. I thought maybe there was a connection with your assignment."

Bull started to acknowledge the dispatcher, but then the first of seven vehicles turned the corner from Bergedo to Acalanes heading in their direction. This first car, a blue Buick, teetered on two wheels as it negotiated the turn. For a second, Bull thought the Buick would overturn, but the driver muscled the other wheels down and then started fishtailing as he tried to regain control. When the Buick passed Bull and his patrol car, the driver, a black male in his late teens or early twenties, stared at Bull wide-eyed and open-mouthed in shocked surprise. Then the other six cars sped past Bull one after the other, tires screeching, radios all tuned to the same station blaring rap lyrics, and each driver gave Bull the same shocked look.

"My, my, my, will you look at that," Mr. Upton said and shook his head in disgust.

"2L31," Bull broadcast on his transceiver. "Start some additional units my way. Seven vehicles just passed by westbound on Acalanes at a high rate of speed. These are probably the same vehicles taken from Save-A-Lot Rentals."

"2L31, are you in pursuit?" the dispatcher asked.

"As soon as I get to my car," Bull replied.

Bull leaped into his black and white and accelerated rapidly to close the gap between him and the stolen vehicles. "2L31," Bull broadcast. "The suspect vehicles just split up. Three are now northbound on 105th Ave. All I can give for descriptions is that they are red, blue, and green sedans and are typical rental cars driven by young black males. I'm westbound on Edes behind the other four cars."

Sergeant Stout came on the radio. "2L75, have 2L31 give his pursuit speed and traffic conditions."

"Ahh, shit!" Bull muttered to himself and slammed his fist on the steering wheel. Bull fumed as he rocketed after the fleeing vehicles. It all concerned CYA. *Covering your ass.* All Stout and other supervisors were concerned with involved liability and CYA in event a crash occurred. Bull darted around a slower moving car as he formulated his radio response. He reflected back to the "old days," when *no one* terminated a pursuit until either the bad guy got away or he ended up wearing handcuffs. Now, if traffic hazards placed the public's safety in *so-called* jeopardy, the sergeant's duty called for him to call off the chase based on the pursuing officer's description of driving conditions. But Bull didn't believe in terminating pursuits because he likened it to admitting defeat and showing weakness. He glanced at his speedometer and saw that it registered sixty-five in a thirty mile per hour zone. When he looked back at the roadway, he had to swerve violently to avoid rear-ending a car in front of him. But he refused to give up on this chase, so he stretched the truth and told Stout what he wanted to hear.

"2L31," Bull broadcast. "Speed forty-five, traffic conditions light."

Now, Tex-Mex jumped into the chase. "2L32, I've got those three 10851's northbound on 105th approaching E.14th." The sound of screeching tires came over the radio as Tex-Mex fishtailed around a corner. "I'm now on E.14th westbound pursuing a blue Olds. Hold on, he knocked over a fire hydrant. Still westbound on E14th."

Several OPD units tried to broadcast on the radio, but with all of them transmitting at the same time, only a garbled chorus of broken sentence fragments sputtered over the air.

". . . eastbound Walnut, brown Dodge. . ."

"2L35, I've got a silver Ford. . ."

"2L34, a blue Chevy just caused a produce truck to overturn

in the 9900 block of E.14th. There's watermelons, tomatoes, apples, bouncing all over the road. . ."

Bull drove northbound on 98th Ave focused on a blue Buick ahead of him. The Buick wove from lane to lane and across the double yellow lines into oncoming traffic trying to evade him. Bull relished the thought of giving this SOB an OPD ass-kicking he would never forget when he caught him. As they approached E.14th, Bull looked ahead in amazement as another OPD unit chased a blue Olds toward him. When they shot past each other, Bull saw Tex-Mex behind the wheel and they both waved and grinned. Twenty-two years in the business, and Bull never pursued a car in one direction and passed another OPD unit chasing a car in the opposite direction.

Now, police vehicles and rental cars zoomed through the streets trying to keep from crashing into each other like bumper cars at an amusement park. Bull darted through an intersection and nearly broadsided another stolen car that locked up its brakes and skidded to a stop mere inches from Bull's right front fender. Bull watched mesmerized as yet another stolen car scythed off a light pole, hurling the pole through the air like a javelin until it pierced the wall of a building. Pedestrians scattered pell-mell in all directions to avoid becoming collision statistics. Sirens filled the morning with a cacophony of competing wails. Citizens simply stopped their vehicles in the middle of the road and watched the insane spectacle unfold. Chasee's and chaser's zigzagged through streets and business parking lots, stopping, starting, turning, reversing, passing, slowing, and accelerating in a madcap montage that rivaled even the best keystone cops silent movie.

~~~~

Jim Foyt drove his company truck into Oakland to make a delivery at a department store. His hangover from a drinking marathon the night before still wreaked havoc on his pounding head, and he had to stop for coffee to clear his mind. Now, he would be late delivering his load of mannequins for the window display, and the store manager would be pissed. But at least the mannequins were fully dressed, which would make up for some of the lost time.

As he crossed the Oakland border, Jim looked ahead and saw a flurry of activity. Police cars careened around corners and blew through stop signs pursuing several other cars. A produce truck lay knocked over on its side, and fruit and vegetables littered the street. One of the pursued vehicles sheared off a fire hydrant and water shot thirty feet into the air. As Jim tried to make sense of all this craziness, a vehicle and a police car chasing it tore through a stop sign on a side street. Jim tried to avoid a collision by turning sharply to his left, but his truck slid on the crushed fruit in the roadway. The car the police car pursued slammed into the truck's passenger side and the truck's loading door popped open. The mannequins tumbled out of the truck's rear bed and skidded through the mashed produce, losing arms, legs, and heads in the process.

~~~~

Lulu Adams and Florence Smith were on their way to the senior citizen center for the morning bingo game. As Lulu drove her older red Lincoln down the street, a police car flashed by with its lights and siren activated, causing Lulu to swerve toward the curb line in a reflex action.

"My Lord!" Lulu gasped. "Po-lice should drive more careful."

Florence made a tsk-tsk sound. "Lulu, you know the po-lice are always speedin' around chasin' these youngsters. But look up there. What's goin' on? Lots of po-lice cars racing 'round the neighborhood with their lights and sirens on. Wonder what they're doin'? Lulu, watch out! Here comes another one!"

Bull pursued the Buick past Lulu's red Lincoln and then carefully wove his way through the detritus that covered the road, swerving to miss watermelons and sliding through hundreds of crushed tomatoes that stained the street a dull, gooey red. Up ahead, a number of fully clothed mannequins lay sprawled in the roadway, and like a bizarre touch of motion picture special effects, tomato slush covered these mannequins and made the scene look like a major disaster just occurred. Bull tried to drive around the mannequins, but to keep up with the Buick, he could not avoid running over a couple of them and severing limbs in the process.

"My, God!" Florence screamed. "That po-lice car ran over

some people and just kept right on goin' like they were rubbish in the street! Look, a leg got torn off, and there's blood *everywhere!*"

Bull swerved left and right to miss other mannequins, but one last human replica wearing a brown print dress was not so lucky. Bull hit it at thirty miles per hour and heard a loud crunch as his tires crushed its torso.

Lulu stopped her car and stared in horror. "Lord, lord, lord! Did you hear that poor woman's bones break? There's bodies all over! There's a head lying by the curb! Po-lice have gone crazy. If they run over people and don't stop, then they liable to start shootin' anytime. My God, Huey Newton was right. Po-lice don't care 'bout no one. We got to get out of here, or we might be next!"

Bull looked two blocks east and stared transfixed at an impending crisis just seconds away. A funeral procession made a turn from 105th Ave. to E.14th westbound, and a motorcycle rent-a-cop stood in the middle of the intersection holding up traffic so that the caravan of mourners could proceed without becoming separated. The stolen Buick took the corner on two wheels, spun out, and crashed into the hearse, causing the hearse's rear door to fly open and ejecting the Dearly Departed's casket to the street, where it skidded along the pavement until it ground to a halt.

Drivers in the long funeral procession slammed on their brakes in rapid succession to prevent a series of rear-end collisions, and the mourners stared in disbelief at this ultimate insult to the dead. The bereaved poured from their cars confused and traumatized by this indignity. Dressed in their funeral finest, the largely black crowd milled around without direction, until several of them focused their attention on the Buick, which momentarily stalled out. It suddenly dawned on them that the driver of this vehicle caused this calamity and deserved to suffer the consequences. Just as the Buick's engine sputtered to life and the vehicle began limping southbound on 105th at a pedestrian fifteen miles per hour, one woman in the grief-stricken throng summed up their collective insight and galvanized the mourners to action.

"Get that motherfucker!" she shouted, and the crowd surged after the Buick like cattle spooked into a stampede.

Two flat tires impaired the Buick's progress, and sparks shot up from the rear wheels as the vehicle scraped along the asphalt. While the Buick crawled forward, the mob of mourners steadily gained ground. Bull drove behind the crowd and tried to make his way through them by activating his siren, but in their feeding frenzy, the impassioned swarm ignored him. Bull saw the suspect look back once at his enraged pursuers, and his face reflected the terror of prey about to be devoured by its predators.

~ ~ ~ ~

Tyrone Davis stood in front of an apartment building on 104th Avenue, which he claimed as his territory for a thriving drug trade he commanded. Several of his foot soldiers stationed themselves around the building, acting as lookouts and runners to distract any Five-O's who might intervene in their lucrative business. And business exceeded Tyrone's expectations. Only a few hours into the day and their earnings already surpassed the previous day's take by several Benjamins. Then the sounds of police sirens and a loud crash caught Tyrone's attention, and he wondered what the hell was going on. A minute or so passed with no further activity, and Tyrone relaxed his fight or flight instinct.

Suddenly, a blue Buick with two flat tires and a crumpled front end rounded the corner and scoured the roadway like a street-paver as it rumbled toward Tyrone. A mob of over a hundred people also turned the corner directly behind the Buick, roaring like banshees as they slowly gained ground on the vehicle. The Buick and mob rampaging in his direction stunned Tyrone, but when he saw a police car, with its red and blue lights activated and its siren wailing close behind, he experienced an epiphany that caused the blood in his veins to freeze in fear. It was *them!* Enraged citizens! After enduring years of frustration, they finally became so fed up with the dealers' rampant drug sales that the police mobilized them to enact vigilante justice and tear them apart, limb from bloody limb. The pharmaceutical entrepreneurs' reaction was totally predictable. They ran for their felonious lives. Unofficial Olympic records for high jumps over fences and 100 meter dashes through yards patrolled by ravenous pit bulls became their lasting legacy.

The Buick finally ended its mad dash, when its engine seized up and a plume of black smoke belched from its exhaust pipe. The mob quickly surrounded the Buick and hurled insidious, dire threats at the driver.

"Someone get a rope!" one man shouted. "Let's hang this desecratin' motherfucker!"

"Bullshit!" another disagreed. "Hangin's too good for him. Let's tie his ass to the bumper of a car and drag him though all of East Oakland. Ain't no asshole gonna knock my uncle's body out of a hearse and live to talk about it!"

Bull got out of his car and cajoled his way through the crowd. He gently restrained one fanatically determined elderly woman from using the spiked heel of her shoe to smash out the driver window.

"All right, folks," Bull said as he attempted to placate the angry posse comitatus. "Appreciate your help takin' this young man into custody, but I'll take over from here."

The encircling ranks reluctantly gave way, and when Bull viewed the suspect's face, he never in his law enforcement career saw someone so grateful to be arrested.

Now, one by one, the pursuits came to a successful conclusion. OPD units took several suspects into custody and the chaotic radio traffic slowly faded away until the mother of all vehicle chases ended not with a bang but a whimper.

~~~~

Once the pursuits came to a halt, Bull, Tex-Mex, and the other involved officers faced the onerous task of mopping up the mess and cogently documenting the holocaust that occurred. Among police officers there is a saying: what takes mere minutes to happen, takes hours to explain, and after ordering a tow for the Buick, Bull relocated with his prisoner to a vacant parking lot to begin the tedious report writing process. From this vantage point, he had an unobstructed view of the urban racetrack where most of the destruction derby took place. The fire department had yet to turn off the sheared-off fire hydrant, and the geyser of water still shot thirty feet in the air, flooding half of the street with a manmade lake. Crushed tomatoes, watermelons, and other produce formed a vegetarian goulash that simmered in the sun. The tomato encrusted arms, legs, heads, and torsos of numerous mannequins covered the roadway like the set of a grade-B, grind-house, slasher movie. Stop signs, light poles, and traffic signals lay strewn about like gigantic, discarded pick-up sticks. And the coffin remained in the intersection at the site of the epic crash, waiting for another hearse to deliver it to its final resting place. Since he was the maestro who orchestrated this mayhem, Bull grinned, puffed out his chest, and felt justifiable pride in providing yet another chapter in OPD's tales of legend and lore.

An unmarked police vehicle entered the parking lot and stopped next to Bull's black and white. Captain Ernie glared at him with undisguised malice. He motioned for Bull to exit his car so they could talk out of the suspect's hearing.

"*You* started all this," Captain Ernie said and swept his arms in a three hundred sixty degree circle to encompass the apocalyptic scene. "*You* turned East Oakland into a fuckin' war zone. The Chief's office has received tens of calls concerning this fiasco. Two little old ladies were hysterical. They claimed that one officer drove over people and then just continued on as if nothing at all happened. . ."

"Captain Ernie, they were mannequins."

"I know, I know, but try explaining that to two LOL's about to have massive coronaries. Irate citizens were even lined up at the mayor's office to complain. But fortunately some citizens applauded our efforts to rid the community of car thieves and racing hoodlums. So, it looks like it's a standoff. But you sure ruined my day, Bull! You know my ulcers can't stand too much of this shit. You know that but you continue to raise hell until I have to gobble Tums all day long just to get through the shift."

Bull suppressed a grin. "Sorry 'bout the trouble, Captain Ernie. But what the hell was I supposed to do? Let seven 10851's just drive away?"

Captain Ernie's stern look softened. "Ahhh, you're right. Guess I'm gettin' too old for this shit."

Bull grinned. "Another day in paradise, Captain."

Captain Ernie cast Bull a don't-fuck-with-me-now look, emptied another roll of Tums into his mouth, and burned rubber driving out of the lot.

5

Bull did not finish his heroic, multi-page report until mid-afternoon. According to the follow-up investigators who later critiqued the epic, its scope and grandeur qualified it as the OPD equivalent of the *Odyssey* or *Iliad*. When Bull finally announced his triumphant return to duty, he expected the dispatcher to cut him some well-deserved slack. Instead, she tersely directed him to report to Internal Affairs, or I-A. Any officer ordered to report to I-A traditionally met with catcalls and mock abuse over the radio from other patrol units, for a visit to I-A meant possible disciplinary action waited for him, and fellow officers thrived on inflicting torment and dread on their peers. So, Bull received the usual pseudo-warnings and comments.

"You'll be *sorry*," one predicted.

"San Francisco PD is hiring," another added.

Whistles and microphone clicks interrupted the routine radio chatter, and some wit chanted the old Dragnet TV show musical theme as a foreboding of doom: "Dum-de-dum-dum." Most officers regarded a visit to I-A with at least mild concern, but Bull took the trip downtown so many times he lost his apprehension, and he looked forward to swapping war stories with the I-A investigators.

~~~~

Internal Affairs—or *Infernal* Affairs as its legion of detractors commonly referred to it–represented anathema to the majority of police officers. Most officers begrudgingly regarded I-A as a necessary evil, but they nonetheless looked upon it with uneasy suspicion. Police departments had their deviants, and I-A existed to rein in problem officers. But the mere existence of I-A did not trouble street cops. Instead, the source of their disdain rested on that rare I-A investigator who took his job as a *calling*.

Working cops loathed and distrusted the overzealous I-A investigator because this *born again* type saw every rule infraction, no matter how trivial, as an incarnate evil that must be quashed without mercy. Most investigators did not act in this manner. In fact, the vast majority of them performed an exemplary job and used common sense as their guiding principle. Occasionally, however, one would slip into their ranks and work incredibly hard to become a genuine asshole.

Lieutenant Carey Scott served as commander of I-A for over a year. At twenty-seven, he was young to hold the rank of lieutenant and even younger to head a unit with such a sensitive mission. Less than average height, with a pudgy build, he had one personality trait that best defined his approach to commanding I-A: a single-minded obsession with enforcing each and every departmental mandate. He viewed himself as a by-the-book man. OPD established rules, regulations, policies, and procedures for officers to obey and follow. He drew his inexorable logic from a simple proposition: if the department did not mean for officers to obey rules and regulations or follow policies and procedures, then why were they established and written down in the first place? His holier-than-thou persona revealed itself in his strict obedience to *all* laws. He did not jaywalk, litter, or cheat on his taxes. Above all, he especially obeyed The Ten Commandments because the Creator wrote them down in *stone*. And to showcase his morality, he had sexual intercourse with his wife *only* in the missionary position. In essence, I-A gave meaning to his life.

Sergeant Rocky Rollins had a different calling. He transferred to I-A only because a knee injury limited him to desk duty until he could return to the streets, and he had sexual intercourse with as many women as he could in so many different positions that it would make the author of the *Karma Sutra* blush. He had Hollywood good looks, charm, and charisma in equal proportions. Just over 6-0 tall, with a slender, athletic build, he also had a swaggering, rhythmic walk that prompted Duke Washington to once remark, "I'll wager that Rocky has some *brother* in him somewhere in the family tree."

After only a month in I-A, Rocky loathed the very air that Lieutenant Scott breathed. He hated the way the lieutenant snuck around trying to catch someone violating some chickenshit rule or procedure. And Rocky did not stand alone in this regard and hope the lieutenant would contract leprosy and rot. All the I-A investigators did. Rocky realized that some rules and procedures were so critical that they had to be followed without deviation. Firearms policies, for instance. But there were others so trivial that *everyone* violated them. To Rocky and the other investigators, they adhered to a principle when they investigated complaints against their peers. If the allegation was serious, they responded with due diligence and dealt with it promptly. But if the allegation was petty or one ignored by most officers, then they relegated it to the round file or dropped it to a minor infraction.

Bull's latest personnel complaint now rested in Lieutenant Scott's effeminate little hands, and he placed Bull at the top of his hit list. To Scott, Officer Bull Brewster represented all that needed weeding out at OPD. His complaint file read like Sherman's March through the South, filled with twenty-two years of depredations. Yes, Scott conceded, Brewster also received numerous commendations and awards for valor, but these accolades did not relieve him of his duty to obey rules and regulations. And now this latest complaint of rude behavior. Imagine telling a woman who just witnessed a horrific suicide that he could do nothing for the victim, who was only a "heartbeat away from checking into Hotel Heaven or Hotel Hell." The audacity! The insensitivity! Well, Lieutenant Scott vowed to himself, Officer Brewster wouldn't get away with this one. He would plot, scheme, and connive. He would track him down like a bloodhound. Show no mercy. Scott became so enthralled with his grandiose self-image as Brewster's Grand Inquisitor that he had to take a deep breath to calm himself before he returned to the matter at hand. Then he furrowed his brows, adopted his patented supervisor frown, cleared his throat, and meant to bark a stentorian command to his I-A subordinates in the adjoining office.

"Sergeant Rollins!" he called out, but a bit of saliva went down his windpipe, causing his voice to inadvertently change to a squeaky, pre-puberty falsetto like a person inhaling helium. Lieutenant Scott had to clear his throat again to achieve the bark he originally intended. "Ah, see me in my office."

Rocky stopped pecking at his computer keyboard, rolled his eyes, and the other two investigators in the office grinned and shook their heads. Rocky's reply revealed his annoyance and disgust. "Yeah, OK."

Lieutenant Scott bristled with indignation. Sergeant Rollins' flippant reply was borderline insubordination. He briefly considered reprimanding him right there and threaten to send him to "dog watch," or midnight shift, in patrol, but then he remembered that Sergeant Rollins was only on loan to I-A until he was fit for full-duty, and besides, he would like nothing better than to return to patrol anyway. He made a mental note to include this episode in Rollins' next performance evaluation.

"What's up, Lieutenant?" Rocky asked, as he entered the office and flopped down in a chair.

Lieutenant Scott fumed at Rollins' informal greeting and fixed him with a penetrating glare. Seconds passed and still he continued his withering scowl, but Rocky returned it with a bored, disinterested look and did not blink. As the stare-down continued, Lieutenant Scott saw to his consternation that *he* was on the verge of losing this test of will, so he averted his eyes in a savior faire manner to make it appear he did not back down. Rocky saw through this subterfuge and returned his volley in this adolescent game of chicken by smirking in a way that let the lieutenant know he *lost*. Rocky enjoyed kicking the shit out of the lieutenant's self-esteem and hoped it would continue, but Scott signaled a détente by returning to the Brewster business.

"Here's the latest complaint on Officer Brewster," the lieutenant said and shoved the folder across his desk.

"Bull got another one?" Rocky said. "Hell, we just finished the investigation about him writing his name on that guy's jacket. Bull must be tryin' to set a record or somethin'."

Lieutenant Scott did not want to risk having Rocky deflate his ego any further, so he couched his next comment as more of a request than an order.

"Uh, try to get on this right away and have it ready for the Chief tomorrow."

Rocky returned to the investigators office. "Well," he announced to the expectant duo. "Bull got another one."

Sergeant Manny Hernandez leaned back in his chair and clasped his hands behind his head. "Old Bull. He's gettin' in so much shit he may as well buy a house on the beach 'cause that's where he's gonna be for a long time."

~~~~

When Bull strutted into the office, Rocky and the others waited in full character for him. Since the lieutenant left the office, his absence gave them a chance to lighten the doom and gloom atmosphere street cops commonly associated with a visit to the *eighth floor*. It offered them an opportunity to show a little levity and reveal that they were not the bloodthirsty headhunters patrol officers made them out to be. So, Manny wore his black cape and Dracula teeth and greeted Bull with the Count's classic line: "I vant to suck your blood!" Bobby placed a scaled down replica of a guillotine on his desk, with a blood splattered, severed doll's head at its base. And Rocky wore a German officer's hat and slapped a swagger stick against his palm. Rocky's German accent needed work.

"Ahhh, Herr Brewster! Ve have been vaiting for you. Please, sit down."

Bull shook his head and grinned. "Guys, guys, at least you could change your skit now and then. This same shit gets old."

Rocky dropped the accent. "Well, maybe if you weren't up here every other day, the novelty wouldn't wear off. Shit, you spend more time up here than you do on the street."

Manny adopted a pained expression. "Bull, did you *really* tell that woman the suicide victim was only a heartbeat away from Hotel Heaven or Hotel Hell?"

Bull assumed a pious look. "It was a moment of divine inspiration."

The three investigators groaned in unison.

"You know, of course," Rocky said, "that *divine inspiration* is gonna cost you. But we'll see if we can soften the blow."

Bull nodded. "All I ask is that you put word in with the Chief to combine my suspension time with my regular days off so I can go to Vegas."

Rocky stacked the necessary paperwork on his desk. "Now, Bull, I realize you have your AB301 rights memorized by this time, but I have to read them to you anyway."

In ten short minutes, Bull finished his statement and they began trading random quips about the latest OPD capers. When Bull related the rental car pursuit and the mannequin and hearse parts, the three I-A sergeants wheezed laughter and tears cascaded down their cheeks. During a lull in the stories, Rocky went to the window that overlooked Seventh Street. The window was open to allow a breeze to enter and filter out the stale office air. Rocky placed his hands on the window sill and let out a high-pitched squeal.

"Whoooeee! You in the blue shorts! You are one *fine* lookin' bitch!"

Bobby gave Rocky a curious glance. "What the hell was that all about?"

Rocky had an enraptured look in his eyes. "I just saw a god-dess walkin' across the street and thought I'd give her a compli-ment and make her day. She was wearin' a skimpy, white halter top and blue shorts so tight I swear I could read the date on a dime she had in her rear pocket. I mean she was *fine!*"

Bull, Manny, and Bobby nodded and went on to other topics.

A few minutes later, Bull started to leave, when a strikingly beautiful Hispanic woman, wearing a white halter top and blue shorts, appeared at the office door.

"Excuse me," the woman said. "I have a complaint to make and the desk officer downstairs directed me here."

Rocky immediately rose to his feet and drawled out an unc-tuous greeting. "Ma'am, I'm Sergeant Rollins. What can I do for you?"

"Well, I was walking across the street from your building, when a man leaned out a window several stories up and yelled something like, 'whoooee', and 'you in the blue shorts', and then called me a 'bitch'! I want to file a complaint."

Rocky's facial expression turned to shock and his voice oozed with empathy. "Why, that's terrible! Did you get a good look at this arrogant jerk?"

"I only saw him for a second or two," she replied. "All I know is that he was a white man, wearing a white dress shirt and tie."

Rocky intensified his look of concern and solicitously guided her to a chair next to his desk. "Now, you just take a seat here, and we'll get to the bottom of this *right this minute*! The Oakland Police Department does not tolerate rude conduct like that."

Bull lingered in the office to see how this academy award winning performance would end. It was all he, Manny, and Bobby could do to keep a straight face, while Rocky played the role of a dedicated, concerned investigator determined to track down the perpetrator who committed this dastardly deed. Fifteen minutes later, the woman signed her statement and left the office *knowing* that Sergeant Rocky Rollins would hunt down the man who maligned her. When he heard the hallway door open and close, Rocky balled up the statement and arced a precision hook shot into Manny's wastebasket. Then he turned to his audience and flashed them a grin of pure triumph.

"Rocky," Bull said in genuine admiration. "That was masterful, a true work of art. But it also leads me to the conclusion that it should be me investigating *you* instead of the other way around."

6

After his shift ended, Bull finished his hour-long workout at the gym and arrived at the Hit 'N Run for his rendezvous with Duke. As usual, the dingy dive close to Jack London Square waterfront crawled with badges from numerous police departments. Bull and his brother and sister officers readily acknowledged that the Hit 'N Run had a reputation as a "cop bar" and they had little difficulty explaining why they gathered there. Cop bars existed because they offered a refuge from prying eyes. Cops congregated at these places to feel comfortable and secure among their own. After being trapped in a uniform and scrutinized all day, they could at last let loose and be themselves. Just cops having a few drinks at their local watering hole and sharing the events of the day.

A few minutes later, Duke entered and wove his way through the maze of tables, stopping frequently to exchange greetings or shake someone's hand. Bull waited at a table in a far corner and Duke made his way toward him. Two Coors bottles stood like sentries at attention on the table top, dripping beads of condensation on their saturated napkins. Bull handed Duke a bottle and held his up for a toast.

"To the illustrious Sergeant Eric Stout," Bull said. "Whose

desperate appeal for help prompted this meeting."

Duke grimaced at Bull's comment, but he clicked Bull's bottle with his own. "Yeah, yeah, amen. I can see you're in denial."

Bull ignored Duke's rebuke, took a healthy swig of beer, and opened the forum for discussion. "You hear about our crazy rental car caper today?"

Duke nodded. "Was it true about the mannequins, funeral, coffin, and mob chasin' down the suspect?"

"All true. No exaggerations."

Duke grinned. "How did Captain Ernie take it?"

"He accused me of starting it all just to aggravate his ulcers."

"Does he still take all those Tums?"

Bull laughed. "Shit, he couldn't survive a day without 'em!"

A short silence ensued and then Duke brought the caucus of two to order. "All right, Bull. Before you imbibe one too many and forget why we're here, let's get down to the nitty-gritty and discuss *your* problem."

Bull frowned. "What do you mean *my* imbibing one too many? You're not drinkin' tonight?"

"I'm on call-out," Duke replied. "Two or three is my limit."

"Understood," Bull said and drained his bottle. "But I ain't got a problem, bro. I just come to work, do my job, and let the chips fall where they may."

Duke held Bull's eyes with a steady stare until Bull squirmed in his seat. Bull hated when Duke turned serious. Bull acknowledged that Duke served as his mentor and trusted his advice. It had been that way since their tour of duty together in Vietnam. But he resented Duke preaching to him. He wanted to stand on his own. But now here he was again, enduring another of Duke's sermons.

Duke continued to fix Bull with a hard glare. "Bull, you got that, 'I don't want to hear this shit', look written all over you."

"Go 'head on," Bull sighed. "I'm listenin'."

Duke shook his head wearily and wondered why he went out of his way to help Bull's sorry, stubborn ass. But then he flashed back to The 'Nam and he recalled why. They forged their bond in that hell-hole and it linked them together as blood brothers. What they endured in that tiny Asian country went beyond what words could describe. They shared intimate knowledge of sacrifices made on a mass graveyard. That bond welded Duke's allegiance to Bull.

"Bull," Duke began. "I'm going to be as candid as I can. I've talked with some people and the consensus is that you're coming dangerously close to being put on a performance deficiency notice. Now, you know what a PDN means. Everything you do will be monitored, scrutinized, and evaluated. Over the years, you've stepped on some toes and made some enemies. But your worst enemy is yourself. When are you gonna wise up?"

"So, what should I do, Duke? Be a yes man? A punk? Hell, I'll match my felony arrest record with anyone in the department. Just because I don't take shit from anyone. . ."

"Ah, Bull, don't give me that crap! I know you're a good street cop. But that's not what we're talkin' about here. You just can't seem to separate being a good cop from violating the department's rules and regs. Like that caper where you wrote your name and badge number down on that dude's jacket. You *knew* while you were doin' it that it was gonna come back and bite you in the ass. So why did you do it?"

"Asshole pissed me off," Bull mumbled.

"What? You don't think I don't get pissed at these assholes? But I like to think that I'm smart enough to see that if I overreact, then I'm fuckin' myself. That's not bein' a punk. That's bein' smart."

Duke let his words sink in and then brought his plea to a close. "You watch yourself, cowboy. If you get put on a PDN, you might find yourself forced into an early retirement. You've got your twenty years in, so you could retire before they try to fire you. But they could make you so miserable that you'd want to get the hell out of here. I know you're not ready to pull the pin, so don't get caught short."

Duke scanned Bull's face and tried to gauge what effect, if any, his words had on him. "All, right. I've done my good deed for the day. Whatever you do from now is on you. I'll get us a couple of more beers."

While Duke waded through the crowd to order another round, Bull glanced at the front door and saw a black Stetson cowboy hat tower over everything around it. The Stetson bobbed forward and Bull watched Tex-Mex weave through the tables and chairs like a running back picking his holes in a defensive goal line stand. Tex-Mex scoped out the premises. He knew the reason why Duke and Bull met there.

"Where's Duke? You survive the trip to the wood shed?"

"He's buyin' beer. Now, don't mention that I told you 'bout him lecturing me. He takes this Ann Landers shit seriously."

"All right, *ese*," Tex-Mex assured him. "I will not let a slip of the lip sink your ship."

Duke paid for the beers and started back to the table. When he saw Tex-Mex, he shook his head and smiled. Bull and Tex-Mex tossing back cold ones set off alarm bells. Alcohol and the two amigos created a volatile mixture that might lead to an explosion. Almost like a chemical reaction. Bull and Tex-Mex soaking up suds could very well develop into tomorrow's I-A caper.

Duke set the two bottles on the table. "You take one, Tex-Mex. I'll go back and get another."

"Why you bein' so generous, Duke?" Tex-Mex asked. "You inherit some money or hit the lottery?"

"No," Duke replied. "I know you two will be on a march tonight, so I figured I'd help out the cause a little."

Duke made good on his contribution, and their table rocked with laughter as they discussed the latest fiascos making front page news in the "OPD Times." The threesome's banter exemplified a maxim that police officers accepted without question: no matter how unbelievably bizarre a caper might seem today, sometime in the future another caper even more bizarre will come along to dethrone it. And since police officers deal with the truly fantastic on a routine basis, they treat the macabre and horrifying incidents they confront with a gallows humor that may be disconcerting to the average citizen. Seen from a psychological standpoint, this cynical view might be construed as a defense mechanism to avoid emotional involvement. They banned only one topic: Kids. But other than this one taboo they made everything else fair game.

So the *sea stories* began, the laughter proved contagious, and soon a dozen or so badges pulled other tables and chairs together and joined in. A late twentyish, blond, female OPD officer, wearing a pair of too-tight jeans that amplified her curvaceous figure, sat down next to Tex-Mex and batted her baby blues in his direction. Eve Lawson had five years with OPD, and the OPD faithful knew she carried a flaming torch for the tall Texan. But Tex-Mex shied away from their becoming an item for fear that another female officer he dallied with might learn of her adversary and initiate a High Noon face-off. So, Tex-Mex tried to ignore Eve, but when her hand wandered south to his nether region and her eyes lit up when she achieved the reaction she sought, the Texan sighed and an old adage came to mind: a stiff dick has no conscience. Eve stoked Tex-Mex's libidinous fire and wanted the Texan to reciprocate.

"I want to hear the swizzle stick story," Eve purred.

"Not again," Bull moaned. "That's an OPD myth that never happened."

"Oh, it happened, all right," Duke said. "I know, 'cause I was there."

A cute female rookie with flawless ebony skin spoke up. "What's the swizzle stick story?"

Duke gave the rookie a look of fatherly concern. "Dear, I don't think you're mature enough to hear such a ribald account of carnal knowledge."

Those in the group who knew the story burst out laughing. Goaded into action by the rest of the group, Duke launched into a spirited rendition that left out none of the prurient details.

"Once upon a time," Duke started his X-rated fairy tale. "Our own Tex-Mex Garcia dated a bartender at a local pub. One night Tex-Mex was off-duty at the bar waiting for her to finish her shift and close the joint. He and I were the only people there, and Tex decided to play a joke on her. So, he stripped off all his clothes and got behind the counter naked. A drunk wandered in for his one-more-for-the-road, took a seat, and placed his order. Tex-Mex fixed the drink, but then the drunk finally noticed that Tex was nude. At first he was taken aback, but then he shrugged it off as only a drunk would do under those circumstances and laid a twenty down. Tex held the drink out to him, but the drunk asked for a swizzle stick. Without missing a beat, Tex lowered the glass and used his dick to stir the drink. The drunk's mouth fell open, he shook his head, looked at Tex's dripping dick, and decided he didn't want that last drink after all. The drunk staggered to the door without taking the twenty, and as he walked outside, Tex shouted out, 'Hey, thanks for the tip!' And that's a true story."

Tex-Mex puffed out his chest and beamed as he savored the

group's adulation. But the cute rookie didn't buy it. Just like a wary citizen, she vehemently questioned the tale's veracity.

Duke frowned at her. "You think anyone could *make up* something like that?"

The group rose and gave Tex-Mex a standing ovation, and he tipped his Stetson in all directions. Now, it was Tex-Mex's turn.

"I know Bull and Duke have heard this one, but does anyone else know the DOA and doll story?"

Duke groaned. "Now, we're *really* sinking to the depths of depravity."

Tex-Mex forged ahead. "Radio dispatched me to a call where a woman hadn't seen or heard from her father-in-law for a couple of days. She had the keys to his house and we went inside together. Everything seemed to be in order. Then we opened the bedroom door and she let out a shocked gasp and covered her mouth with her hand. And there he was. In all his glory. Naked, lying face down on top of one of those full-size, plastic blowup dolls that are available at sex novelty stores. An autopsy later showed he'd suffered a heart attack. Probably had the Big One just as he got his jollies. And he was still *fully inserted*! The woman just stood there takin' it all in, too paralyzed in shock to move or speak. Then my bad boy alter ego took over and I couldn't resist. I gave her a comforting hug, tried to put a positive spin on the situation, and said, 'At least he passed away happy'."

The female rookie's mouth dropped open. She sat glued to her chair, too stunned to mount a retort, until she broke from her trance and joined the others in uncontrolled laughter. Now, more cops gravitated toward their tables like spectators drawn to an open mike night at a comedy club, and Bull took his turn.

"I was workin' a swing shift one night and radio dispatched me and a cover unit to a family beef. The husband had been drinkin' and the wife had a small bruise on her cheek. He was a real asshole, but she didn't want him arrested. Now, you gotta remember that OPD's policies were way different *back in the day*. Not like the zero tolerance we have today for domestic violence. She told us she'd handle it, so we made out an assignment card and got the hell out of Dodge.

"An hour later, radio dispatched us back to the same family fight, and when we arrived, we heard this God-awful shrieking. We broke into a run, thinkin' that the asshole was beatin' her half to death. But when we got there, she sat on the couch inside, as calm as could be. I went to the bedroom and saw that one side of the asshole husband's facial pigmentation had been burned off, so that one half of his face was black and the other half bright pink. She told us she waited until he passed out and then poured a pot of boiling tapioca pudding on his face. She knew we had to arrest her 'cause it was a felony, but as we escorted her outside, she said, 'I bet that pinto bean lookin' motherfucker won't ever jump on me again!'"

The large group roared its approval. Justice had been served. Street justice! The female rookie stood and raised her glass in a toast.

"Forget three strikes and you're out," she bellowed. "Any asshole who commits a heinous crime should be eligible for the *pinto bean enhancement clause!*"

The bar shook from an avalanche of applause, and the ad hoc vigilante assemblage rose to their feet with a thunderous chorus of "aye-aye's" that made the rookie's proclamation unanimous.

They quaffed more drinks, told other tales, but slowly the bullshit session gradually lost steam and wound down. Eve saw her chances of luring the Texan to her bed diminish, and she pressed a note into his hand that gave her phone number, address, and a single word—*Anytime*. She said her adieu and by 8:00 P.M. only the original three desperados remained at the table. Duke stood and stretched.

"Time for the Dukester to get-to-steppin'."

Bull gave Duke a conspiratorial leer. "Duke, the night is young. It's a good night for a march. You could call in sick."

Duke replied firmly. "Not tonight. I've had my three. Got to get me some sandman time. With my luck, I'll get a call-out." He paused, narrowed his eyes, and gave Bull a long look. "Hope you remember our talk."

Tex-Mex broke in before Bull could answer. "I'll look after Bull and make sure he stays out of trouble."

Duke snorted as he turned to leave. "Shit, you lookin' out for Bull is like puttin' a fox in the hen-house to guard the hens!"

When Duke reached the door and looked back, Bull and Tex-Mex already left their table and bellied up to the bar to order another round. He could hear their hearty laughter even after he walked outside.

7

The two mavericks reached their third watering hole after leaving the Hit 'N Run, when boredom set in and brought Bull's incubating mischief into a full-blown contagion. Tex-Mex had his sights focused on a flirtatious blond, who threw him come-hither looks that stirred his dormant loins to peak hormonal production. He was about to recite his well-rehearsed opening seduction lines, when Bull intervened and pulled him back from Aphrodite's DEFCON-2 level of love readiness and proposed another, more challenging recreational pursuit.

"Forget that platinum bimbo," Bull said. "You can add her to your trophy collection some other time. Let's do something *really* off the wall for a change. Something that will generate an 8.0 on the originality Richter scale and solidify our reps as totally gonzo dudes."

Tex-Mex was not easily dissuaded once he had his quarry in the cross-hairs. "Bull, I got this one in the bag. In less an hour, I'll be dick-deep. What can you suggest that will beat that?"

Bull placed his hand under his chin, rested his elbow on the bar, and assumed a Rodin's Thinker pose. "We could *convince* a couple of working girls to take a night off from the 'ho stroll on MacArthur and take them out for a night on the town. No sex.

Just introduce them to another slice of Americana to expand their cultural horizons."

Tex-Mex let out a long whistle. "Damn, Bull, that was *deep*."

"Well, what do you say?"

The Texan looked beyond the bar's three dimensional realm in a thousand yard stare, as if contemplating the *true* meaning behind Bull's proposal, and he formulated a question infused with a vital, pragmatic concern.

"Just *why* are we going to do this?"

Bull's profound reply countered the Texan's pragmatism with the infinite wisdom of the Socratic Method.

"Because we *can*."

Spurred to action by Bull's dogmatic assertion, Tex-Mex galvanized his enthusiasm into an immediate response. After draining the rest of his beer and saying farewell to the spurned, frowning bimbo, he led Bull to his classic '57 Chevy, with more horses under the hood than a rodeo, and the two chivalrous cavaliers sped off on a mission to rescue two courtesans from carnal activities that *might* further besmirch their reputation. But first they stopped off at a local convenience Stop and Rob to pick up a twelve-pack of barley and hops to fuel their creative engines.

Bull opened a can of Coors and handed it to the Texan. "I know *just* the two debutantes who would benefit most from attending our coming-out party."

~~~~

Chi Chi Esparanza and Ebony Jones proudly proclaimed their status as two veteran working girls, who staked out the 10000 block of MacArthur Boulevard as their turf. Both were in their late twenties with long arrest records for prostitution on their professional resumes. While neither would ever be considered a contestant in a beauty pageant, they did exude an earthy sexiness that their customers sought to satisfy their kinky lusts. On this warm July night, they squirmed into snug, skin-tight shorts that left their butt cheeks to wiggle and bounce in wide open grandeur for potential Johns to drool over as their lewd and lascivious eyes scanned this sexually explicit smorgasbord. As they performed the 'ho stroll, Chi Chi and Ebony kept their eyes open for both Johns and the police, especially undercover vice officers who regularly patrolled MacArthur Boulevard making arrests for solicitation. When the emerald green '57 Chevy slowed down and pulled to the curb, the two working girls approached the open passenger window, prepared to begin the bargaining process to sell their product.

Ebony leaned down to look inside the Chevy. "Hi, baby! You two lookin' for a double date. . .Brewster! What the fuck you doin' out here?"

Chi Chi poked her head through the window. "And Garcia! Two PO-POs up to no good. We know you ain't workin' no vice sting. Shit, every 'ho out here knows both of you. So, what's your game?"

Bull's demeanor collapsed in sham shock. "Ain't no game. Damn, Chi Chi, you got a case of the paranoids!"

Tex-Mex tried to explain. "It's just that we thought you and Ebony would like to take a break from your, ah, work, for awhile."

Confusion clouded the two women's faces.

"What the fuck you talkin' 'bout *take a break?*" Ebony said. Then in an instant her confusion disappeared and a sly look took its place. "You two got a scam goin', huh? You want to use us for somethin', huh?"

"Ebony," Chi Chi said. "Come on, let's get away from these two scheming motherfuckers. We got to make our coin tonight."

The two women started walking away, when Bull called out to them in a singsong falsetto. "Oh, laaadies! Hold on a second. Chi Chi, how 'bout when I got you out of that soliciting case a few months ago? If you want to continue doin' business with me, you're gonna have to repay your debts."

"And Ebony!" Tex-Mex added. "Remember when I tossed away that little bit of weed your brother was holding? That would have been his third case, and you know where he'd have gone if I hadn't made that weed disappear."

Both women stopped and slowly retraced their steps. Weary looks of resignation signaled their surrender.

"What?" Ebony asked. "What do you want us to do?"

"Better not be something too freaky," Chi Chi added. "I've known both of you for years, and the word on the street is that you're a little too scandalous to be PO-POs. Especially you, Garcia. We've heard *stories.*"

"Damn, Bull," Tex-Mex said. "Even out here in the land of the working girls I can't get away from my reputation."

"So, what is it that you want us to do?" Ebony asked.

"I know you're not gonna believe this girls," Bull replied. "But all we want is to take you out and show you a good time. Do some crazy shit that will have you laughing your asses off. All expenses are on us. And no sex. You both deserve a night off." Bull paused a moment to make eye contact to lend his words more credence. "Just think of this as an adventure where nothing is off-limits, and we have the chance to become legends in our own time."

Chi Chi narrowed her eyes to wary slits. "Uh-huh," she replied and traded knowing looks with Ebony. "All, right. We owe you, so we'll go along with this party as long as it doesn't go too far. And me and Ebony drink Johnny Walker Black."

~~~~

After a quick stop for libations, the four celebrants bombed down E.14th Street, the main corridor that runs through the heart of East Oakland, when they encountered their first adventure of the night. They passed by the Quarter Pounder Diner, which overflowed with racing vehicles of all types, some of them loaded on trailers, towed there, and put on display. A large crowd milled about in the parking lot, making bets and bargaining for the right to race their cars at a mutually agreed upon drag strip. Even the side streets teemed with racing junkies, who made side wagers and argued heatedly among themselves.

"Street racers," Bull said. "Getting ready to convoy out to a race site. Racing for big bucks, pink slips. Wouldn't be so bad if all they did was race, but everything turns to shit when there's a disagreement about who's the winner or some asshole doesn't pay off his bet. Then someone ends up gettin' shot. Happens all the time." Bull paused and pointed out the window. "Hey, Tex-Mex. Speedy's here with his Dodge. Chi Chi, Ebony, you see that Dodge loaded on that trailer in the middle of the lot? Word on the street is that the owner, a dude named Speedy Henderson, has never lost a race."

"How come you PO-POs can't stop him?" Ebony asked. "Shit, you can see 'em all here in this lot. Why not ride in here with your lights and sirens on and clear him and rest of these niggas out?"

Bull chuckled. "It's a little more complicated than that, Ebony. Something to do with the Constitution, due process of law, shit like that. You know, Tex-Mex used to race out here years ago before he joined OPD. He was one of the street racing elite. Shit, all the racers knew this '57 Chevy on sight. And this was before he *really* modified this Chevy into the fastest thing on four wheels. Right, Tex-Mex?"

Chi Chi turned and fixed the Texan with a scolding glare. "See, Ebony? What did I say 'bout Garcia bein' scandalous? Shit, he ain't no better than these niggas out here runnin' wild in the streets!"

"Hey, I'm retired from racing," Tex-Mex said, and then added with a twinkle in his eye. "Of course, I *occasionally* come out of retirement if the stakes are high enough."

Ebony matched Tex-Mex's twinkle with one of her own. "Well, what about tonight, Garcia? You two said nothin's off-limits and we have a chance to become legends or some kind of shit like that. How 'bout it? Un-retire your ass and let's go do some racin'!"

Chi Chi chimed in. "Now, that's a motherfuckin' good idea!"

Tex-Mex glanced over at Bull and watched his shit-eating grin spread.

"You know this could cost us some days on the beach," Bull said.

Ebony looked back and forth between Bull and Tex-Mex. "What beach? Days on what fuckin' beach?"

"Nothin', Ebony, nothin'," Bull replied. "Just po-lice talk." Bull playfully slapped the back of Tex-Mex's Stetson. "All right, Mario Andretti, let's go find us a street race!"

Tex-Mex backed the Chevy slowly into the shadows of a dead-end street in an industrial section close to the Oakland Coliseum. An old abandoned car sat on four flats on the other side of the street, and a stray cat lurked underneath the chassis, its eyes glowing like yellow embers in the dark. The Texan let the engine idle and turned up the radio to listen to the Righteous

Brothers wail away to, "You've Lost That Loving Feeling," on a local Golden Oldies station.

"It's spooky down here," Chi Chi slurred. "How long we have to wait for the racing to start?"

"Yeah, and we're running out of Johnnie Walker," Ebony added.

"The waitin's over," Tex-Mex replied and nodded to a three block long procession of racers and their spectators as they drove slowly past their darkened hideaway. "We'll stay here until they get the race set up, and then I'll unleash this bad boy and see if Speedy's Dodge can catch it."

As Tex-Mex and his racing crew waited in ambush, four vehicles were set to go at 81st Avenue and San Leandro Street. Guards blocked the side streets to prevent any traffic from entering the impromptu drag strip, and the drivers lined up, revving their engines to intimidate each other and add a redundant dose of drama to the already over-hyped scene. A large crowd formed at the 92nd Avenue finish line. Other spectators stretched down both sides of the street and conducted side bets to heighten the suspense. Speedy Henderson was the clear favorite. His 500 cubic inch Dodge behemoth resembled a mechanical beast, whose revved-up engine sent shock waves rumbling out in all directions. When the designated starter gave the go signal, large plumes of white smoke rose from the starting line as the vehicles broke traction and shrieked away toward the finish line several blocks away.

~~~~

A few blocks behind the race's starting line, Tex-Mex eased his *slightly modified* Chevy out of its hiding place and stealthily stalked the four oblivious prey. The guards posted to prevent traffic from entering San Leandro Street did not expect a vehicle from this dead-end street, and the Texan crept to within striking distance until he floored the accelerator, and the Chevy's front end bucked into the air like one of the Four Horses of the Apocalypse trying to throw its riders. The Chevy blasted forward liked a guided missile, and the engine's roar and the hurricane rush of wind blowing through the open windows drowned out Chi Chi and Ebony's screams. The lines in the street streamed past in a blur, a Morse code of dots and dashes which could only be deciphered as three words: mach two speed.

The other four racers shrieked over the roadway, the combined sound of their engines exceeding the wail of a jet preparing for takeoff. They jockeyed back and forth for the lead until Speedy punched the gas pedal and the Dodge's 500 cubic inches responded like a rocket shrugging off the last vestige of gravity before entering the stratosphere. With only a few blocks to go, Speedy had his unbeaten Dodge firmly in command and locked into victory. The whine of his engine reached a crescendo until it seemed that his monster machine would leave terra firma and become airborne.

Then an eardrum-puncturing mechanical scream eclipsed the combined roar of all four racers, and Tex-Mex's *slightly modified* '57 Chevy blasted past them like they were kids competing in a soap box derby. Speedy stared in shocked disbelief as the Chevy's driver haughtily tipped his black Stetson toward him and delivered the *coup de grace* by accelerating beyond what he or any other racer thought theoretically possible. And as they flashed past, both Chi Chi and Ebony stuck their hands out the windows and gave the one finger salute to Speedy and the other vanquished foes.

Tex-Mex didn't reap any monetary prize for his victory, but Oakland's street racing aficionados witnessed a former king from the past back to reclaim his rightful crown.

~ ~ ~ ~

The four victors' laughter continued unabated, as Tex-Mex took a detour off the main roads to elude any outraged racers, and with no further ceremonial fanfare, he slipped back unnoticed into retirement. The Johnnie Walker evaporated and a twelve pack of Coors replenished the beverage supply, but now they had to come up with another diversion to maintain their soaring spirits. Bull recalled that they were close to the golf course. Golf would provide the two "diamonds in the rough" with a more refined image.

"You girls ever go golfing?" Bull asked.

Blank looks from both of them. Ebony took a stab at an answer. "You mean where you use sticks to hit a little white ball and try to put it into some holes in the ground?"

"You got the idea, Ebony," Bull replied. "And that's what we're gonna do next."

Tex-Mex seemed doubtful. "You sure? Where we gonna get balls and clubs?"

"Details, details," Bull said. "You forget that Galbraith Golf Course is on my beat, and any self-respecting beat man would have access to the club house, even when it's closed. In other words, I have a key."

Chi Chi's first swing at the ball on the driving range was a colossal miss that spun her around in a corkscrew and caused her to fall on her ass. Ebony broke into a hysterical spate of guffaws that caused her to collapse next to Chi Chi. After *much* trial and error, the two aspiring LPGA card holders managed a few weak dribbles, slices, and hooks that ricocheted off trees, signs, and the clubhouse until Ebony somehow got faced in the wrong direction and launched a towering drive that soared over the surrounding fence and broke a window in a nearby business.

"Hmmm," Bull intoned. "Maybe we ought to postpone golf lessons for another time. Ebony's last drive may have set off a burglar alarm, and we'd be hard pressed to explain to the beat officer what in the hell we're doin' out here in the dark hitting golf balls through windows. Besides, I've got a better idea."

Bull unlocked the golf cart storage yard, and he and Tex-Mex took passenger seats in two carts piloted by Chi Chi and Ebony which zoomed over the asphalt pathways between holes. Yet another twelve-pack of beer restored their supply of refreshments, and they played follow the leader, tag, hide and seek, and bumper cars all over the course. Their shrill cries and raucous laughter resonated over the rolling greens. When the four duffers exhausted the challenges that the golf course pathways had to offer, Tex-Mex suggested they stage drag races in the streets of the commercial area only a block away, and they sped off into the darkened, deserted streets.

~~~~

Mo Pearson and Nate Fuston were two burglars who made a nice living plundering multiple businesses in the commercial area that Oakland and the city of San Leandro shared next to

Galbraith Golf Course. Mo and Nate's MO was simplicity personified. They removed water meter covers from their places in the pavement, threw them through windows, and then entered and took all the accessible business machines. Thus, they became known as the Water Meter Bandits.

As the two golf cart teams tore through the industrial park, Mo and Nate backed their stolen Chevy van into position in front of their next victim business. Mo readied himself to launch the concrete cover through the large plate glass window, when he heard shouts and hysterical laughter coming from somewhere close by. He paused for a moment and listened carefully but the sounds ceased. After assuring himself that he must have imagined the sounds, he heaved the cement slab like a shot-put, and the resulting crash resounded through the silent streets.

~~~~

"Ebony!" Chi Chi shouted. "I'm gonna catch you, you little 'ho!"

Ebony steered the golf cart around a corner, with Tex-Mex hanging on like a man dangling from a roller coaster, and screamed back over her shoulder. "Oh, yeah? Well, bring it on bitch! Ain't a day in hell you're gonna catch my black ass."

During a brief lull in the girls' barrage of insults, Tex-Mex heard the unmistakable sound of glass shattering and brought their cart to a halt by reaching over and applying the brake.

Chi Chi and Bull pulled up next to them and stopped. "What's the matter, you two give up. . ." Bull said, but he grew silent when he saw Tex-Mex's raised hand and the intense look on his face.

Both Ebony and Chi Chi still giggled, but then Ebony saw Tex-Mex and Bull's expressions.

"What is it? What's the matter?" Ebony asked.

At that moment, there was another sound of breaking glass as the two burglars kicked out the remaining shards of window blocking their entry. Bull and Tex-Mex glanced at each other and simultaneously whispered the obvious.

"Water Meter Bandits!"

"Wha. . ." Chi Chi started to say.

Bull put his forefinger to his smiling lips and whispered.

"Now we're gonna have some *real* fun. Girls, we are hereby deputizing you as honorary PO-POs about to take some bad guys into custody. Chi Chi, just ease up real slow to this next corner, until we can see what's goin' on. Then just do what we say. You too, Ebony. All right, let's go."

At first, Mo and Nate were too busy hauling typewriters and computers out of the business and stacking them inside the van to see or hear the two golf carts approach them. Mo returned to the van with his third business machine, when he caught a glimpse of something moving toward them. For a second or two, what he saw didn't make sense. It looked like two golf carts with two men and two women aboard them. But Mo's common sense overruled his eyesight. What the hell would four people on two golf carts be doing in the middle of a business park at 11:30 at night? But with every yard the carts got closer, the more Mo decided that his eyesight might be 20/20 after all, and he dropped the computer he held and immediately broke into a sprint. Nate heard the computer crash to the pavement, saw the carts' and riders' ghostly apparitions, and dropped the typewriter he carried and fled in the same direction as Mo.

Chi Chi and Ebony didn't hesitate a second. They floored the pedals to the floorboard, and an electric whirring sound competed with the sound of the suspects' shoes pounding the asphalt.

"Get 'em, Chi Chi, " Bull cried out. "*Andale, andale!*"

"Run 'em over, Ebony!" Tex-Mex screamed. "Run those assholes over!"

Mo's mind raced. Who were these people? They couldn't be PO-POs. Cops didn't do stakeouts in golf carts! But if they weren't cops, then why were they chasing them? Whoever they were he had to get the fuck out of there. Shit, he was a three-striker. One more felony conviction and he would be going away for life. But now Mo's legs felt like Jell-O. He wobbled as he ran, and that black bitch driving one of the golf carts stayed right on his heels, talking a lot of smack as he reversed direction into the business' rear parking lot.

"Yeah!" Ebony shouted. "Got you now, motherfucker. Where you goin'? Huh? You ain't goin' nowhere. I got your punk ass in my sights!"

Chi Chi echoed Ebony's war cry. "Hey, *maricones*! Hey, *putos*! You can run, but you can't hide!"

~~~~

In the parking lot behind the business Mo and Nate burglarized, there was another van parked in a secluded corner. Inside this van, Tony Perkins straddled his latest Miss Right For Tonight, who he picked up at a local bar to add another notch to his cocks-man resume. His courtship ritual lasted all of half an hour until he convinced this easy lay, whose name he already forgot, to accompany him in his love mobile to consummate a one night stand. Their foreplay lasted long enough for Tony's Johnson to harden, and he pounded away at Miss Anonymous' tunnel of love. So passionately did they make love that the van rocked from side to side, and their moans and lusty love talk made them blissfully unaware of Mo and Nate's arrival on the scene. Tony concentrated on the orgasm only seconds away. Closer, closer, he could feel it start to build.

CRASH! And the plate glass window splintered in a shrill explosion.

Tony stopped in mid-stroke and listened, but no follow-up noise distracted him from his single-minded obsession. He joyfully returned to jackhammer this succulent piece of poon-tang, and what's-her-name responded by letting loose with a primal groan that excited him into a series of savage thrusts that took him to the edge of ecstasy. . .

SLAM! Chi Chi inadvertently plowed the golf cart into Tony's van with such a seismic jolt that the crash tore the star-crossed lovers apart from their coital embrace. At the same time, Tony heard women shouting dire threats, men laughing and cursing, and sounds of someone moaning and gasping for breath. Thinking that he faced mortal danger, Tony's only thought centered on his own self-preservation, and he burst through the van's rear double doors to flee, leaving his beloved what's-her-name to fend for herself. Tony joined the wild parade of fleeing burglars and police posse in golf carts circling the parking lot, and his naked appearance, combined with his erect appendage, gave the scene a double dose of surrealism that caused the crooks, cops, and 'hos to stop dead in their tracks and gape at this *dues ex machine* dropped into their midst. For a few moments they stood dumbfounded as they watched Tony sprint around the lot like a randy Greek sculpture brought to life, but then Mo and Nate recalled their criminal act and the years in prison that awaited them if they were captured, and the chase resumed as before.

But now fatigue put an end to their mad dash. Nate's total exhaustion caused him to collapse in the lot, and Chi Chi stopped the cart and stood over him with a look of triumph planted smugly on her face. The Water Meter Bandit slowly regained his senses and stared up at her with sudden recognition and disbelief.

Nate pointed at Chi Chi. "Hey! You're one of the 'hos on MacArthur!" Then he turned to Bull. "And you're that big PO-PO that fucks with the D-boys at Carney Park. What the fuck is goin' on. . ."

Chi Chi gave the burglar an indignant glare. "I *used* to be a 'ho! Now, I work with the PO-POs to send motherfuckers like you to the joint!"

Shortly after Nate Fuston's Olympic sprinting career came to an abrupt end, Ebony and Tex-Mex *literally* ran down Mo Pearson and set in motion what would turn out to be, after his conviction for first degree burglary, the rest of his life spent in state prison. The indentation from the cart's front wheel showed clearly visible on the back of his shirt, and he groaned and fought for breath, as the first OPD units arrived on the scene in response to the business' silent burglar alarm.

These OPD units and Sergeant Gus Gerard, the District 5 Supervisor, happened on a strange sight. Two drunk, off-duty officers had the much sought after Water Meter Bandits in custody. Two *well-known* MacArthur Boulevard prostitutes, also drunk, accompanied the two off-duty officers. Two golf carts mysteriously found their way to this parking lot. And a naked man attempted to conceal his *au natural* condition by hiding behind some shrubbery.

Sergeant Gerard was less than pleased at what he saw. He shook his head many times and wandered the crime scene talking to himself as he beseeched the heavens why Bull Brewster and Tex-Mex Garcia felt the need to persecute him so late in his OPD career. Although not a religious man, he raised his hands skywards and muttered, "Why me, God, why me?" How would he explain this mess? What the hell would happen next? What would happen next came in the form of a San Leandro officer, who drove up and asked for the supervisor in charge. Sergeant Gerard reluctantly stepped forward.

"Hey, Sarge," the San Leandro officer said. "I saw all the commotion over here and wondered if what you guys have goin' has anything to do with an alarm we had a little earlier. A window was broken at a business on our side of Doolittle Drive. We found this golf ball on the floor inside."

Sergeant Gerard took the ball and examined it as he would a miniature crystal ball he could gaze into and make all this madness go away. Then he nodded his head knowingly and turned to face Bull and Tex-Mex, who both took an inordinate interest identifying constellations in the night sky. A twisted smile grew on Sergeant Gerard's lips as he handed the ball back to the San Leandro officer.

"No, I don't believe this ball has anything to do with our investigation here. Sorry."

But the San Leandro officer took in the whole street scene, and a flicker of doubt crossed his face. The two guys in civilian clothes looked more than half-gassed, and the muscular one bore a striking resemblance to the OPD Day Watch officer who patrolled this area next to the San Leandro border. The two females had "hookers" written all over them, and he wondered if the two golf carts had a connection with the broken window. But it wasn't until he glanced at a row of shrubbery at the rear of the lot and saw the naked man standing there that he had enough good sense to realize that he should leave this mess to OPD to sort out, and he cheerfully waved goodbye and departed this OPD Twilight Zone to return to his safe little city.

After the San Leandro officer drove out of earshot, Sergeant Gerard turned his full attention to the two besotted centurions.

"Bull, Tex-Mex, how. . ." Sergeant Gerard began but then stopped as he grasped futilely for words.

He tried again. "You two. . ."

A third time. "What the hell were you. . ."

Chi Chi frowned. "What's the matter with *him*? Why's he so pissed? Shit, we caught the two assholes, didn't we? We ought to get a medal or somethin'."

"Enough!" Sergeant Gerard roared, and the veins in his forehead appeared ready to burst. He took a series of deep breaths and gradually his pulsating arteries returned to a normal enough condition that an aneurysm did not seem imminent. "Maxwell, Godfrey, drive Tex-Mex and Bull's, ahem, friends back to MacArthur where they belong. Conners, have the golf carts towed back to Galbraith. And you, trying to hide in the shrubbery! Get your naked ass back in your van and get the hell out of here!"

The sergeant waited until Chi Chi, Ebony, and the nude Adam and Eve replicas disappeared from view. Then he turned his wrath on Bull and Tex-Mex. "You two! Write your supplemental reports but make no mention of the two women, the golf carts, or that naked guy and his girlfriend. Just state that you. . . that you just happened to be driving by, heard the glass break, and took appropriate action. And next time do your drinking with your *friends* in San Leandro or Alameda, but *not* in Oakland!"

~~~~

The Water Meter Bandits' apprehension never made it to the hallowed halls of I-A. Rumors circulated that Bull and Tex-Mex used some kind of unconventional, unorthodox means to capture the burglary suspects. But the sergeants in the Criminal Investigation Division were so relieved that the burglars' reign of terror finally ended that they cast a collective blind eye to the numerous discrepancies they encountered in their follow-up investigations. And what they *heard* seemed so outlandish that it took on the essence of a Big Foot tall tale that they mentioned only in hushed whispers. However, it did become a staple for cop shoptalk at the Hit 'N Run for years to come. Bull and Tex-Mex dodged a bullet on their night out with two representatives from Oakland's demimonde, but they would have to confront another specter when they arrived for work the next morning.

8

Four hours after Duke left Bull and Tex-Mex at the Hit 'N Run, the phone rang at his residence and he fumbled in the dark to turn on the table lamp. He lifted the receiver to his ear and had to clear his throat before answering curtly. "Yeah?"

"Sergeant Washington?" the caller said. "This is Officer Hill working the desk. I have a call-out for you. You got a pen handy?"

The message was brief. A SIDS death. Sudden Infant Death Syndrome. Duke copied down all the relevant details and instructed the desk officer to have his homicide partner, Sergeant Mary Sanders, meet him at the scene. He hung up and sat on the edge of the bed as he tried to shake the sleep from his mind. His wife Brenda stirred on her side of the bed, fluffed her pillow, and drifted back to sleep. Duke yawned, ran a hand over his head, and thought about what lay ahead.

Duke would rather undergo a root canal procedure than investigate a SIDS death.

A child's death, especially a SIDS, made each case a heart-wrenching ordeal. Invariably, the parents' grief caused them to speculate if they were somehow responsible. Some felt a subliminal guilt that might affect them for the rest of their lives. Hysteria also made the cases difficult to investigate. Investigators had to use considerable tact lest an inadvertent word or action be misconstrued by the child's relatives as insensitive or improper. Many SIDS cases remained unsolvable. There was simply not enough evidence to determine the cause of death. Yet because of an array of suspicious circumstances that surrounded many SIDS cases, OPD procedures mandated Homicide Division to investigate every SIDS case to determine if it involved foul play.

Duke glanced at the clock. Ten after midnight. Only two hours of sleep. He faced another long day. He rose to his feet and trudged to the bathroom. Twenty minutes later, he knotted his tie, put on a sports coat, and started to leave, when Brenda's drowsy voice stopped him.

"Let me know if you can't pick up Cynthia from school, Duke."

Duke reversed his way back to Brenda's side of the bed and kissed her lightly on the cheek. "I'll let you know, sleepyhead."

~~~~

Duke listened to the police radio as he maneuvered his unmarked car through the sparse, early morning traffic. It was almost 1:00A.M., and shootings, stabbings, and general mayhem dominated the airwaves. The emergency calls followed one after another in an endless stream of human anguish. The dispatcher's urgent requests for officers to respond to multiple crises made the carnage palpable. Just another night on the front lines of Oakland, California, violence capital of the Bay Area. Duke fought off a yawn and took a cautious sip of the Doggie Diner coffee he purchased on the way to the SIDS scene. The fiery brew scalded his mouth and throat, but the caffeine rush started to melt away his fatigue.

He reluctantly wound his way through the war zone on his way to the call-out, but at least he had Mary Sanders as his partner in this investigation. He liked working with Mary. Although only twenty-eight years old, with just seven years on the PD, she already established her reputation as an excellent investigator on a fast track for promotion to lieutenant. Known for her street smarts, uncanny intuition, and crafty interrogation techniques, she also had a *bad-ass* attitude that prompted her fellow officers to label her with the moniker, Mary "Don't Take No Shit" Sanders. She used her rapier-like wit to put many a suspect *or* officer in his place. It also didn't hurt her path to advancement that she was an ebony beauty with a dynamite body. Duke had to put up with some minor marital discord when Mary became his partner. One look at Mary put even the most trusting wife or girlfriend on instant alert for any hint of hanky-panky.

Duke finished his coffee as he rounded the corner to the cul-de-sac where the SIDS death occurred. It was a quiet court in an opulent area of the Oakland Hills, and the flashing amber lights from several police vehicles and an ambulance gave the neighborhood a carnival ambience. Duke's investigative eye scanned the scene and he nodded approvingly at what he saw. The officers had the yellow crime scene tape in place. An officer stood guard at the residence's front door to prevent unauthorized entry. Two other officers conducted a door-to-door canvas of nearby houses for information. And the field technician's arrival on the scene told him that the crucial task of gathering possible evidence was well under way. Everything seemed in order. Duke parked his car and met the sentry at the front door.

"Hey, Porter, the district sergeant here?" Duke said.

"Yeah, Sergeant Janovich is inside," Porter answered.

Duke stepped inside the house and noted that the front room appeared clean and nicely furnished. At the end of the hallway, Sergeant Janovich stood with his arms crossed over his chest, and he peered intently into a well-lit room and had a concerned look on his face. Duke noted that he'd lost a little more hair and gained some weight since he last saw him. The ravages of middle-age, Duke empathized. Bill greeted Duke with a brief smile and a handshake.

"Something told me you'd get this one, Duke," Bill said.

"No rest for the weary, Bill," Duke said. "So, what do we have here?"

Bill provided Duke with a brief summary of what occurred. The parents, Judy and Patrick Dempsey hired sixteen year old Karen Holtz to baby-sit their fourteen month old daughter, Dawn, while they went out for dinner and a movie. The baby-sitter attended the same church and they knew her well. The parents returned home at about 11:00 P.M., and the baby-sitter told them she put the baby to sleep in the dayroom downstairs.

The mother checked on the infant and found her not breathing and unresponsive. The father phoned 911, and the fire department and ambulance arrived a few minutes later and declared the baby DOA.

Duke recorded this background information in his notebook and then sought Bill's input.

"Ok, what's your take on this?"

Bill took a deep breath and the concerned look returned to his face. "I don't know about this one, Duke. Couple of things jumped out at me when I first looked over the scene. I think you'll see what I mean when you get into your investigation."

A pretty red-headed paramedic, wearing a standard blue jumpsuit, exited the dayroom and joined Bill and Duke in the hallway. She handed Duke her preliminary report.

"Guess you'll want to see this," she said.

"Thanks, Janie," Duke replied.

"I haven't seen you since the double murder at the Holiday Inn last month, Duke," Janie said. "Where you been keeping yourself?"

Duke glanced up from the report and smiled. "Out of trouble, Janie, out of trouble."

While Duke scanned the report, Janie and Bill conversed quietly. Then Duke pointed at the body diagram and turned to Janie with a questioning look.

"That's right," Janie confirmed. "Two small burn marks on the infant's chest. Unknown what caused them. No other signs of body trauma or abuse. Cause of death unknown at this time."

Duke nodded and returned the medical report to Janie, and he and Bill went to the end of the hallway where they could discuss the investigation in private.

"What about the parents and the baby-sitter?" Duke asked. "What do they have to say?"

Bill glanced at the stairway leading to the second floor, where an officer stayed with the parents in the master bedroom, and lowered his voice. "Well, you can imagine what the parents are going through. They say the baby appeared in good health, with a clear medical history, and they have no idea how the burn marks got on the child's chest. They have nothing but good things to say about the baby-sitter. The girl's supposedly a straight-A student, never been in trouble, a devout Christian, and this is the fifth or sixth time she's baby-sat for them. They don't have any idea what happened here tonight, Duke."

"And the baby-sitter Karen. . ." Duke began, as he leafed through his notes searching for her last name.

"Holtz," Bill said.

"Holtz," Duke repeated. "What's her story?"

Bill paused before answering. "Well, she's been very cooperative. She gave a complete account about what happened after the parents left and claims no knowledge about the burn marks."

Bill stopped and Duke sensed that he experienced trouble expressing something bothering him. "What is it, Bill?"

"Duke, it just seems like she's not all that concerned that the baby died while in her care. She's just so blasé about the whole matter. Like when I finished interviewing her and asked her to wait in the kitchen until you arrived, she went right in there and immediately started doing her homework. It was like, 'Oh, the baby died? Well, I've got to finish my math'."

Sergeant Mary Sanders interrupted Duke's return comment. She walked briskly toward them, taking confident strides that exuded a cocky temperament. Her dark blue pants suit fit snug at the hips and revealed a butt that most women would die for. Her complexion was flawless, her cheekbones high and well-rounded, and her lips full and sensuous. She knew men watched her and she enjoyed the approval in their eyes. Mary thought about making a witty introductory remark, but the two men's troubled looks cautioned her to forego her usual trademark banter. She intuited that this would not be a routine SIDS case in any sense of the term.

"Well, Duke," Mary said. "I can tell by your demeanor that we've got something going on here, right?"

Duke shrugged. "Maybe, Mary. Or maybe I'm reading too much into this."

After briefing Mary on the case, Duke looked toward the dayroom and dreaded what would come next. Even though he conducted dozens of homicide investigations, he had an aversion to viewing and handling dead children. He could not overcome this phobia. Since he was the lead investigator on this case, Duke had to initiate the first steps. He reread his notes a third time and then nodded to Mary that they should begin.

Mary and Duke entered the room and stood to the side,

while Jenny Colon, the evidence technician, snapped photographs and took measurements for the scene diagram. The tiny body lay on its back in a crib decorated with brightly colored decals. Several stuffed animals and plastic toys hovered motionless above the crib, suspended from a rack attached to the headboard.

A fresh diaper covered the baby's genital area. The infant's eyes were closed and the burn marks on her chest clearly visible. Everything appeared in order. There were no medications or other ingestible substances within reach, which could have caused an overdose or poisoning. Nothing in the crib that could have caused choking or suffocation.

Jenny stepped away and packed her equipment. "I'm finished now Mary, Duke. You can examine the baby."

With Mary's help, Duke performed a thorough visual scan of the body, and as with Janie's medical report, they found no signs of trauma other than the burn marks. The child's flesh was cold to the touch and rigor mortis started to set in. Duke's hands felt clammy and betrayed a slight tremble that he tried to hide. He returned the infant to the mattress and replaced the diaper.

"Maybe the autopsy will turn up something," Duke said.

"Maybe," Mary repeated.

Mary watched Duke step away from the crib. He stared at the infant. After working with Duke for more than a year, Mary knew her partner's idiosyncrasies. When she spoke, he jerked his eyes toward her in a startled, reflex action.

"You want me to conduct the interviews, Duke?" Mary asked.

Duke nodded quickly. "Thanks, Mary."

Mary smiled and squeezed his arm. "Come on, let's go see the parents."

They heard a woman sobbing as they neared the bedroom where the parents waited. Through the open bedroom door Mary and Duke saw the mother lying in a fetal position on a king-sized bed. The father sat on the edge of the bed holding his head in his hands. Duke greeted the uniformed officer standing just outside the door and knocked lightly on the doorjamb. The father rose to his feet. He had grief sculpted into his face.

Mary took control and outlined how the investigation would proceed. She combined both a sympathetic and professional approach that quickly put the parents at ease. A subsequent Q&A

concerning the baby's health history and a recap of the night's events failed to reveal any further leads. Mary concluded by assuring the parents that they would do everything they could to determine the cause of their child's death.

Mary led the way downstairs. "Well?"

Duke shook his head. "The parents didn't have anything to do with this."

"Agreed," Mary said. "So, that leaves you know who as our person of interest for whatever happened. How do you want to handle this? Want to take her downtown?"

Duke shook his head. "If we take her downtown, then she's liable to stonewall us, and placing her in a formal interrogation setting puts *Miranda* in motion. So, let's just feel our way along and hope we get lucky. If nothing develops, we can take her down later." Duke let a slight grin surface. "Besides, I've always been in awe of your interrogation skills, Mary. Hell, if you put your mind to it, you could make the Mafia Godfather violate the Omerta Code and confess."

Mary smiled and arched her eyebrows in a don't-bullshit-me-now-look, but she nodded her agreement that they conduct the interview here first. Ever since the *Miranda* warning took effect, police officers had to advise suspects of their rights to remain silent and seek legal counsel if they became the *focus* of a criminal investigation. But if officers steered clear of questions that dealt specifically with the criminal act, then this borderline questioning was permissible. And Mary would attempt this nuanced interrogation.

"Well," Mary said, "time to go see the star of the show."

When Mary and Duke entered the kitchen, the uniformed officer had his attention fixed on a late night TV movie, and Karen Holtz busied herself with her homework. The officer muttered a brief greeting and excused himself, and Mary began the interview. Just as she did with the parents, Mary explained what the investigation entailed, and as she continued, Duke formed an impression of the girl. Very pretty with bright blue eyes. A slim, athletic figure. Long brown hair pulled back in a ponytail. And she smiled continually and nodded her head often to show Mary that she listened carefully and meant to cooperate. Duke concluded that Karen Holtz had a wholesome quality that radiated a girl-next-door persona.

Mary ended her introduction by dropping her professional police image to foster a casual, friendly attitude. Duke smiled to himself at Mary's familiarity tactic and admired the way she succeeded. Make the girl feel at ease. Engender a bond of trust. Establish herself as a friend. And then get the girl to divulge information that she would not have otherwise given. Mary's skill at this tactic made it seem as though she and the girl were friends catching up on old times.

Mary sat down next to the girl and used the textbook on the table as an opening to begin the interview. "I hear you're a straight-A student."

"Yes ma'am," Karen replied. "Both my freshman and sophomore years. I just hope I can keep it up until I graduate."

Mary engaged the girl in small talk about her school activities and learned that Karen attended Skyline High School. Mary informed Karen that Skyline was her alma mater, and they established an instant rapport. They compared anecdotes and discussed teachers they both took classes from, and the conversation seesawed back and forth for a short time. Duke stood to the side, leaning against the kitchen sink, watching Mary lay the groundwork. He confirmed the impression that Bill Janovich confided to him earlier. This girl seemed completely unaffected by the infant's death. During a brief lull, Mary gestured toward the open textbook Karen had in front of her.

"So, what kind of homework are you doing now?"

Karen picked up the book to show Mary the cover. "It's a book on CPR, cardio pulmonary resuscitation. It's part of a health class I'm taking this semester."

"That's great," Mary said. "How's the class going?"

A slight frown broke through Karen's sunny façade. "It's going OK, but I have my doubts about whether CPR will actually work."

Duke saw an inkling of interest register in Mary's eyes.

"Really?" Mary asked. "Where'd you get that idea?"

Karen's frown deepened. "I don't know. It just seems farfetched to me. Like something you see on TV or in the movies. I mean, it's hard to believe that you blow into a dead person's mouth and press on her chest, and she'll come back to life."

Karen looked away as she explained her reasoning, and Mary shot Duke a glance to determine if he caught the pronouns the girl used, and his quick nod assured her he had.

Duke tried to plot Mary's strategy. He calculated what her next tactic would be. Like a game of chess. Move and counter move. Trying to stay one step ahead. Mary had a glint in her eyes that told him she was on to something. He watched her facial expression change as she launched another avenue of approach. Her voice took on a different inflection to reassure, to dissolve any apprehension, to subtly probe through casual discourse. Mary infused her words with an airy confidence.

"Karen, CPR works, believe me. You just keep practicing the proper techniques and maybe you'll have the opportunity to save someone's life."

Karen's response tumbled out too quickly to retract. "Oh, I've been practicing on my own."

Mary leaned toward the girl with a puzzled look. "You have? How have you been practicing?"

Karen started to explain, but in an instant a premonition of doubt wrinkled her forehead, causing her to break eye contact with Mary and stop. "Well, I. . . " Karen began and then lapsed into silence.

Duke saw this pronounced hesitation and knew Mary did too.

Mary smiled and leaned back in her chair. Duke knew that her interrogator experience cautioned her to back off to keep from spooking her quarry.

"Karen, can I see the textbook?" Mary asked.

Karen seemed distracted and vaguely uneasy as she handed the book over. She stared at the TV as Mary thumbed through the pages. Mary stalled for time until she could think of a new ploy to coax more information from the girl. Mary handed the book back.

"By the way, Karen," Mary asked casually. "Where did you get a mannequin to practice CPR with?"

Karen put her left hand to her cheek and leaned her elbow on the table as she opened the book and idly flipped through the chapters. A few seconds elapsed before she finally answered.

"I, uh, couldn't borrow a mannequin, so I just used one of my old dolls."

"A doll?" Mary asked. "No wonder you don't think that CPR will work. Practicing CPR should be as realistic as possible.

Don't you think so, Karen?"

Duke watched Mary interrogate suspects many times before. She was tenacious, relentless. Once she had the scent, she never backed off. The moments passed. Karen did not answer. She sat hunched over at the table, resting her head in her hand, staring at the book, absentmindedly twirling the end of her ponytail with her other hand.

"Karen?" Mary said and waited for an answer.

The girl continued to play with her hair. Duke sensed that Mary faced a fragile impasse. She needed to adopt a new tactic or she would lose the concessions she already gained. Maybe a more intimate bond would open the way. A closeness. Where secrets are shared between confidants. Mary left her chair and knelt on one knee until her face closed to within mere inches of the girl's bowed head. She held this position until Karen slowly raised her head and riveted Mary's eyes with her own.

"Karen?" Mary repeated in a barely audible voice.

"I didn't really use a doll," Karen whispered.

Duke saw a sudden comprehension flash in Mary's eyes, and then they narrowed to near slits as she burrowed into the girl's crumbling defensive system. Searching for the cerebral tunnel that would lead to the truth. Trying to locate the trigger that would release the words she *wanted* to tell them. Mary followed the scent to the girl's lair. And waited.

Mary's kept her voice soft yet firm. "Karen? Is there something you need to tell me?"

Karen's face did not betray her. She displayed no furtive, telltale facial tics which would have conveyed apprehension. Her face remained a blank slate. Devoid of emotion. Without compassion. No guilt. No remorse. She spoke in a straightforward, monotone manner as if she recounted to them an everyday, mundane experience that she had earlier that evening. She revealed what occurred to the two police officers because it constituted an act that held no more significance to her than if she crushed an insect that got in her way.

"I just wanted to find out if CPR really worked. I was curious, that's all. So, I decided to practice CPR on baby Dawn. I didn't want to hurt her. That was the last thing I wanted to do. But to do CPR she had to stop breathing. So, I tied a plastic bag over her head to cut off her air. I read somewhere that this was a painless way to die. All I had to do was hold her hands so that she wouldn't tear the bag. When she wasn't breathing anymore, I started CPR. I did it just like I learned, but it didn't work. I tried over and over but it just wouldn't work. I was getting really angry because what they taught us didn't do what it was supposed to do, and I was mad at them because they were causing baby Dawn's death. So, I had to think about some other way to get her breathing again, and I remembered that you could shock someone back to life. I got an extension cord, shaved off one end, plugged in the other end, and put the wires on Dawn's chest. . ."

Karen became so involved with giving an accurate account of what happened that she failed to notice Mary and Duke's reaction. Not until her story ended and her tumult of words trailed off did she finally turn her attention to the two homicide investigators and see the horror reflected in their eyes.

~ ~ ~ ~

The investigation continued throughout the early morning hours and into the day. Duke surmised that it would remain for the courts to decide if Karen's admission would be ruled a spontaneous statement, or if they should have advised her of her *Miranda* rights. Mary and Duke arrested Karen Holtz for murder and sent her to juvenile detention. Duke held no illusions about the case's final disposition. He knew that the justice system had its quirks, and this was especially so in the juvenile justice system, where the offender's youth played such a huge role in the outcome. Plea bargaining also played a major role in determining what the final charge against Karen Holtz would be. So, whether the DA's office decided to prosecute her for murder or some lesser charge was up to them. Duke knew that he and Mary did their jobs and now the case rested in someone else's hands.

It was dark when Duke started driving home. He loosened his tie and stopped at a liquor store and bought a can of beer. Departmental policy strictly forbade the consumption of alcoholic beverages while operating a city vehicle, but he reasoned that one "road dog" wouldn't harm anyone. He took a sip of the ice-cold brew and listened to the barrage of radio calls dispatched to OPD units and the resulting sirens that split the evening's stillness. Just like last night. And nights in the future.

Duke tried to sum up what he learned from this murder case. He heard of amorality before, but he never witnessed an example. Until Karen Holtz. What's worse, he reasoned in an abstract way. An amoral person who commits a heinous crime and doesn't know it's wrong? Or a sociopath who knows it's wrong but just doesn't give a shit? Good question, he thought. He mulled this over for a few seconds, drained the last dregs of his beer, and then concluded that the sociopath presented the lesser of the two evils. At least the sociopath would understand *why* the court sentenced him to life in prison or the death penalty.

The amoral person would not have a fucking clue.

8

Bull and Tex-Mex's *march* with Chi Chi and Ebony took a savage toll. The morning after, Bull groaned to himself. Why did there always have to be a morning after? He struggled into his uniform and then paused in front of the full-length mirror on the wall next to the men's locker-room door to assess the damage. A sign on the wall above the mirror read in capital letters: GEN-TLEMEN, TAKE PRIDE IN YOUR APPEARANCE. He looked at his reflection and a strange caricature of a police officer stared back at him. Sagging circles of wrinkled skin hung like pendulums beneath his bloodshot eyes. His badge lost its silver sheen and seemed infected with some kind of tarnished, smudged fungus that he did not have the strength to polish off. His navy blue shirt and pants were rumpled and so linty that they appeared to develop their own form of dandruff. His paratrooper boots were scuffed beyond redemption. But in fact, Bull felt so hung-over that he could have been wearing a pink tutu and he would have cared less. He bore the brunt of a litany of sarcastic remarks, when he staggered into the line-up room.

One officer grimaced and shook his head. "Damn, Bull, you have AIDS or somethin'?"

Another wit added. "Bull, did you get run over by a herd of

elephants?"

Bull ignored his tormentors and took his customary seat along the rear wall. He took a glance a few seats over and saw that Tex-Mex suffered the same ravages as he did. Bull bowed his head and silently prayed to the Sacred Saint of Hard Drinkers Everywhere: just get me through this day, he begged, and I'll never drink again. But then he winced, when faint stirrings from his church-going past took hold, and he decided that this rash, exaggerated vow might be viewed as a minor blasphemy, and he wisely amended it: never again, oh Sacred Saint, at least *not for a while.*

Captain Ernie stood at the podium and read off the beat assignments, discussed relevant patrol issues, and then opened the forum to questions and comments. Officer Rita Sims raised her hand and Captain Ernie nodded toward her in acknowledgement.

"Captain, what's the scuttlebutt about an off-duty shooting outside the Hit 'N Run last night?"

Captain Ernie paused before answering and shifted his blistering gaze back and forth between Bull and Tex-Mex. "There's an ongoing investigation into that matter, but that's all I'm at liberty to say at this time."

After his parting salvo to "lock up the bastards," Captain Ernie passed by Bull and Tex-Mex in the hallway. "See me in my office," he growled.

Bull looked to Tex-Mex for a hidden meaning behind the captain's *invitation,* and the Texan's return glance confirmed Bull's concern that Captain Ernie heard about their march the night before. The two aspiring AA candidates scaled the stairs to the captain's office at a snail's pace and knocked on the door. Captain Ernie's gruff response bade them entry.

"You two go on a march last night?" the captain's question translated as an accusation, and the two rogues waited for the other shoe to drop. "Thought so. Both of you look like death warmed over." Captain Ernie fixed them with a hard stare. "You know, *someone* shot out the street lights across from the Hit 'N Run last night. You two know anything about that?"

Both Bull and Tex-Mex sighed in relief that news of their escapade had yet to reach Captain Ernie's ears.

"Wasn't us, Captain Ernie," Tex-Mex said with conviction.

"We were there 'til 'bout nine," Bull said. "But we weren't involved in any shootin'." Of course, he didn't add that they engaged in a street race, vandalized a business by breaking a window, and *borrowed* a couple of golf carts. . .

"Hu-huh," Captain Ernie grunted. "Well, all the fingers seem to be pointing at you two. You say you didn't do it. OK, I can buy that. Now, you both know that back when OPD had a sense of humor, firing a few rounds at some street lights was something that the higher echelon brass would just wink at. A kind of boys-will-be-boys thing. Not anymore. When the legislative gods made negligent discharge of a firearm a felony, the rules of the game changed overnight. You do any shootin' now, and the department will hang your ass out to dry. I *hope* you understand."

"Captain," Bull said. "You know we've done a lot of shit in the past. But we've always owned up to it if we were caught. And Captain Ernie, we didn't do *any* shootin' last night!"

Captain Ernie gave them a long look and then dropped the subject. "Go ahead and hit the street. But make your first stop Engine 29. Ask the firefighters to give you a few hits of oxygen to clear your heads so you'll be able to earn your salary today. And then get out there and lock up a few bastards!"

~~~~

After inhaling more oxygen than a pair of deep sea divers, Bull and Tex-Mex drove to a small, secluded city park facing the estuary. They pulled their black and whites next to each other and made plans to stay there until they were reasonably sure they were going to survive, or the dispatcher sent them to an assignment, whichever came first. For the first hour, the bacchanalian gods granted them mercy and they received no calls. The salty, cool morning breeze swept through the park and helped clear their heads, and they leaned back against their headrests and closed their eyes. They just climbed over the first hurdle to hangover recovery, when the dispatcher's usual bored, monotone voice rose an octave as she broadcast the next call, and Bull and Tex-Mex's eyes snapped open at the same instant.

~~~~

Kathy Winters looked forward to this day all week. As a first grade teacher at Sobrante Park Elementary School, she joined her class riding the bus to the San Leandro Bay Park along the Oakland estuary for a nature excursion on the shoreline. She hoped that seeing birds and animals up close would give the children a greater appreciation and understanding for the wildlife they studied in the classroom. It promised to be a memorable day.

Kathy sat in the seat just behind the bus driver, and from this position she monitored the children's behavior. Packed with twenty-eight excited six year olds, the bus transitioned into a bedlam of shouts, laughter, and high-pitched squeals of animated delight. Occasionally, Kathy had to caution a child whose play became too rough, but she enjoyed this excursion as much as the children.

The bus just crossed the Hegenberger overpass to the Highway 80 freeway, when Kathy first heard the low rumble of a semi-truck gearing down. As the bus approached the freeway off-ramp, she also heard the screech of the semi's brakes lock up. Kathy became aware of a large object taking shape in her peripheral vision. She jerked her head to the right and saw the enormous semi bearing down on them. At the last instant, a child screamed and Kathy's reflex action caused her to raise her arms in front of her face.

The semi broadsided the bus with a massive crunch, sending a neck-snapping jolt through the length of the bus. The bus lurched and then tipped lazily, and for an extended moment or two it seemed to teeter on two wheels. Then the bus continued to tip and Kathy watched the roadway approach in slow motion until the bus' fall gradually gained momentum and the street became a gray wall rushing toward impact. The bus slammed against the pavement with a stunning blow, followed by a grinding, screeching sound of asphalt scraping the bus's metallic skin and Kathy blacked out.

~~~~

"All units, all units," the radio dispatcher broadcast. "A 901A involving a school bus and a semi truck just occurred in the 400 block of Hegenberger. There are reports that children are on board and the bus is on fire. Units to respond?"

Bull had his car in gear and jetted out of the park even before the dispatcher finished transmitting. Tex-Mex followed a second behind him. They were only a few blocks away and Bull stomped the accelerator into the floorboard, making parked cars, trees, and buildings a blur as he flashed past. The wind whipping through the open window and a surge of adrenaline helped flush the hangover out of his system. A rising column of black smoke billowed into the sky as Bull rapidly closed the distance to the collision scene. He arrived seconds later and felt chest pangs, when he saw the bus resting on the driver's side, with flames crackling from the rear engine. Chaos ruled the scene. People milled about in confusion, shouting for someone to phone the fire department, screaming that there were children trapped inside, pleading for someone, anyone to do something. But the fire kept the crowd back. They knew the bus could explode at anytime and any rescuer unfortunate to be caught inside. . .

In an instant Bull leaped from his car and sprinted toward the bus, pushing and shoving the crowd aside. He hoisted himself to the top of the bus without hesitation, as flames whooshed toward him. He tried the door first, but the force of the collision bent and jammed it closed. Then he used his short baton to smash out a window and wedged inside. The interior was in shambles. Tiny bodies lay twisted, tangled, and heaped one atop the other. Arms, legs, heads all in a jumble, with lunch boxes and thermos bottles strewn about like pieces of detritus. The children's cries of pain and wails of fear filled the bus' interior with a cacophony of despair.

Bull flung himself into the rescue. He picked up a hysterical little girl and passed her out the window to Tex-Mex, waiting on the street below. The Texan's long arms gathered her in and he handed her off to a citizen, who in turn rushed her to safety. A small boy was next, but a gust of flame pushed Bull back inside. He paused for a moment and tried again.

"Tex-Mex! Another comin' out!"

"Go ahead, I'm here!"

Two out, many more to go. He picked up a third child and pushed her out to Tex-Mex. One child after another. And all the while, Bull murmured soothing words of comfort. "It's OK, little guy. Everything's gonna be all right. Don't worry. OK, I got you.

Here we go, out the window. Come on, honey. Don't be afraid. There you go, out the window."

The fire intensified and tentacles of flame flicked out like a serpent's tongue along the length of the bus. Again and again Bull retreated back inside to avoid explosive bursts, like an open oven disgorging blasts of super-heated air. Bull waited for these flames to diminish and then resumed his herculean efforts. One after another the children emerged from the inferno. Now, the bus filled with thick, black smoke, and Bull had to feel his way along the seats to locate yet another child. He groped, found an arm, and lifted a girl to the window. A leg led him to another girl and he hoisted her out the window. A foot belonged to a screaming little boy who made it to safety. How many more? How many more? Bull heard Tex-Mex call his name.

"Bull! The fire's gettin' worse! The bus is gonna blow!"

But Bull continued his methodical task. Search. Find. Lift. Push out the window. And do it again. He began to hallucinate as he went about his robotic mission. He became obsessed with time. Not enough time remained. Not enough time to watch a morning sunrise or an evening sunset. Not enough time to sip an ice-cold brew on a hot summer day. Once he had all the time in the world to do whatever he wanted. Now, he could feel time running out. The last grains of sand emptied from his life's hourglass and he could not stop them. In his mind's eye, he watched them pour out of the narrow funnel stem into the container, where the other grains of used up time vanished into eternity.

"Goddamn it, Bull!" Tex-Mex pleaded. "Get the fuck out of there!"

Tex-Mex's frantic warning shocked him back to reality, and he redoubled his efforts. He raced now. He raced the heat, smoke, and flames that engulfed the bus. His breathing became increasingly labored, and he coughed up thick coal black soot that smothered his lungs. His huge arms felt like heavy lead bars hanging from his shoulders. Another child out the window. Still another. Feeling his way through the blackness. Was that all of them? A moan led him to a boy he pushed out to Tex-Mex. Then he gathered Kathy Winters into his arms and struggled to lift her out the window. The female bus driver followed. After lifting children, the two adults taxed his endurance to almost total exhaustion. Two more lives spared. How many more?

He climbed over the seats in a final search and found nothing. Maybe some grains of time remained after all, he thought, as he fought his way back to the window. He started to climb out, but a sudden whooshing sound and a wall of fire forced him back inside. Another try and a spike of flame like a lightning bolt drove him back again. He readied himself for what he reasoned would be his last chance to save himself, when he heard racking sobs a few feet away and he clawed his way back through the debris, determined not to leave this last one behind. He felt an arm and pulled a girl to his chest and waded back through the wreckage to the window. Bull flung the girl out and hoped Tex-Mex would be there to catch her. Then he summoned what little strength he had left and hoisted himself out of the window. Raging flames darted all around him, and he hurled himself to the street below. He landed in a heap and Tex-Mex dragged him by one arm across the road to safety just as the bus detonated in a towering fireball that sent a heat wave blasting out in all directions.

The street convulsed in turmoil. The fire department arrived and trained hoses on the bus's flaming carcass. Police cars dotted the landscape. Rescuers spread the injured out in the parking lot of the Hyatt Hotel, which faced the collision scene. A dozen or more ambulances waited for paramedics to complete their triages before transporting the injured to hospitals. Police officers, firefighters, paramedics, and citizens swarmed over the area, giving medical attention and comfort to the injured.

Bull and Tex-Mex knelt next to a fire engine with oxygen masks strapped over their faces. Except for a few minor burns and lacerations, Bull's injuries would not require emergency medical treatment. Tex-Mex remained unscathed. But both were totally spent by their efforts and for several minutes they greedily sucked oxygen to clear their lungs and heads. Tex-Mex finally broke the silence.

"Did we get 'em all out?" he wheezed.

Bull nodded, too wasted with fatigue to answer.

"Hell of a way to get rid of a hang-over," Tex-Mex said.

Bull grinned at Tex-Mex through the mask and then gave a nod of his head that turned the Texan's attention toward Captain Ernie, who made his way toward them. After conferring with several emergency personnel along the way, the irascible

Daywatch Commander planted himself in front of Bull and Tex-Mex and shook his head in feigned disgust.

"Look at you two. Uniforms all torn and dirty. Faces covered with soot and grime. Your leather gear scuffed and peeling. What kind of example are you setting for OPD? And Bull, your hair is half burned off!"

Bull reached up and felt his head and then stood and looked at his image in the fire engine's side mirror. The fire singed the left half of his crew down to his scalp, giving him a lopsided look that had a comical effect. A sudden coughing fit caused him to remove his mask and spit a large glob of phlegm to add to a growing puddle of mucus at his feet.

"You two catch a ride with an ambulance and get checked out at the hospital," Captain Ernie ordered and then chuckled. "Damn shit-disturbers! Do you have a personal vendetta against me? First that circus pursuit yesterday that had me wallowing in paperwork all day long. And now this! I'll have to spend the better part of this shift writing up decoration recommendations for your two sorry asses. Not to mention, of course, that some citizen got the whole incident on video tape, so you're gonna be national heroes and celebrities too. Well, what do you have to say about ruining my day?"

Bull thought for a moment before answering. "Captain, can I trade my decoration for having my I-A complaints wiped off my record?"

Captain Ernie's words dripped with sarcasm. "Ahh, Bull, you missed your calling. You should have been a con artist." Then he turned serious. "You two did a hell of a job. You got all the kids, the teacher, and the driver out of that flaming wreck, and the paramedics say they're all gonna be fine. A few with moderate injuries, but nothing life-threatening. And it's about time a citizen videotaped police officers doing something positive for a change. Now, we can tell our critics and detractors who vilify us for our misdeeds to kiss our collective asses! All, right, get on up to the hospital. Oh, and when you get off-duty today and make your nightly pilgrimage to the Hit 'N Run, try to resist the temptation to commit some bullshit act that will generate another I-A complaint. And even if you say you didn't do it, leave those fuckin' street lights alone! Costs the city big bucks to replace them."

Tex-Mex let a mischievous grin develop below his Pancho Villa mustache. "Captain, aren't you going to end your speech by tellin' us to go lock up some bastards?"

"Fuck you, Tex-Mex," the captain said and turned on his heel and walked away.

~~~~

Captain Ernie did not exaggerate. Their exploits turned into a media sensation, and reporters and newscasters besieged them with requests for interviews and TV appearances. The video footage depicting the rescue became a newscast staple that ran and reran continuously for days. Media moguls pushed most negative law enforcement issues to the papers' back pages or neglected them altogether. Bull and Tex-Mex's smiling faces graced the covers of national magazines, and the two heroes basked in the limelight and capitalized on their newfound fame by humbly accepting as many free drinks as they could, while their celebrity status commanded the tribute. Everywhere they went their glasses never remained empty. Politicians heaped accolades upon them and they had photo-ops with the mayor of Oakland and the governor of California. The public treated them like rock stars and women gravitated toward them as if they were irresistible sex symbols. Tex-Mex's list of ex's grew exponentially. Women fawned over Bull like a giant, cuddly Teddy Bear. They had their vaunted fifteen minutes and then some and a magical climate prevailed.

9

A day later back in the bastion of Internal Affairs, however, another kind of magical climate prevailed. Lieutenant Scott sat in his office and attempted to sum up the Brewster investigation so that he could see the *big picture*. To achieve this intense magnification of Brewster's wrongdoings, he sought to reduce complex issues to their *lowest common denominator*. He didn't know what that phrase meant, but he heard other people refer to it frequently, and he repeated it as often as possible whenever it seemed appropriate. He noticed, however, that when he used the term, some people gave him strange, perplexed looks and seemed baffled at what he attempted to say. Of course, Scott smugly interpreted their puzzled response as verification that they were unable to comprehend his superior intellect.

So, he ruminated, what comprised the lowest common denominator of the Brewster big picture? He thought long and he thought hard, but the Brewster big picture remained blank. Lieutenant Scott *willed* the Brewster big picture to reveal itself in all its Cinemascope grandeur, but his mind rebelled and stubbornly resisted. He heard of writer's block before, but he had thinker's block and it unnerved him. Panic set in as he tried to retrace his line of thought. What the hell had he been thinking about before he lost himself in the big picture and lowest common denominator? Ah, yes, it finally came to him! The Brewster investigation!

Now, he was back on track. But he had to reluctantly admit one glaring fault of his own. He envied Officer Brewster's sudden rise to fame. In fact, he was literally St. Patrick's Day green with envy. He just could not understand all the fuss over the incident. OK, he conceded, so OPD's answer to a Marvel Comics super hero rescued a bunch of kids from certain death. So what? Anyone could do *that*. It didn't take any brains to jump into a burning bus. Hell, if Brewster had any brains, he wouldn't have jumped into that bus in the first place. He still remained a thorn in OPD's side because of his flagrant disregard for the department's rules and regulations. Plus, he had no ambition. Twenty-two years and still a lowly police officer? What kind of career was that? Frankly, Lieutenant Scott concluded, Brewster belonged in the loser's hall of fame.

In Scott's view, the command staff embodied OPD's elite in its law enforcement mission. Street cops just caught crooks, solved everyday citizen problems, and responded to emergencies. The command staff, on the other hand, devised new, *cutting edge* organizational models to make the department more *professional*—God, he loved those terms! Command served as the philosophical backbone of the department. In fact, street cops merely acted as workers who carried out management directives. Scott often thought of street cops as just a necessary evil. If the command staff could only find a way to take them out of the loop, then the department would run *so* much smoother. There would be no more personnel complaints, no nagging problems with officer involved shootings, no union strife. He had so many *progressive*—another great term—ideas that he often went off on tangents that took him away from his primary job. Therefore, he reluctantly tore himself away from his real passion of theorizing theoretical theories and returned to the Brewster problem.

Lieutenant Scott held the "smoking gun" that he hoped would lead to Brewster's demise: the preliminary investigation of an officer involved off-duty firearms discharge that occurred outside the Hit 'N Run bar. He had reliable information that Brewster and his constant sidekick, Tex-Mex Garcia, were at the bar during the time the shooting took place. At last! A felony! He now had the golden opportunity to rid OPD of two quasi-criminals in one fell swoop!

But Scott had one minor problem. Lack of evidence. And the big picture once again began to fade. There were no witnesses and no shell casings left at the shooting scene. *Ergo*, he inductively reasoned and deductively surmised, that meant the shooters used revolvers! *And*, he had spies who informed him that both Brewster and Garcia favored revolvers as off-duty weapons. If he was shrewd enough, Lieutenant Scott schemed, he could twist and distort the I-A findings so that they would establish adequate probable cause to name Brewster and Garcia as the shooters. He only needed to manipulate the "facts," he thought slyly. A little bit of *creative investigation* would go a long way to render them culpable. And *voila!* The lowest common denominator and the big picture at last came into clear focus.

~ ~ ~ ~

Police Chief Gerald Carter sat at his desk in his office on the eighth floor. He was fifty-five years old, with a florid facial complexion and gray, thinning hair. He had the distinction of having the longest tenure as Chief of Police of any large metropolitan department in California. Given Oakland's renowned volatile political climate, his fifteen years at the helm constituted a remarkable achievement. Though known as a strict disciplinarian, street cops also knew him as a fair Chief who had their *backs* when the shit went down.

He studied Captain Ernie Stanton's Medal of Valor recommendations for Officers Bull Brewster and Tex-Mex Garcia. He watched the citizen's video tape of the rescue several times and grew more astounded at the courage both of them displayed each time he viewed it. What a pair of *cajones* it took for Bull to climb into that flaming wreckage! He knew Bull for over twenty years. He even worked the same district with him as a newly promoted sergeant, when Bull was a raw rookie just out of the academy. He smiled at some of the capers Bull pulled off over the years. Did he deserve the punishments he received? Without a doubt. But he also did some mighty fine police work along the way. Of course he would approve the Medal of Valor for both of them. That was a given.

His real dilemma stemmed from all the I-A complaints Bull piled up along with his commendations. He couldn't just ignore these complaints. That would send the wrong message to the rank and file that all they had to do was perform some heroic act and he would forgive their transgressions. On the other hand, what would happen if he recommended discipline and the media got hold of it? The City Fathers would cry bloody murder, and the TV channels and newspapers would have a field day! But more to the point, what was the *right* course of action?

Sometimes he thought it more important to make a difficult decision based on principle rather than the strict letter of the violation. He was not so naïve to assume that *every* officer followed each and every departmental order. Like accepting a free cup of coffee, for instance. OPD policy strictly forbade accepting any gratuity, no matter how small. But he knew it went on every day, and as long as officers handled it discretely and it did not escalate to accepting outrageous freebies, he turned a blind eye to the transgression and expected his command staff to do the same.

Unfortunately, one command officer did not adhere to this principle, and Chief Carter regarded him as OPD's Achilles' heel and a colossal pain in the ass. Just like the overzealous Inspector Javert in Dickens' novel, *Les Miserables,* Lieutenant Carey Scott was an evangelical fanatic determined to hound out of OPD anyone who disobeyed *any* rule or regulation. The man did not have one iota of common sense. And now he submitted this investigation implicating Bull and Tex-Mex in an off-duty shooting. Chief Carter read Scott's report three times and *still* could not understand what the idiot said. It read like a science fiction short story, filled with obfuscations, euphemisms, distortions, contradictions, exaggerations, double entendres, outrageous embellishments, and any other term that could be construed as the art of literary deception. Chief Carter thought it a masterpiece of innuendo, and the most blatant misrepresentation of facts he ever encountered.

How could he have ever promoted such an incompetent? The fact that Scott placed number one on the lieutenant's written exam was probably the deciding factor. The lucky bastard undoubtedly guessed right on every multiple choice test question and then somehow fooled the oral board into believing that he had leadership and managerial abilities. Hell, he couldn't lead a Cub Scout troop or manage a paper route! But what really bothered Chief Carter was his self-perceived pride in being able to identify a person's character flaws. Well, he obviously missed the proverbial boat with this half-wit. He finally reached the decision to reassign Lieutenant Imbecile at the very first opportunity, and now that opportunity arrived.

Chief Carter picked up his phone. "Lieutenant Scott, see me in my office, please."

Lieutenant Scott marched to the chief's office with a self-satisfied smirk on his face. He surmised that the chief read his Pulitzer Prize-winning report on the Brewster case and he visualized the *axe* falling on the chopping block to decapitate Brewster's head. He glowed with pride at his skill in writing reports, using four and five syllable words he culled from his thesaurus, when a one syllable word would have been more appropriate. He didn't know how to use these big words to develop a cogent account of a police incident, but he thought that anyone reading his reports would marvel at the big words and think he was academically gifted. In fact, his penchant for bombastic language made his writing seem as though an eight year old child plucked words at random from a dictionary and then scribbled them onto a page to form incoherent sentences. Scott's confidence soared as he knocked on the chief's door.

"Come in and have a seat, Lieutenant."

Scott readied himself for the coming accolades.

Chief Carter studied the lieutenant's report. "I've gone over this investigation and concluded it is a very thorough piece of work."

Scott's lips formed a slight smile. "Thank you, sir."

"I'm particularly impressed with your tautological presentation."

Scott's slight smile turned to a slight frown. Tautological? Scott scrolled through his vocabulary, but he came up empty. He would have to look that word up later. Lots of syllables. Be great for his next report.

"You also tend to obfuscate your central points."

Obfuscate? Wow, another great word, Scott thought. He didn't know what that word meant either, but he beamed a broad smile to let the chief know he appreciated the praise.

Chief Carter returned the smile because he realized that this intellectually challenged cretin did not have the slightest idea that he just called him a moron. He could continue this game of Insult The IQ Disabled for the rest of the day, but then he remembered he had several appointments to keep. So, he dropped his vocabulary down a few notches to a See Dick and Jane Run level so Scott would understand him.

"Lieutenant," Chief Carter explained, "what I'm trying to tell you is that your report is a pile of shit."

The chief's words stung Lieutenant Scott like a slap in the face. He tried to compose himself, but his shock at the chief's rebuke registered in the form of a very loud fart he barely held back since he entered the office. The fart's noisy exit totally crushed his ego and rendered him unable to speak. He sat perfectly still until the pungent aroma drifted up and caused him to wrinkle his nose.

Chief Carter looked at him with disgust. He wanted this man as far away as possible. And he knew just where. Crime Analysis, or in OPD common parlance, The Land Of The Living Dead.

"Lieutenant Scott," Chief Carter delivered the *coup de grace*, "I'm transferring you to Crime Analysis, effective Monday. Before you leave I-A, however, you will resubmit this report on the firearm discharge without *any* mention of Officers Brewster and Garcia. There is absolutely no evidence to connect them to the shooting. In addition, you will also make a finding of Counseling and Training in the case where Brewster wrote his name on that asshole's jacket. And I do mean asshole! You saw that suspect's rap sheet. He has more priors than Bull has personnel complaints, for Christ's sake! And, I want the same finding made on the rude conduct complaint concerning the suicide. One more thing. Bull Brewster has *forgotten* more about being a street cop than you would ever hope to know, even if you were to live as long as Methuselah. Now, go back to your hovel of an office and do as you're told!"

Still unable to speak, the future commander of The Land Of The Living Dead shuffled like a zombie through the dissipating gas and returned to his tomb. Chief Carter grinned as he watched him go and then sprayed a copious amount of air freshener to remove the last vestige of the lieutenant's remains. Then he turned his attention to Bull and Tex-Mex. It was time for a little sit-down with them. On their turf.

~~~~

Bull and Tex-Mex were into their third beer at the Hit 'N Run later that evening, when Bull glanced toward the door and his jaw almost dropped to the floor. He gave the Texan a hard nudge to get his attention, and they both watched Chief Gerald Carter enter, buy a beer at the bar, and then start toward their table.

"Bull, Tex-Mex, mind if I join you?"

Bull started to stand and then sat back down awkwardly. "Be our guest, Chief."

Chief Carter sat down and took a swig from his bottle. "Just wanted to congratulate you two on the bus caper. Twenty-eight kids, a teacher, and the driver owe their lives to you. Hell of a job."

"Thanks, Chief," Tex-Mex mumbled. "Uh, how did you know where to find us?"

"Oh, I just took a peek at your complaint folders and noted where most of your I-A investigations begin," the chief replied with a grin.

Bull and Tex-Mex averted their eyes. Chief Carter continued smiling, but he was pleased to see that his barbed comment hooked both of them.

"Look, you two," Chief Carter said. "I don't see any sense beating around the bush, so I'll just say what I have to say and be done with it. Tex-Mex, this concerns Bull, but you keep your ears tuned in too. Bull, I rejected two I-A findings that would have resulted in you spending more than a few days on the beach. I'll be frank and admit that my reason for doing so was the bus incident. As far as I'm concerned, your I-A slate is wiped clean. But, if you get into any more shit, then the entire process will start all over again. Do I make myself clear?"

Bull nodded but remained silent.

With his mission completed, Chief Carter relaxed and dropped his Chief of Police posture. "You know, Bull, you're getting pretty ingenuous with your I-A capers. Writing your name and badge number on a citizen's jacket? That gets an A-plus for innovation."

Bull grinned and looked away, and Tex-Mex burst out laughing.

Chief Carter continued. "Of course, my all-time favorite was the baby alligator caper. That was one true Einstein Theory of Relativity genius. How many days on the beach did I give you for that one, Bull?"

"Seven," Bull laughed.

Then the Chief slashed a rapier-like question at the Texan. "And you, Tex-Mex. For years I've wanted to know if the swizzle stick story is fact or fiction. Come on, 'fess up."

Tex-Mex nodded and he, Bull, and the chief laughed so hard they were close to tears. A second beer led to a third as they dug up long buried memories, and for a brief time the chief set aside his title as commander and became one of them. For a while. But when Tex-Mex pushed away from their table to buy another round, Chief Carter wisely declined.

"That's it for me. By the way, if this evening turns into a march, have a little mercy on the citizens of Oakland and take taxis between the many watering holes you'll patronize. Traffic collisions are up over last year, so I'd appreciate you not adding to the increase."

For a few seconds the table remained silent as they watched Chief Carter walk out the door.

10

Just after Chief Carter left the Hit 'N Run, two young men in a new, dark green Toyota Camry cruised the funky streets of East Oakland, scouting the terrain for potential targets. Rondell White and his younger brother Larry had the tape player's amps maxed out, and the Camry shook with pulsating hip-hop tunes. Rondell drove and had his best *gangsta lean* going, nodding his head in rhythm to the heavy, booming beat. He took a hit from his joint and felt the weed start to take hold. His growing euphoria made him feel in sync with the world. He chilled to some sounds, toked on some killa Thia Stick, and watched the sun sink slowly over the horizon. This was Rondell's favorite time of the day, when approaching darkness signaled the beginning of night's catalytic shift to the excitement and danger he craved.

While Rondell yearned for action, Larry gripped the 9mm Smith & Wesson pistol he held in his lap. He turned the pistol over repeatedly and ran his fingers over the long, smooth barrel, caressing the hard cool steel like an animate object. After he fondled the heavy handgun for a minute or two, a noticeable bulge formed in his groin and spread rapidly. Then he took hold of the pistol, stroked its rounded, curved lines, and closed his eyes. He daydreamed for a brief time, and only when Rondell changed the cassette in the tape player did he open his eyes and take stock of his surroundings. He shifted in his seat and toyed with the pistol, pointed it out the window at pedestrians and uttered soft gunshot sounds as he took aim.

Rondell glanced at Larry and his anger flashed. "Fuck you doin', Larry?! If the PO-PO happen up on us and see you fuckin' with that gat, we gonna be in some deep shit!"

Larry fixed Rondell with a hard look. "I got my eyes on, blood. You just drive and I'll take care of the PO-PO if we get stopped."

"Nigga, stop playin'!" Rondell shouted. "The only time you think you bad is when you got a gat in your hand. Here, give me the gat. Give me the goddamn gat!"

Larry's expression turned sullen, but he handed the pistol over. Rondell snatched the pistol and slid it under the seat. He scowled at his younger brother and recalled all the times he had to wade in and help Larry when he took on something he couldn't handle. But as soon as Larry got a gat in his hand, he became a *bad-ass* nigga. Shit, he had half a mind to stop the car and give Larry a little ass-whippin' just to remind him who was in charge. Ever since they were kids Larry was always a little scary. He always *talked* about takin' care of business. But if the shit went down, it would be Rondell who would have to bail him out.

Rondell flexed his arm and chest muscles. Firm and tight, good to go. He was twenty-five, a little over six feet tall, with a slender, athletic build, medium brown complexion, hair in cornrows, with a smooth baby face. The girls called him Pretty Boy. But his youthful looks belied a mean streak that frequently erupted in uncontrolled fury. He'd been in and out of trouble since he turned thirteen, did some juvie and county time for a variety of minor, chicken-shit beefs. But now he graduated to major crimes and dragged Larry along with him. Even though he regarded Larry with undisguised contempt, he felt uneasy about involving his younger brother in heavy shit. He couldn't explain why, but he sensed that it had to do with watching out for him. He looked at Larry and saw a twin of himself. Except for being two years younger and having a short natural hair style, Larry mirrored Rondell's image.

There were times when Rondell questioned why he took this deviant road, and he had lucid visions that his criminal path would someday come to a dead end. But until that time, the maelstrom of criminal life sucked him into its vortex. He thrived on the gangster mentality. No quarter given, none asked. Violent crime hooked Rondell like dope snagged an addict. Acting out his sadistic impulses and carnal lusts gave him an insatiable rush. It let him vent his hostility and satisfy his need to inflict pain. It was like playing God, having the power to take away the one thing people valued above all else. Their lives.

Rondell turned to Larry. "You down for tonight, blood?"

"Why you trippin', Rondell?" Larry replied. "We already talked this shit over. No need to go over it again. Know what I'm sayin'?"

"Just wanted to make sure, blood. Don't want you backin' out at the last second. Know what *I'm* sayin'?"

Larry scoffed. "Nigga, please, ain't no one backin' out."

"Shit, Larry, I seen the way you acted when I popped those three white bitches. Started moanin' and shit, walkin' 'round in circles, didn't know what to do."

"Fuck you, Rondell! It's just that there was no need to do it. We could have snatched that old lady's purse away from her, no problem. Instead, you go crazy and kill 'em. What you gonna do? Kill everyone we rob?"

Anger lit up Rondell's eyes. "I *told* you the older bitch disrespected me. Like I wasn't holding a gat on her and wasn't shit. Like I was playin'! I wasn't gonna let that old bitch get away with that. So, I popped her. And I popped the other two 'cause they were witnesses and it didn't matter anyway. Fuck 'em! Fuckin' white bitches deserve to get popped for what they done to niggas for the last four hundred years. Besides, if any motherfucker gives me shit, I'm gonna lay him in his grave!"

Larry shook his head. "Well, we went from doin' a stretch of time at Pelican Bay to takin' a hot shot at Quentin if the PO-PO track us down."

Rondell's mood lightened and he laughed. "Forget it, blood. PO-PO ain't gonna get us. But I'll tell you what. I won't pop no one else unless it's necessary, if you'll stop hangin' your gat out the window playin' like you're doin' a driveby. You down with that? All right, let's go take care our business."

~~~~

Barry and Carol Rawson and their two children, eleven year old Clay and ten year old Cora, drove home from a pizza parlor dinner, following Clay's twilight Little League game. The dinner broke up at about 8:30 P.M., and the night's excitement and too many pieces of pizza had both children dozing off in the rear seat. The Rawsons pulled into the driveway of their affluent home high in the Oakland hills, but they failed to notice the dark green Camry glide to a stop with its lights out a few doors down from their residence. Clay bounded from the car first, dashing to the front door, squirming and crossing his legs.

"Dad, mom," Clay cried out. "Come on, hurry! I have to pee!"

Carol Rawson sighed. "Didn't I tell you to go before we left the pizza parlor?"

"I know, I know, but hurry!"

"Hold on, Clay," Barry said, as he shook Cora awake and helped her out of the car. "We'll be there in a sec."

While Carol fumbled in her purse for her keys, Rondell and Larry White crept up quietly behind them.

Rondell's harsh voice shattered the silence. "Brake yourselves, Brady Bunch!"

The Rawson family whirled around and saw the two men wearing ski masks and gloves, pointing pistols at them sideways in stereotypical gangster fashion.

"What. . ." Barry started to say but stopped when Rondell raised his pistol less than an inch from his face.

"Listen up, motherfuckers, and listen good," Rondell said. "Open up that door quick, bitch, or I'm gonna splatter your man's brains all over this porch."

"All right, all right," Carol replied. "I'm trying to find my keys."

While Carol frantically searched her purse, a puddle spread around Clay's shoes.

Larry laughed softly. "Hey, man, little Jose Canseco done peed his pants."

Carol finally located her key and tried to insert it into the lock, but her shaking hands would not cooperate. Cora started to cry.

"Open the door, bitch!" Rondell hissed. "Open the fuckin' door!"

When Carol at last succeeded, Rondell and Larry shoved the

family inside. Clay's tears joined Cora's and their chests heaved with racking sobs.

"All of you on the floor," Rondell ordered. "Face down."

"God, oh God," Carol pleaded.

As the Rawsons complied, Larry placed his pistol in his waistband and used duct tape to bind Barry's hands behind his back. Barry attempted to bargain with the two men.

"Listen, please. Go ahead and take whatever you want, but I beg you not to harm my wife or kids. I'll even show you where the safe is. . ."

Rondell placed his pistol against Barry's temple. "You ain't gonna show us nothin'. What you *are* gonna do is lie there quiet and still like a good motherfucker and don't cause us no problems. Your woman will show us where the safe is."

While Larry watched over the three bound captives, Rondell forced Carol to lead him to the safe. A few minutes later, Rondell and Carol returned with a pillow case containing money and jewelry. Rondell handed the pillow case to Larry to inspect.

"Hmmm, not bad," Larry said. "Enough to last us for awhile."

Rondell's smile showed through the mask. "We got us something else besides money and jewelry, blood. Got us some tender white pussy, too. I could go for some. How 'bout you?"

A forlorn look crossed Carol's face and she hung her head. "Oh, please, please. . .I've done all you've told me to do. But please not that. Please. . ."

Rondell adopted a mocking, reassuring tone of voice. "Come on, mommy. It won't be all that bad. Bet you haven't had any black dick before. We'll show you a good fuck. Better than your peckerwood husband. So, come on and take off those clothes."

With her head still hanging limp upon her chest, Carol lost her composure and began to cry. "Oh, please. . ."

Rondell's voice hardened. "Ain't gonna tell you again. You do what we say, or we take little mommy here and do her. The choice is yours."

Carol stifled a sob and raised her head. "All, right. I'll do anything you say. Just don't touch my daughter."

As Carol removed her clothes, Larry made comments like a play-by-play announcer.

"Nice titties. Big booty for a white bitch. Pussy's a little too bushy, but I think I'll be able to find my way inside."

Rondell took a quarter from his pocket. "Let's flip to see who goes first. I call heads. Hmmm, tails it is. The pussy's yours, blood."

Larry cackled with glee, forced Carol to her hands and knees, and moved behind her. Then he unzipped his pants and the rape began. He moved her around the room in a circle, slapping her buttocks repeatedly, and the fleshy smacks competed with Carol's sobs in a din of despair. Barry turned his head away and shed tears of rage. Cora and Clay closed their eyes and whimpered helplessly. All the while, Larry kept up a torrent of verbal abuse.

"Hey, blood, this white bitch got some *good* pussy. Nice and tight. Wait 'til you get your dick in here and you'll see what I'm talkin' 'bout!"

Rondell's laughter cut through the room. "Yeah, but keep slappin' that ass, man. That's it. But harder! I like the sound of that ass bein' slapped. That's it, sting those cheeks!"

The rape and humiliation continued ad nauseam. Barry clenched his teeth and endured. His fury consumed him. His wrists burned from trying to loosen the layers of duct tape, struggling to get free. His efforts intensified until sweat soaked his clothes. Then he felt the tape give slightly, and he increased his exertion until his arms ached. Another straining movement and the tape loosened even more. He worked the tape back and forth until there was an audible snap and his hands burst free. Without thinking, Barry sprang to his feet and launched himself at the animal defiling his wife. His flailing fists found their mark on Larry's face and head, inflicting a gash to his cheek and stunning the rapist into a dazed confusion. The sudden turn of events startled Rondell, but he quickly recovered and placed the pistol against Barry's head. The ensuing gunshot put an end to his life.

The gunshot, Carol's hysterical shrieks, and the childrens' muffled screams soon brought lights blinking on throughout the neighborhood. Rondell struggled to get Larry to his feet and guided his woozy brother to the door.

"Come on, blood!" Rondell said. "We got to get the fuck out of here!"

Rondell pushed and pulled Larry outside, while Carol's shrill wails now brought neighbors to their porches and windows. Carrying the pillow case in one hand and his pistol in the other, Rondell managed to shoulder Larry into the Camry and they sped off into the night.

~ ~ ~ ~

It was call-out time again, and Mary Sanders arrived on the scene first. The crime's savagery shocked her. It became clear that the suspects stalked the Rawsons to their residence and planned the rape from the start. And race played a significant role in the suspects' MO. But they did not plan the murder. Mary concluded that the suspects' intent was far more hideous. They wanted to inflict emotional and psychological trauma that would transcend even death. Terror, fear, and survivor's guilt were their objectives. Mary imagined the children watching and listening to their mother being degraded in the worst possible way. What will those children think of black men in the future? Will the mother ever be able to overcome what happened here tonight? And the husband. Hearing the sounds of rape and racial slurs. Feeling the guilt and emasculation unless he acted. The rage and blind fury escalating to the point where the suspects' barbarism provoked him into a suicidal mania.

Mary held no illusions. She realized every race, ethnic group, and nationality had the capacity for racism. The dynamics of ethnocentrism were as alive and powerful today as they were in the past. Whites were responsible for more than their share of atrocities. Slavery. Imperialism. Segregation. Institutionalized racism. Lynchings. All played a part in an intentional policy to subjugate blacks and other minorities. But it angered and saddened Mary, when blacks did the same kind of shit as a personal vendetta for past injustices, or as a form of self-loathing, where they blamed whites for their own pathetic failures in life.

Mary stood in the hallway watching the technician gather evidence, when Duke entered the house and took a position by her side.

"Duke, we've got a bad one here."

"Yeah, I heard," Duke replied. "A couple of real vicious assholes."

"Not much to go on," Mary said. "Suspects wore ski masks, gloves, left nothing at the scene except a 9mm shell casing and the duct tape they used to bind the victims. Even the duct tape and casing are clear of prints, so that means they wore gloves whenever they handled them. There are some blood stains left by one of the suspects when the husband attacked him, so at least we have that and the semen from the rape exam."

"Any witnesses among the neighbors?"

"Lots heard the shot, screams, and saw a dark, four-door sedan drive away at high speed. Nothing else." Mary paused a few seconds. "Duke, this one bothers me. These two suspects are predatory rapists, and I'll bet they won't stop until they're caught. But I also have to own up to something. It bothers me that these two assholes are black. I know I shouldn't feel this way, but it's like I have a sense of guilt because I'm black too."

Duke gave Mary an understanding smile. "Yeah, you're right. You *shouldn't* feel that way. These suspects are more than racist rapists. They're out-and-out evil sociopaths. Evil has no color, Mary. Evil is color-blind. These two suspects just happen to be black. And I think you're absolutely right. These assholes will never stop until they're caught. Or killed."

11

Rocky Rollins relaxed at home nursing a beer while he watched the last few innings of the A's/White Sox game. The game really didn't interest him. He turned it on to pass the time until Mary arrived home. She phoned earlier and advised him that she would be home late again tonight. Another homicide. But at least this one turned out to be a mom and pop murder/ suicide that allowed Mary and Duke to close out the case. Not a *who done it* like the past few. Since this was her last night on call-out, tomorrow she would have a six week reprieve until the cycle started over again. They both looked forward to living like a normal couple for a while.

This last call-out week had been tough on Mary. Recent changes in her personality troubled Rocky. Mary's once feisty, cocky persona seemed subdued, pensive, and withdrawn. She brooded for long periods and lashed out at him for innocuous re- marks he made in jest. At first, Rocky thought she felt fatigued from the multiple call-outs that limited her sleep. But during the past few days, she made subtle comments about the homicide cases that told him they bothered her. He tried to draw out her feelings, but she told him that she would work out her mood swings on her own. Rocky only hoped that Mary would not suffer any lasting emotional scars.

The front door opened and Mary entered with a flourish. After removing her Glock .40 caliber pistol and holster from her belt, she entered the living room, where Rocky wrapped her up in his arms.

"Hmmm," Rocky murmured, "love that perfume."

"Shit," Mary huffed. "Had to practically pour it on me to drown out the smell of that mom and pop scene. They'd been dead a few days."

Rocky made exaggerated sniffing noises. "Now that you mention it, I do detect a slight whiff of Channel Death Lotion on your person. Didn't Duke have one of those smelly cigars he keeps handy for such occasions?"

"No, he was out," Mary said and wagged her head side-to-side ghetto queen style and pushed him away. "And *thanks* for the romantic comment. I'm headin' for the shower, so I'll be able to pass your sniff test."

Rocky leered at her. "Want some company?"

Mary put her pistol and holster on the coffee table, placed her hands defiantly on her shapely hips, and cocked her head to one side.

"Company, huh?" she sneered. "I know what you mean by *company*. We start out by takin' a shower and end up sharing bodily fluids."

Rocky arched his eyebrows. "Is that a bad thing?"

Mary smiled coyly and took a few seductive steps toward the bathroom. "Now, I'm not sayin' if it's good or bad. All I'm sayin' is that's how you keepin' me company in the shower will end up. So, why don't you stop the bullshit and bring your little white boy self in where you belong."

Then it was hissing jets of hot water, dense steamy fog, thick lathered soap suds, and brown and white slippery skin joined together. Lips and tongues shared their passion, and his fingertips caressed the skin of her firm buttocks and found the crevice that caused her to tremble with anticipation. His erection pressed against her abdomen, and she used the frothy soap foam to stroke it until it was rock hard. They moved to the shower stall floor with her on top and the rhythmic cadence began. Slowly at first and then steadily more urgent, driving thrusts under a cascade of water that drenched their clinging bodies. Undulating hip movements that rippled sensuously. Grinding pelvic bones that locked together for deeper penetration. And soft moans that signaled the beginning of the end. The primal dance gained momentum until the moans grew to groans and a tidal wave of orgasmic ecstasy swept over them. The frenetic motion slowed and then stopped. They collapsed against each other, breathing heavily, her lips caressing his ear.

"Now, that's what I call keepin' me *company*," Mary whispered.

~~~~

Later, Mary and Rocky cuddled in bed, when the phone rang and Rocky answered and handed Mary the receiver. "It's Duke."

Mary frowned. "Duke, this better be important, 'cause I've spent an entire week with you and I'm tired of your ass."

"Sorry, Mary, but this couldn't wait. The ballistics report came back on the Rawson 187. The same 9mm that killed him was also used in the triple in the condominium complex."

Mary's frown turned to a grimace. "Now, I *know* they won't stop until they're captured."

"There's more, Mary," Duke added. "I went through the BOLO's from other departments, and a double 187 in San Mateo a few days ago caught my attention. I contacted San Mateo PD and found that the MO for their case similar to ours. Two female whites robbed, raped, and then shot and killed in a home invasion. The weapon was a 9mm. I'll bet ballistics will confirm that our two savages did that one too."

"OK," Mary sighed. "I know you didn't call me up just to tell me this. What's up?"

"Yeah, you're right," Duke replied. "The lieutenant wants us to go to San Mateo early in the A.M. tomorrow to compare our cases with theirs. So, I thought we'd leave here about 5:00 to avoid the commute traffic. I'll buy breakfast. Sound OK to you?"

"Yeah, yeah, see you at 5:00," Mary grumbled. "But hell, it's not like I have a choice, right?"

Duke laughed. "See you at 5:00, Mary."

Mary hung up and turned to Rocky. "Looks like our beloved sociopaths are responsible for two more murders in San Mateo. Duke and I are going there tomorrow to compare our cases."

Mary gritted her teeth. "Those two motherfuckers are really on a killing spree. Oh, what I wouldn't give to get them in my sights and blow their fuckin' balls off!"

Rocky assumed a look of sham surprise. "Well, I'm certainly glad that you're in touch with your anger."

Mary gave him a cold stare.

"Sorry, babe," he backtracked. "Just tryin' to loosen you up a bit. You know you shouldn't take this shit personally."

Mary relented and laid her head on his shoulder. "Yeah, you're right. But I've seen what those monsters have done, and it's difficult *not* to take it personally. If you could have seen that mother and her two kids after what those two niggers did. . ."

"Hey, hey, come on, babe," Rocky said. "Let it go for the rest of the night. Don't dwell on it. You know, it's still early. How 'bout goin' out for Chinese at the Maple Garden? We can celebrate my transfer to the narcotics squad."

Mary mulled over the suggestion. "No, not tonight, Rocky. I just want to lay here with you."

Rocky placed his hands apart mimicking the scales of justice. "Let's see, Kung Pao Chicken or holding you. Mongolian Beef or holding you. I don't know. . ."

Mary smiled. "You incorrigible brat!" Then she gave him a coquettish look that promised something more. "Besides, maybe you can keep me *company* again."

"Hmmm," Rocky replied. "You know, I wasn't really hungry for Chinese after all."

12

The last week in August heralded Officer Becky Farmer's first day on Day Watch after transferring from swing shift, and she felt the typical discomfort of being a relative stranger among a group of veterans who knew each other for years. She received a few curious stares when she entered the line-up room, and she saw one male officer mouth the words, "who's she?" to another officer, who shook his head and shrugged his shoulders. But as a four year vet, she knew the seating protocol and steered clear of the rear rows where the "old salts" traditionally sat. Instead, she veered to the front "rookie rows," took a seat, and the "salts" nodded their approval. Her first day's status gained a few points.

At thirty-three, Becky would not be considered *pretty* in conventional terms, but most people found her attractive, with long brown hair she pulled back into a bun while working. Her most appealing attributes were a warm, friendly smile that she flashed readily and often, and her bright blue eyes that immediately captured people's attention. Her principal problem, on the other hand, stemmed from her weight. While not obese, people who wanted to speak kindly of her remarked that she had a *full* figure. Over the years, she experimented with diets of all types with limited success. The thirty or so pounds she shed always seemed to find their way back, until she grew weary of the battle of the bulge and resigned herself to her size fourteen.

"Morning," Captain Ernie announced from the podium. "Today is Monday, August 30th, and I'll be the Watch Commander. Before I continue, I'd like to welcome Officer Becky Farmer to the watch. She transferred over from District Two Third Watch. Glad to have you aboard, Becky. You'll be doubled up with Officer Brewster for the first few days so he can show you around the district."

A number of obligatory groans, cat-calls, and whistles greeted the captain choosing Bull as Becky's guide, and Tex-Mex spoke up and summarized Day Watch's feigned antipathy for the captain's lack of critical judgment.

"Captain Ernie! How could you do that to this poor, innocent child? Bull will corrupt her so thoroughly that she'll think she's had a tour of Sodom and Gomorrah instead of our beloved District Five."

Laughter cascaded over the line-up room, and another would-be prophet carried the Biblical theme even further. "Lo though I walk with Bull Brewster through District Five's valley of death, I shall fear no evil. . ."

Bull bristled and defended himself. "What am I, the Rodney Dangerfield of OPD? I get no respect!"

A wag with R&B aspirations sang a falsetto version of Aretha Franklin's golden oldie. "R-e-s-p-e-c-t, that's what it means to me. . ."

Throughout the uprising, Captain Ernie smiled and shook his head. Then he raised his hands to restore order. "All right, all right, let's settle down. Bull, why is it that whenever I give you an assignment other than catching crooks, your peers go after you like the Sioux did after General George Armstrong Custer at the Battle of The Little big Horn?"

More howls of laughter erupted.

Bull haughtily ignored his detractors and turned to Becky Farmer with his right hand raised as if taking a vow before testifying in court. "Officer Farmer, I will provide you with all the professional assistance at my disposal. You will have to pardon and forgive these ruffians, for they know not what they do. Please accept my humble apology for the common riffraff the City of Oakland has been forced to hire as police officers in these troubled times."

Becky rolled her eyes and shook her head, while Captain Ernie and the others convulsed in laughter at Bull's attempt to rise above his usual street talk and speak proper English. Once the tumult subsided, Captain Ernie went on with line-up and then dismissed them with his copyright remark to "lock up the bastards!"

Bull drove their black and white as they wound their way through the morning commute traffic. "So, what'd you do before joining OPD?"

"I taught high school English at Oakland Tech," Becky replied.

"High school teacher!" Bull said and let out a long, slow whistle. "At Oakland Tech? I *know* that was a tough job. When I go into one of the high schools, it's like I'm running a gauntlet of abuse. The kids start chanting, 'Fuck the police! Fuck the police!' And I don't mean a few kids. The majority of them do it. I try to stay away from the schools as much as I can."

"Yeah, I know," Becky agreed. "I've witnessed that kind of disrespect more times than I care to count."

"How come you quit teachin'?" Bull asked.

"Oh, I started feeling more like a guard than a teacher. Most of the kids were OK, but there were some who made teaching *very* difficult. So, I started looking around for another line of work. I got to know Mary Sanders, when she was out here working patrol, and she suggested I consider OPD."

Bull let out a laugh. "So, you have Mary 'Don't Take No Shit' Sanders to blame for gettin' you in this mess, huh? Couple of more years and you'll be burned out here and want to go back to teaching."

Becky studied Bull for a few seconds. "You know, Bull, I've heard a lot about you during my brief four years at OPD. Even when I was in the academy, all of us recruits heard the many, crazy Bull Brewster stories. You're damn near a living legend. But the *one* thing I never heard was that you don't like police work. Oh, you, Tex-Mex, and others put on cynical airs and bad-mouth policing, but deep down you cherish every aspect about being a cop. From putting on your uniform in the morning, to chasing car thieves and dope dealers through backyards, to going to the Hit 'N Run after work and drinking a shitload of beer and enjoying the camaraderie and bonding that goes on among police officers. You love all of it. I see right through you, Bull. You're an easy read."

Bull glanced over and noted the suggestion of a smile on Becky's lips. He didn't offer up a retort. There was no need. Because she was right. She had him pegged and dead to rights. Captain Ernie assigned *him* to show her around the district, point out the hot spots and landmarks, and in the first ten minutes, she had *him* analyzed and ready for therapy. He liked her immediately.

Becky decided to salvage what was left of Bull's ego and served the ball to his side of the court. "Well, what's first on the agenda?"

"What else?" Bull replied. "Coffee for two at . . ."

But the radio dispatcher had other ideas.

"2A31, 2A31, respond to 269 Isleton on an unknown disturbance. An elderly man asked for OPD, said he had a problem, and then hung up. No answer on the call-back. Your incident number is 1021."

"2A31, copy the call," Becky answered.

Bull jogged his memory. "That's old man Beckman's house. He's lived in jive five for forever. Wonder what's goin' on there?"

When Becky and Bull arrived at the Isleton address, seventy-two year old Henry Beckman stood in his front yard with a perplexed look on his weathered brown face. He turned as if to go back inside his residence, but then he stopped abruptly and faced back toward the street. When the police cruiser coasted to a stop, his smile spread when he saw that Bull was one of the two officers.

"Hey, Mr. Beckman," Bull greeted him. "What's goin' on?"

Mr. Beckman's smile remained, but he still seemed confused. "I don't rightly know how to 'splain it to you, Officer Bull."

"Well, you just take it slow and easy," Bull said. "Oh, and this is Officer Farmer. This is her first day workin' out here in East Oakland."

Mr. Beckman nodded affably to Becky and then went on with what he had to say. "Couple of months ago this here young lady, calls herself Lil' Bit, told me that she was homeless and needed a place to stay."

"Hu-huh," Bull grunted in response.

"So, I decided to help her out and let her stay with me 'cause I stays here by myself and gots plenty of room. Anyway, everything was goin' OK for a while. You knows how things go between mens and womens, and pretty soon we was havin' relations in bed and all."

Mr. Beckman stopped for a moment and averted his eyes, when he remembered Becky's presence, but then he picked up where he left off.

"Like I said, things were goin' OK, but then this mornin' she gits up and goes to the bathroom and locks the door. This was more than an hour ago. After a while, I hears her moanin' and carryin' on. Well, the moans got louder and louder, and I got worrieder and worrieder, until I decides to call the po-lice. I figured she got hold of some of that dope, so I decided to wait out here until y'all came."

"All right, Mr. Beckman," Bull said. "We'll go check on her and see what we can do. Do you know if she has any weapons in the bathroom?"

"Naw, sir, Officer Bull. I didn't see her with nothin' when she went in there."

Mr. Beckman led Becky and Bull inside and pointed to the closed bathroom door. Becky and Bull heard a moan. Bull put his ear to the door heard another moan, but louder this time. Sounds of splashing water followed, and Bull turned the doorknob and found it locked. Bull knocked on the door.

"Lil' Bit? This is Officer Brewster of the Oakland Police Department. Mr. Beckman asked us to check on you. Are you all right?"

A faint voice answered. "I'm takin' a bath, Officer. Be out in a minute."

Bull banged his fist on the door. "Lil' Bit, we don't have time for any shuckin' or jivin'. Understand? Now, you either open this door right now, or we're gonna bust it down!"

More moans and water splashing sounds followed, and then the door burst open and a slender, naked black woman lurched past Becky and Bull, stumbled into the adjacent bedroom, and flung herself on the bed face down. Bull and Becky traded puzzled looks as they tried to make sense of the situation. Becky moved to the woman's side and checked her for signs of trauma or drug use. Then a dark stain spread from the woman's groin to the white sheet underneath her. Bull went into the bathroom and saw streaks of blood lining the bathtub's rim. Becky covered the woman with a sheet and joined Bull at the bathroom doorway.

"Look at the blood trail, Bull," Becky said and pointed to the numerous drops leading from the toilet to the tub.

Bull's face reflected his bafflement. "Abortion?"

Becky moved inside the bathroom and lifted the toilet lid with her short baton. The water inside the bowl was dark crimson and blood splatters covered the nearby vanity and sink. Then she saw bloody scissors on the vanity next to the toilet and finally replied. "I hope so, Bull." Becky used her baton to sift through the murky toilet water. Part of an umbilical cord surfaced.

"Jesus, Becky," Bull said. "You don't think. . ."

Becky didn't answer at first. "Better request an ambulance, Bull."

Bull broadcast into his transceiver. "2A31, start us an ambulance and the fire department code three."

Becky and Bull stared down at the toilet.

"She flushed the baby down the toilet?" Bull whispered.

Becky's answer betrayed her denial. "I don't know. . .I don't know if it's possible. The hole is so small. But if the baby was premature. . ."

Then both of them heard a barely audible whimper. From close by. And then again but cut off in mid-cry. Coming from the clothes hamper. The whimpers stopped. Bull opened the hamper's lid and lifted out a layer of dirty clothes. And there he lay. Covered with afterbirth and part of the umbilical cord still attached. The baby did not move and showed no sign of breathing. Bull picked up the infant and started performing CPR as he moved to the front room and laid the baby on the couch.

Becky broadcast on her transceiver. "2A31, 2A31, we need an ETA on the ambulance and the fire department!"

Bull used two fingers to depress the infant's tiny chest and then covered the nose and mouth with his own mouth and gave two puffs of air. He repeated the procedure. Fifteen chest compressions and two puffs of air. No response. Again. And again. There was a slight cough and the baby regurgitated into Bull's mouth. He turned and spit out the debris, saw the infant's chest expand on its own, and the cries of life began. Above the baby's wails, Bull heard Mr. Beckman chant the same refrain over and over.

"Good God Almighty, good God Almighty. . ."

They heard sounds of rapid footsteps approaching on the walkway outside and then the front screen door opened and slammed shut. Janie the paramedic moved to Bull's side and gave him a gentle nudge to move him out of the way.

"Hey, Bull," Janie said. "We'll take over now. Go get cleaned up. Your face is a mess."

Bull stood and backed away to allow Janie and her partner room to work. Becky handed him a towel to wipe his face. Then a second ambulance crew and fire department personnel overran the small house. Janie and her partner had the infant breathing fine by the time the ambulance transported him to Children's Hospital for further evaluation. A second ambulance took the mother to another hospital for observation.

Sergeant Stout arrived on the scene and approached Bull and Becky, smiling and shaking his head. "Are you the guardian angel of all Oakland's kids, Bull? Another commendation? See me in my office a half hour before the shift is over, so you two can look over the commendation paperwork. OK?"

After Sergeant Stout drove off, only Mr. Beckman, Becky and Bull remained at the house.

"Mr. Beckman," Bull said, "you mean to tell me that for the last two months you didn't know that Lil' Bit was pregnant?"

Mr. Beckman gave Bull a sheepish smile and lowered his eyes. "Well, Officer Bull, I done had my 'spicions. I ain't gonna lie. 'Specially when she wouldn't let me see her in the light naked and all. She made me turn off the light when she came to bed, said she was 'barassed. When we had relations, I noticed she had a big belly, but I just thought she was a healthy young woman and didn't ask her 'bout it."

Bull grinned. "So, are you and Lil' Bit finished?"

Mr. Beckman's grin matched Bull's. "Yes, sir, Officer Bull. I'll get me an older woman next time. They more reliable."

Bull put his patrol vehicle in gear. "You take care, Mr. Beckman."

They were silent for a while as Bull merged into traffic. "Well, how's that for your first assignment in the district?"

Becky deflected the question with one of her own. "First the bus caper and now this. What are you going to do with all your commendations, Bull?"

"I'm just trying to balance things out, Becky. For every I-A complaint I get, I'll expunge my record with a good deed. I figure the process will work in reverse, and the department will have to give me back all the pay they've taken from me for my suspensions over the years. Hell, I might even be able to pay my bar tab at the Hit 'N Run!"

"How many days on the beach have you had, Bull?"

"I'd need a calculator to add 'em all up." Bull glanced at Becky out of the corner of his eye and decided to let it all hang out. "You like Mexican food?"

Becky laughed. "Look at me, Bull. It's obvious I've never seen a type of food I didn't like."

Bull gave her a raised eyebrow look. "Well?"

Becky cocked her head to one side. "You asking me out?"

"Well," Bull mused, "if your answer is no, then no, I'm not askin' you out 'cause I hate to be rejected. But if your answer is yes, then hell yes I'm askin' you out!"

"Where we going?"

"Where else?" Bull said. "Cha Cha Cha. Home of the most potent margaritas in Oakland. And the food ain't bad either. So. Is it yes?"

"Of course it's yes," Becky replied. "But, there's just one thing."

Bull's eyes narrowed. "What?"

"If I have more than two of those potent margaritas you bragged about, you may have to guard your chastity more than a fifteen year old boy in a house of ill repute."

"Ah, promises, promises," Bull scoffed. "This Friday night sound good?"

"As good as it gets," Becky answered.

Bull grinned as he made the turn into the Children's Hospital driveway. It would take about half an hour to fill out the paperwork for the protective custody hold on the baby and finish the report, and then they would meet Tex-Mex for their meal break at the Days Inn Coffee Shop.

13

Tex-Mex waited at the Days Inn Coffee Shop for Becky and Bull. He staked out their favorite booth and ruminated over his increasingly complicated love life. He finally succumbed to temptation and let Eve Lawson have her way with him. Ever since that night at the Hit 'N Run, when she played digital gymnastics with his Johnson, his Rock of Gibraltar will power began to crumble. He tried to hold out against her feminine charms, but he at last capitulated to the weaknesses of the flesh. Like the Garden of Eden fable where Eve tempted Adam with an apple, the latter-day Eve seduced the Texan with a much more pungent piece of fruit, commonly known as *poon-tang*. And like his Biblical brother before him, Tex-Mex could not resist temptation. Not that it was all bad Tex-Mex readily admitted. In fact, romping with that blond, buxom babe became so enjoyable that he added her to his pussy reservoir in the unlikely event of a poon-tang drought.

Yet Tex-Mex bemoaned his enduring dilemma. To keep his many love options open, he had to juggle multiple romances at the same time. For Tex-Mex womanizing evolved into a way of life, his *raison d'etre*. He functioned like a honeybee going from pussy to pussy, dipping his genital proboscis to spread his love potion among as many of the female gender as possible. He was born to this calling and accepted it without reservation. And being a police officer enhanced his opportunities for sexual liaisons. Tex-Mex recognized that the uniform, badge, gun, baton, handcuffs and other police tools of the trade served as sexual stimuli to some women. Rock stars had groupies. Professional athletes had their camp followers. And police officers offered a stable of studs available to women whose sexual proclivities leaned toward *rough trade*.

These sexual fantasies even had some Freudian implications inherent in them. Although the Texan could not articulate these psychological theories, he translated them into common sense, pragmatic terms: whatever worked. In essence, Tex-Mex operated under the guise that *anything* that helped him get within striking range of his intended target he adopted as a welcome weapon in his seduction arsenal.

The Texan also knew that virtually every citizen gave police officers *the look*. People gave them *the look* for a variety of reasons: fear, admiration, distrust of authority, wannabe envy, hatred bred from prior negative contacts, and DARE IT BE SAID, females attracted to the power, danger, and charisma police officers represented. Books, movies, and TV fostered this image, and Tex-Mex and other officers exploited it whenever they crossed paths with little hotties who wanted to step over the line and test the macho mystique.

At times, however, the women Tex-Mex bedded pushed the exploration envelope just a wee bit too far to satisfy their carnal lusts. One freaky deviant wanted him to wear his gun belt and hat, handcuff her hands and ankles to the bedposts, use his baton as a dildo, and then insert the barrel of his unloaded pistol into her vagina and dry fire while she writhed in masochistic ecstasy. But the Texan balked at such kinky demands. Like the meat and potato, beer drinking man, who is the antithesis to gourmet food and wine snobs everywhere, Tex-Mex remained true to the pussy-lickin' and pussy-fuckin' tried and true Old School tradition. Lickin' and fuckin' were where his talents lay, and any woman wanting a reincarnation of Marquis de Sade would be better served looking elsewhere.

Another problem Tex-Mex experienced dealt with chance encounters with his multitude of ex's, who prowled the streets searching for the man who swore his everlasting fidelity to them and then vanished like a fart in the wind. Always on the alert, he constantly glanced over his shoulder to spot trouble and escape before some prior paramour pounced on him, forcing the Texan to concoct some wild tale to explain his disappearance. The ex's developed into a telemarketing nightmare, constantly phoning OPD to leave messages to their wayward Lothario. The Jilted Ones even called in fake requests for police services, asking for OPD's answer to Valentino by name to respond to their life and death crises. OPD dispatchers learned to screen and evaluate calls to determine if they were actually legitimate or a ruse to lure Tex-Mex to rendezvous with women whose abiding motto was Hell Hath No Fury Like A Woman Scorned. The ex's even infiltrated public venues and coffee shops, in particular, were prime ambush sites. An aspiring assassin merely scouted the territory until she found the Texan's distinctly numbered car parked in the restaurant's lot and then moved in for the kill.

~~~~

After leaving Children's Hospital, Becky and Bull joined Tex-Mex at the Days Inn to discuss the Texan's latest career move. Bull and Tex-Mex served together in District Five for so many years that citizens regarded them as fixtures in the community like any other notable landmark. The Texan's decision to terminate their partnership distressed Bull.

"So, you're really gonna do it, huh?" Bull asked.

"Yeah," Tex-Mex replied. "If they grant my transfer request. I'm tired of patrol. All the bullshit family beefs and never-ending reports are startin' to get to me. Narcotics should be a refreshing change. Rocky Rollins just transferred there from I-A. Maybe I'll get him as my supervisor. Besides, I need to disappear and become invisible for a while."

Bull grinned. "A-ha! *Now,* the truth comes out. I told you all your pussy foraging would come back to haunt you someday."

Tex-Mex shrugged. "Comes with the territory."

"Are your conquests hounding you, Tex-Mex?" Becky asked facetiously.

Tex-Mex shot Becky a dismissive look and ignored her comment. Bull was about to take a sip of coffee, when his eyes widened and focused on the front door. Tex-Mex saw Bull's sudden change of expression and whirled around to assess this looming threat.

"Isn't that Juanita, your ex. . ." Bull said.

The aforesaid Juanita's lips contorted into a vengeful smile, as she marched her voluptuous anatomy resolutely toward their booth. Her spiked high heels made rapid clickity-clack sounds like a machine-gun on the terra cotta floor. Tex-Mex at first cringed like a cornered cur, but then he went into survival mode and started to slide across the seat for a hasty departure. But his intrepid adversary traversed the distance to their table in record time and anchored herself firmly in front of the Texan to block his escape. Becky monitored this confrontation with the savvy of a battle-scarred veteran of many skirmishes between the sexes. She sized up Juanita, saw the glint in her eyes, and knew Tex-Mex had his hands full.

The wary Texan started his doomed defense with a lame line. "Hey, Juanita, how's it goin'? Long time, no see. Want to join us?"

When Tex-Mex started to rise, Juanita stopped him with a hand on his shoulder and pushed him back down. "Long time, huh?" she snapped back. "How about three months long time!"

Bull lowered his head and took inordinate interest in studying his coffee cup. This mutual give and take of words fascinated Becky and she eagerly waited for Tex-Mex's return volley. People in nearby booths cast curious glances in their direction.

"Well, I. . ." Tex-Mex stammered.

"*Pinche cabron!*" Juanita spit back. Then her voice took on a mocking, lyrical tone that recited the history of their short, troubled relationship. "'*Oh, baby, you're the only woman in my life.*' Deny you said that! Go ahead, liar! '*Someday we'll get married.*' Bull shitter!"

Bull tried to think of a way out of this mess, when he turned toward the front door and a look of even greater shock replaced the previous one.

"Jesus, Tex-Mex, *another* ex!" Bull croaked.

Tex-Mex heeded Bull's warning, jerked his head toward the door, and saw yet another nemesis stomping her way to their table. This second ex was Carmen, a dark hued, thirty-five year old Costa Rican lovely. When she came to a dramatic halt with her arms crossed over her bulging bosom, Carmen's smoldering gaze rested first on Tex-Mex and then shifted to Juanita, whose fiery demeanor matched her own. Carmen looked up and down at Juanita, Juanita's defiant stare returned the challenge, and the Texan's adrenaline mechanism kicked into high gear. Just when Tex-Mex was about to give new meaning to Sun-Tzu's theory of *tactical retreat*, Carmen cut through the uneasy truce by asking the Texan a very succinct question.

"Who the fuck is this bitch?" Carmen said and nodded at Juanita.

Juanita laced her retort with equal venom. "Who the fuck are you calling a bitch? You *pinche mayate!*"

Now, Bull rose from his seat and attempted to adjudicate the escalating conflict just as he did thousands of times in the past on the street. Becky remained seated, awed by this age old tale of the eternal triangle and love gone awry. And this docu-drama had a rapt audience, for every pair of eyes in the restaurant turned in their direction for this latest episode of "Cops and Their *Femme Fatales.*"

"*Mayate!*" Carmen screamed and advanced on Juanita. "I'll show you who the *mayate* is, you *pinche puta!*"

Tex-Mex tried to calm the enraged vixen. "Carmen, take it easy."

"Carmen!" Juanita shrieked back. "So, this is the bitch who wanted you to handcuff her to the bedpost, use your club like a dildo, and shove your gun up her cunt!"

"What!" Carmen's shrill soprano split the air like an atom being halved. "You told *her* about *that?*"

And the fight was on.

Tex-Mex became the first casualty, when Carmen threw Juanita against the table, knocking the Texan's coffee cup into his lap and scalding what could be construed as the *trophy* the two women battled over.

"Oooowww!" Tex-Mex's emasculated howl bounced off the walls, causing *every* male customer in the café to clutch his groin in instinctual empathy.

Becky roused herself from being a spectator and joined Bull trying to restore order. Carmen and Juanita hurled salt and pepper shakers and sugar containers at each other like grenades, and the sound of shattering glass joined the women's vile curses to transform the coffee shop into a chaotic bedlam. One male customer's Denver Omelette became an avant-garde fashion statement on the front of his three piece suit. An elderly woman in the restroom heard the wild melee, assumed a terrorist attack was in progress, and shuffled out of the ladies room from her interrupted toilet duty with her bright pink panties clinging to her ankles. A clergyman's wraparound white collar took a direct hit from the contents of a broken ketchup bottle, giving him the appearance of a chaplain wounded in battle. And all the non-combatant customers, cooks, and servers streamed out of the restaurant, running amok trying to escape the war zone.

When the Days Inn manager heard the uproar from his office, he cautiously poked his head into the coffee shop and witnessed the five combatants ruthlessly destroying it. Two police officers fought two shrieking, hissing wild women, while a third officer lay curled into a fetal position in a booth, using his hands to cover and protect what remained of his manhood. The manager backed out of the doorway and dialed 911. But the dispatcher insisted on asking a prepared list of bureaucratic questions which the manager thought totally irrelevant. After attempting several times to interrupt the dispatcher's rote spiel, he became so frustrated that he cracked open the coffee shop door, held the phone receiver inside, and let the dispatcher hear the calamity for herself. Bull's booming base voice came through loud and clear.

"You're under arrest, Juanita! Stop digging your nails into my throat!"

East Oakland erupted in a wail of sirens as the dispatcher broadcast the one call that sent police officers rocketing at warp speed through city streets with total disregard for all traffic laws. *940B Officers Need Help!* From far and wide the howling black and whites converged on the Days Inn intent on rescuing their brother and sister officers. But then Tex-Mex inadvertently keyed his portable radio transmitter, and the resulting broadcast caused responding officers to increase their speed beyond what even a raving maniac would drive.

"Drop the knife, Carmen!" Tex-Mex shouted. "Drop the goddamn knife!"

Tex-Mex's latest significant other, Officer Eve Lawson, responded along with the legion of other saviors hell-bent on exceeding Bonneville Flats land speed records to effect the rescue. She heard the desperation in the Texan's voice and vowed to smite whoever threatened his well-being. Eve was the first officer to arrive on the scene, and she flung open the door and charged inside. Here she stopped for a few seconds to decipher what the hell was going on. Bull, Becky, and Tex-Mex grappled with two women, who alternated between attacking each other and taking their vengeance out on the officers, who tried to stop their clawing, scratching, kicking, punching, hair pulling, and biting. Eve heard shouts, cries of pain, and curses in Spanish. Then Bull glanced toward where she stood.

"Tex-Mex!" Bull roared and pointed. "It's a future ex!"

Tex-Mex swiveled his head in Eve's direction and instantly abandoned all hope of survival. He found himself caught in the crosshairs of cupid's deadly crossbow and surrendered to absolute despair.

Eve felt a sixth sense moment of total clarity when the Texan revealed the *truth* written indelibly on his face, and she laser-beamed a cruel smile that burned its way to the center of his two-timing heart. Eve researched her romance novel, soap opera conventional wisdom and did the math. These were not just two anonymous women who wandered into the coffee shop and started a fight. No, these two ho's were members of his hoochymama faithful, which meant that the Texan's claims of complete fidelity to her deserved considerable more scrutiny. Eve replaced her prior concern for Tex-Mex's safety with the need to show him that she was not a fool. Her malevolent smile intensified and she launched herself into the fray. Quite by *accident*, she later claimed, her first shot of pepper spray caught Tex-Mex dead between the eyes.

"Ahhhhh!" Tex-Mex screamed in agony only a few decibels lower than his earlier howl, when the steaming hot coffee scalded his dick and balls.

Unfortunately, as any police officer will attest, when they use pepper spray it has a nasty habit of affecting not only its intended target, but also anyone else in close proximity. Soon, all the combatants wheezed, coughed, and shed tears, while Eve stood aside with a self-satisfied smirk that spoke volumes about her state of mind. Seconds later, the rest of the OPD posse swarmed into the coffee shop to bring the raging riot to an end.

A relative calm returned to the café, but it resembled a ground zero site after a nuclear detonation. Responding officers handcuffed Juanita and Carmen and deposited them in the prisoner transport wagon for their ignominious trip to jail. Although Bull's throat gouges were minor, they made him look like he'd had a close encounter with Dracula. Tex-Mex's boiled private parts did not require medical attention, but he had to take a leave of absence from his amorous pursuits for a while. Except for being doused with pepper spray Becky remained unscathed. But she marveled at the universality of lust dramas, for even police officers did not develop immunity to the unrequited love syndromes that pervaded the rest of society. Bull summed up the escapade's ramifications to Becky on their way back to the PAB to change their torn and stained uniforms.

"There we were minding our own business and those two bitches came in and started a big mess. Mark my words. We'll end up being the bad guys in this caper. I can smell another I-A investigation and more days on the beach comin'."

14

Mary Sanders sat at her desk in the homicide office, plowing through paperwork, trying to find something, anything that would provide a lead on the serial murder cases. It was an early afternoon in late August's *dog days* and the scorching sun baked the office's outer wall, negating whatever cooling effect the air conditioning had indoors. Mary fanned herself as she sifted through the piles of reports, memos, and field contacts that engulfed her desk. She placed a request in the Daily Bulletin for FC's on any newer, dark green Toyota Camry two weeks earlier, and stacks of them accumulated with more coming in everyday. Patrol officers stepped up their proactive work, but nothing solid turned up yet.

Mary focused on two types of evidence that appeared more promising. First, they had the expended shell casings and bullets from the 9mm pistol used in the murders. Officers confiscated handguns every day, and if the killers blundered into an incident where officers seized their weapons, then a ballistics test would identify the pistol used in the murders. The second type featured biological evidence. The rape exam recovered semen, and the injuries incurred by one of the suspects during Barry Rawson's ill-fated attack on him provided blood samples taken from the car-

pet. But in either case they had to have the weapons or the suspects' biological samples before they could make a connection.
And since the suspects wore gloves during the crimes, the investigation to date did not include fingerprint analysis. Mary also
placed a description of the jewelry taken in the Rawson case in
the Daily Bulletin, requesting that officers detaining anyone who
possessed any similar jewelry items transport that person to
homicide for questioning.

Duke made the rounds of pawn shops and advised them to
contact OPD if someone pawned or attempted to pawn jewelry
taken in the murder. In addition, he circulated a Special Bulletin
stipulating that officers debrief all arrested suspects, whatever
their crimes, to determine if they had any knowledge concerning
the murders. He also encouraged officers to dangle the carrot of
possible reduction to a more lenient charge or drop the charge
altogether if the suspect provided reliable information. And of
course he asked all officers to spread the word among their
snitches.

Mary and Duke continued their painstaking efforts to develop leads in the case, but it wasn't until Mary received a phone
call from Becky Farmer that they got their first real break.

"Hey, Becky, good to hear from you," Mary said.

"Listen, Mary, I think I've got something for you on the Rawson case."

"I'm all ears," Mary answered.

"I made a walking stop on one of the working girls in the
10000 block of MacArthur, and she wore a ring you described in
the DB. I have her detained and I'm assuming you want to see
her."

Mary's pulse quickened. "Does a bear poo-poo in the woods?
You bring that little 'ho to homicide and don't spare the horse-
power!"

~~~~

When Becky arrived at homicide with the prostitute, Mary
and Duke waited expectantly. But despite their eager anticipation, they used a favorite investigative tactic: they feigned disdain and disinterest in a person about to be interrogated to put
the subject on the defensive and give the impression that homi-

cide sergeants had far more important fish to fry than one measly, insignificant 'ho. As Becky walked the young woman through the office, Mary barely raised her head from a report she pretended to study and pointed to one of two interrogation rooms to place her in. After Becky secured the woman in the room, Mary and Duke pumped Becky for information about the stop.

"I've known Angel Bennings for over two years," Becky said. "She used to work West MacArthur. She's on active probation, and one of her requirements is that she not frequent known areas of prostitution."

Mary examined the ring and saw Carol Rawson's initials engraved on the inside of the band. "What'd Angel say about where she got the ring."

"Well, I didn't want to press her for details because I didn't want to compromise your investigation, but she mentioned that some guy gave it to her for turning a trick."

Mary beamed. "What'd I tell you, Duke. The power of poontang. Our boy faces multiple murders, but he throws caution to the wind and puts the rest of his miserable life on the line for a piece of ass!"

Duke shook his head and grinned at Mary's feminist interpretation of men's weakness for the fair sex and went to enter Angel's name in the computer to obtain her CORPUS read out.

"Becky, what kind of little 'ho we got here," Mary asked. "Is she gonna roll over and tell us what we want to know, or does she have a jailhouse mentality that we have to overcome?"

Becky laughed. "Oh, Angel tries to talk bad, but she's all bark and no bite. So, just do your thing, Mary, and you'll get what you want."

After waiting half an hour to let Angel Bennings stew in her own nervous juices, Mary and Duke entered the windowless five by eight room to conduct the interrogation. While Duke set up the tape recorder and note pads, Mary gave Angel a cursory once over: light complexioned black, or "high yellow" in black vernacular, twenty years old, slight build, wearing a natty blond weave. Except for a prominent scar on her right cheek, she was pretty in a sultry, sensual way. She eyed the two investigators warily and her defiant posture exuded *bad attitude* in every one of her mannerisms.

Mary smiled to herself at Angel's bad-assed nigga front and

took the seat next to her. "Angel, I'm Sergeant Sanders and this is Sergeant Washington."

Angel gave Mary a sullen nod but did not reply.

Mary continued. "You were stopped by Officer Farmer today because you were loitering in a known prostitution area. You're on active probation for prostitution, and one of the court's stipulations is that you not frequent these areas. You were also in possession of stolen property because the ring you were wearing was taken in a robbery that occurred a week ago. Possession of stolen property is a felony, and a conviction for that charge would place you in state prison for two to four years. These are the charges that you are being held for. Do you understand what I've just told you?"

Angel nodded again.

Mary's answer showed her contempt. "Angel, the tape recorder can't *hear* you nod your head. You have to give a verbal reply."

Angel cleared her throat and sneered. "Yeah, yeah, I understand. But what about my rights? Ain't y'all supposed to read me my rights?"

Duke leaned forward and assumed the good cop role. "Angel, sure we can read you your rights. Sure we can. *If* that's what you want. Or, we can handle this. . .informally. You see, we're not overly concerned with your being in possession of that ring, even though *if* we wanted to, we could charge you with possession of stolen property and make it stick. After all, you were wearing the ring. But, who we're really after is the person who committed the robbery, and the logical suspect is the person who gave you the ring. Understand?"

Angel radiated a cocky, street savvy smile. "So, what you be sayin' is you want to make a deal, right?"

Mary leaped back into the verbal duel. "Only if you come across with information that can be verified. We're not interested in bullshit stories."

Angel laughed derisively. "Girl, you are a trip. Sittin' there tryin' to act all bad. Female PO-PO. You ain't about shit! Bring yo' sassy black ass out to the streets and us 'hos will turn yo' pussy out!"

Mary shrugged indifferently. "What did I tell you, Duke? Even before we came in here, I said this little high yellow pussy-pusher didn't have a lick of sense and would end up doin' state time. OK, Angel, you play it your way. We'll charge you with probation violation and possession of stolen property, and you can have your day in court."

Mary and Duke picked up the recorder and notepads, left the room, and closed the door behind them. Within seconds, Angel banged on the door, imploring them to listen to her.

"Hey, lady po-lice! I was just playin'. I'll talk to you. Hey, lady po-lice, you hear me?"

"Little high yellow pussy-pusher?" Duke mimicked.

Mary grinned. "Apropos, don't you think?"

Ten minutes later, Mary got back in character and flung open the door and stood in the doorway with her hands on her hips. "You finished wasting our time, Angel?"

Angel's sullen expression softened into a look of contrition. Mary and Duke took their same seats, turned on the tape recorder, and the interrogation began. After asking basic questions about the incident's date, time, and location, Mary zeroed in on the particulars.

"So, how'd this whole thing go down?"

"A dude gave me the ring for a trick I laid on him."

"You have a name for this dude?"

"Naw, he was drivin' by and stopped me while I was doin' the 'ho stroll. First time I ever saw him. He wanted some extra stuff done, but didn't want to pay what I wanted, so he offered me that ring. I saw right off it was a real diamond, so I took it. Then we went to the Mission Motel, did the thing, and he split."

"What kind of car was he drivin'?" Duke asked.

"I ain't much on rides. Can't tell one from another. But this one was new and dark green."

After almost an hour, Mary and Duke exhausted their questions, and Angel grew tired of the repetitive queries and became restless and irritable.

"OK, we're through here," Mary concluded and gave Angel her business card. "Officer Farmer will give you a ride back to the east end. No charges will be filed at this time. If you get any more information, let us or Officer Farmer know. If your info is any good, we'll do what we can to help you out of any soliciting beef you get arrested for in the future. OK?"

Angel rose from her chair and paused. "One more thing. You

know how niggas always be talkin' a lot of smack? You know, tryin' to impress everyone 'bout how they be playa's and all that? Well, this mothafucka was all 'bout bullshit. I seen through him straight away. He had this nine he kept showin' off to me. Tellin' me how he don't back down to nobody. How he'll bust a cap in a nigga's ass just for mean-muggin' him. I played him on, but I could tell that mothafucka was so scary he'd run from his own shadow. And a dumb mothafucka too! Give me a ring he stole in a robbery? Mothafucka do somethin' like that deserve to get caught."

After Angel Bennings left the office, Duke stated the obvious. "The assholes made their first mistake."

"There'll be more," Mary added. "Angel was right. Any suspect who pays for a piece of ass with a ring taken in a robbery-rape-murder is not loaded with too many smarts. Sooner or later, our hero will be back on MacArthur lookin' for some more poon-tang." Mary smiled and gave Duke a condescending look. "Ah, you men. Your brains rank a distant second to what's hanging between your legs when it comes to making critical decisions."

15

The OPD cafeteria buzzed like a beehive in the usual early morning activity. The non-uniformed personnel, or as blue-suits called them, "building rats," hurriedly picked up their coffee, juice, and snacks prior to their shifts. While they queued up to make their purchases, a few Dog Watch patrol officers gulped caffeine at a rear table, trying to stay awake until they finished their late paperwork. Sergeant Rocky Rollins poured himself a cup of Joe and joined the line. A familiar voice caused him to turn around.

"Where's your Danish, Rocky?" Tex-Mex asked.

Rocky's face lit up when he saw his old beat partner. "Hey, Tex-Mex! No more Danishes for me, man. Mary's been on my case about my love handles."

Tex-Mex grunted. "Figures. Wives, girlfriends, mothers, sisters, they're all out to reform us."

Rocky laughed. "Heard you got yourself in the shit again. The Days Inn rumble in the jive five jungle?"

"Yeah," the Texan answered. "That's why I transferred out of patrol. I was gettin' too easy to find out there."

"Well, you're out of that rat race now," Rocky said, as he paid for their coffee. "You're gonna be workin' for me in narcotics. It'll be like old times. Come on, I'll show you the nuts and bolts of our operation."

When Rocky and Tex-Mex entered the interior office, heads swiveled in their direction and the hazing began. A short, stocky black officer in his mid-thirties raised his eyes to beseech the heavens.

"Oh, God," Officer Harold Osgood moaned. "Why have you forsaken our esteemed narcotics unit? What did we do to incur your wrath that you sent Tex-Mex Garcia to wreak havoc on our humble domain? Now, there will be tornados, hurricanes, pestilence, famine, tsunamis, and wild fires. Please, God, have mercy on our souls!"

A tall white officer in his early forties took a sample Days Inn menu from his desk and placed an imaginary order. "Let's see," Officer Bill McGuire pondered. "I think I'll order the Days Inn special: one Carmen omelet with extra hot chili *temper* on the side. No, wait. How 'bout a Juanita eggs over easy, with a handcuff, bedpost, baton, dildo sauce!"

A hulking, thirty-five year old Latino officer with long, premature gray hair placed a huge arm around Tex-Mex's shoulder. "Don't you listen to these *putos*, bro," Officer Jose Lima assured him. "They're just a couple of *maricones* who don't recognize a kick-ass streetcop when they see one. Oh, by the way, would you introduce me to the hottie who wanted you to dry-fire your .40 cal in her pussy? Sounds like the kind of girl I want to take home to meet mom."

The office erupted in laughter, Tex-Mex joined in the levity, and the other narcotics officers gathered around him to shake hands and welcome him into the unit. While the sarcastic quips continued, Lieutenant Hal Allen, the Vice squad commander, entered the office unnoticed. He wore a sport coat, tie, and slacks that clashed with the casual attire of the other narcotic officers.

"Well, I'll be damned!" Lieutenant Allen exclaimed. "I knew the narcotics squad was going downhill, but I never thought the brass would have the balls to send Tex-Mex Garcia to us. Who's next? Bull Brewster?"

"I guess someone made a mistake, Lieutenant," Tex-Mex replied.

The lieutenant shook the Texan's hand. "No need to be so formal, Tex-Mex. You can either call me Hal, or if you don't feel comfortable with that, LT will do fine."

During this introduction, two black narcotics officers saun-tered into the office and laid their carry bags on their desks. In his late twenties, of medium height and build, and clean shaven, Aaron Cook was quiet and reluctant to joke around. Sean Morris was Aaron's exact opposite. As flamboyant and outgoing as Aaron was withdrawn and quiet, Sean was in his mid-thirties, tall with an athletic build, and his signature trait were the out-sized pieces of jewelry, or *bling*, that he wore and flashed around. But one factor defined the two of them: they were always to-gether, both on-duty and off. The other narcotics officers stand-ing one-liner alluded that they were Siamese Twins but didn't realize it.

"Yo, Tex-Mex!" Sean shouted. "You gonna show us how to buy dope, *ese*? And you *habla* too! Man, you're gonna be a natural gettin' them slingers!"

"Not me, Sean," Tex-Mex replied. "I'll never match you. This is your world. I'm just glad to be a small slice of it."

Sean burst into laughter. "LT? You hear him? Shit, he jumped right in doin' the dozens!"

Lieutenant Allen raised his hands to quiet the commotion. "All right, all right, let's settle down so we can start the day."

He motioned the squad into his small office, and while the officers lounged around, Lieutenant Allen organized the day's operations. He opened a few file folders and studied their con-tents for a few seconds.

"OK," he began. "What do we have goin' today?"

Rocky spoke first. "I'll break Tex-Mex into the routine by giv-ing him the grand tour of our facilities and introduce him to our procedures. Probably take a few days until he's up to speed and ready to operate."

The LT nodded his approval. "What about our joint operation with the Feds and the Alameda County Task Force workin' Hol-lywood Hawkins? What's shakin' with that?"

Sean spoke up. "Not much, LT. After we came up empty on that last search warrant, there's nothin'. No snitches. Not even any rumors floatin' around the streets."

"What about that shipment of black tar heroin that Hawkins was supposedly expecting?" the LT asked.

"That info dried up, LT," Aaron said. "It was like poof! And it was gone with the wind."

"Well, keep on it Sean, Aaron," the LT ordered. "Maybe something will turn up and we'll catch a break. You two meeting with DEA this morning?"

"Yeah," Sean replied. "We're gonna catch up with Agent Burke out east. He's got a snitch that might help us out."

"OK, and who's got court today? You, Harold?"

"Yeah, the Ramirez case."

"OK, Harold, but contact the DA and see if you can be put on phone stand-by. And where are we getting our wheels today?"

"Atkins Chevrolet," Rocky replied.

"Again?" Jose whined. "Those Chevys are pieces of shit. When are we gettin' some Dodges?"

The LT grinned. "Your cousin still manage the Dodge dealership, Jose?"

The rest of the squad burst out laughing as Jose tried to deflect the insinuation.

"Come on, LT!" Jose pleaded. "You know that ain't got nothin' to do with it. I ain't gettin' no kick-back or nothin'. Dodges are just better cars."

"Blah, blah, blah," the LT said and covered his ears. "All right, let's hit the bricks."

~~~~

The following week Tex-Mex eased into the operational fold. Jose drove the Chevy loaner as they made their way out to a surveillance site in the Campbell Village housing projects. This would be his first test as a buy officer, and Tex-Mex felt out of place cruising the streets in a civilian car, dressed in civilian clothes, without a protective vest and the psychological well-being the blue uniform and a marked car provided. The uniform and vehicle let *everyone* know who you were. The good people, the bad guys, and those in between. Tex-Mex reasoned that he would get used to his undercover role, but for now he felt like a fifth wheel. And working narcotics had other perils. In addition to being exposed as police officers to bad guys, they also faced the danger of being taken for dealers by rival drug dealers, or mistaken as suspects by fellow officers. More than a few undercover officers suffered serious injuries or been killed in these debacles.

"What's with this Campbell Village surveillance?" Tex-Mex asked.

"Routine rock house," Jose replied. "Not a heavyweight, but not a lightweight either. We've been on it now for a couple of weeks. We're set up in a vacant apartment across the street. We monitor what goes on, record it in our reports, and make some buys when we can. Pretty cut and dried. When we get enough probable cause, we'll take it to a judge for a search warrant and bust down the door."

"That's it?" Tex-Mex asked.

Jose gave him a puzzled look. "What? You expected wild car chases like in patrol? Man, most of what we do is sit, drink coffee, and watch people. A lot of times the dealers get suspicious and won't sell to us. That's why we get new faces like you to make buys 'cause the rest of us have gotten burned from too much exposure."

"So, what's happening today?" Tex-Mex asked.

"We'll watch for a couple hours so you can confirm how the routine works. You've been out with Rocky on other surveillances, so you know how it goes more or less. Then I'll get hold of Rocky to see if he wants you to take a shot at a buy. OK, here's our apartment building. We'll park in the rear lot and head on up to the third floor."

Jose and Tex-Mex set up their equipment inside the vacant apartment and began the tedious surveillance. For the next two hours, they used binoculars and a camera to record the steady stream of buyers who frequented the drug residence. They noted down license plate numbers and kept a log of arrival and departure times. During lulls in the activity, Jose and Tex-Mex discussed vice policies and the latest departmental rumors.

"What's the deal with Hollywood Hawkins?" Tex-Mex asked. "How come we can't nail him?"

Jose shrugged. "Shit, the average beatcop knows as much as we do. It's a big mystery. LT thinks we've got a mole somewhere in our operation. But nobody's got a clue who it might be. Every time we write up a search warrant, there's no dope, guns, or money when we serve it. So, for now Hollywood Hawkins sells dope with impunity. None of our snitches have come up with anything. And his competitors are scared shitless. That last Funktown dealer found at Castlemont High School with the rebar stuck up his ass is the third 187 in the last month. Shit, everyone knows Hollywood's responsible and is sending a message to his rivals, but there's no evidence to prove it. But fuck it. We got our own gig here. So, you ready to do your thing?"

"You mean make a buy?"

Jose rolled his eyes. "No, I mean are you ready to swish up to the Chief's office and ask if it's OK for you to come out the closet! Of course I mean make a buy, *maricon!*"

Tex-Mex laughed. "Yeah, sure."

"All, right. Let me get hold of Rocky and get his OK. Rocky, you copy?" Jose broadcast over his portable radio transceiver.

There was a few seconds delay before Rocky's reply sputtered over the airwaves. "Yeah, what's up?"

"OK for you know who to get a little buy time?"

"Up to you," Rocky said. "If he's ready, turn that bad boy loose!"

"OK, done deal," Jose said. "How 'bout in twenty minutes? I'll monitor the action from my spot if you'll take position to respond as cover. OK?"

"You got it. Tell Serpico not to mess up his cherry buy."

Both Jose and Tex-Mex laughed. "He copied. I'll let you know when he's on his way."

Jose put a fresh battery in the transceiver. "OK, you've been watching how the buyers approach the rock house. There's no big mystery how to make a buy. You've heard all the drug lingo on the street, so you know what to say and what not to say. The main thing is it's just like an acting audition. Just play the role and everything else will fall into place. I'll be checking how the shit goes down, and Rocky and Bill will be right around the corner in case anything goes wrong. You ever wired up before?"

"Rocky showed me how to wear it and how it works," the Texan replied.

"There's nothin' to it *if* there are no glitches," Jose said. "But every once in a while, the damn thing malfunctions and we lose contact. Here, let me help you put it on." As Jose assisted Tex-Mex assembling the radio wire inside his shirt, he instructed Tex-Mex on emergency precautions. "OK, in case something goes wrong and the wire *is* working, you'll use a verbal signal to let us know you need immediate cover. Just say, 'Damn, it's hot today!' and we'll come runnin'. Now, if you give the verbal signal and we don't come, then that means the fuckin' wire is out of whack, and you'll have to give a visual signal. In this case, just take off your Stetson and that'll be the sign. Got it? Just remember, if something doesn't feel right, just give us the verbal or visual signal and we'll be on you like stink on shit. Until you get the hang of this dope buying business, officer safety is the number one priority. *Comprende?*"

Tex-Mex placed his Glock in the small of his back. Then he nodded at Jose and started toward the door.

"Hey, Tex-Mex!" Jose called out, and the Texan paused and looked back. "Sort of like your first day in field training a few centuries ago, huh?"

Tex-Mex grinned back. "Sort of."

"Well, go kick some, you Pancho Villa looking, bad-ass *cabron!*"

Tex-Mex closed the apartment door behind him and waited in the hallway for the elevator to arrive. A muscular black kid in his late teens swaggered to a stop a few feet away. He wore the standard ghetto uniform. Baseball cap cocked sideways, over-sized, un-tucked T-shirt, and sagging jeans that hung well below his exposed underpants. The youngster took a side glance at him as if to size him up, and Tex-Mex returned the teen's insolent stare without breaking eye contact. He learned long ago that gang-bangers regard avoiding a stare-down as a sign of weakness.

"S'up?" the youngster challenged.

Tex-Mex shrugged. "You, homes."

The teenager glared at him for a moment, but then the elevator door opened to defuse the confrontation. Tex-Mex made it a point to enter and leave the elevator first to make a statement in the testosterone pecking order. As he left the building, he felt the teen's eyes burning into his back.

He made the short walk to the rock house in less than a minute. Tex-Mex tried to keep his mind clear of doubts. He reassured himself that he could pull off this charade. Just as he did with the sullen teenager in the building a few moments ago. His role called for him to play a tweaker buying rocks. But the closer he got to the door, the more his doubts resurfaced and eroded his confidence. He rehearsed his opening lines. Then rehearsed them again. But they sounded false. With each step he took, his words sounded more and more like a cop's bad imitation of a dope fiend. Now, he made his way up the walkway leading to the front porch. He knocked on the door. He waited. Footsteps approached. Window shades peeked apart. The deadbolt unlocked. The door eased open.

Then total shock.

The face that stared back at him was a mirror of his own. Eyes bulged wide. Mouth gaped open in disbelief. Both men had instantaneous recognition. An arrest that went bad a few weeks before. A foot chase and a violent struggle. A knife attack that barely missed opening up the Texan's midsection and spilling his guts on the ground. The suspect's subsequent escape. Reunited as adversaries. Here. Now.

The face-off lasted only a fraction of a second, and then the struggle resumed as if it never stopped. Tex-Mex lunged forward to block the door from being slammed shut. The two men pushed and shoved for control of the door. Voices shouted inside and the door collapsed inward. Tex-Mex's momentum caused him to lose his footing and fall to the floor. The fall saved his life. Multiple gunshots erupted in a fusillade that would have riddled him if he still stood. A short silence followed as Tex-Mex reached for his Glock and sighted it towards the apartment's interior.

~~~~

Jose finished the last of his coffee when Tex-Mex arrived at the rock house. He focused his binoculars on Tex-Mex as the door opened. A sudden flurry of movement caught Jose by surprise. Muffled grunts and the sound of violent struggle came over the wire. Jose broadcast the emergency over his transceiver.

"Rocky! Bill! Tex-Mex's in trouble! 940-B! 940-B!" Jose sprinted toward the door, when he heard the long volley of shots fired and he broadcast again. "Shots fired, Rocky, shots fired! 940-B!"

Rocky changed radio frequencies to alert OPD units on the west end's primary channel. "All units, all units! 917 Campbell. 940-B! 940-B! Plainclothes officers on the scene. Shots fired!"

~~~~

Tex-Mex lay proned out on the living room floor. He swept his pistol from side to side but nothing moved. Except for the sound of sirens wailing in the distance, the house remained eerily quiet. Then Tex-Mex heard running footsteps and a door banging open, and he leaped to his feet and ran to the rear of the apartment. He had a brief glimpse of the rock slinger climbing the rear fence. He brought his Glock to a firing position, but the suspect disappeared on the other side before he could sight in. Tex-Mex knew there was at least one other suspect who did the shooting, but he did not see this person. All his prior training told him to err on the side of caution and proceed slowly to insure that the shooter was not waiting to ambush him. But he already lost this same suspect once before and did not intend to lose him again. He launched his lanky body pell-mell through the rear door and matched the rock slinger fence for fence, yard for yard.

~~~~

As the shrieking sirens of OPD's cavalry drew closer, Rocky, Bill, and Jose thundered up to the open front door with pistols drawn. Both Bill and Jose tried to enter the house at the same time, but their beefy bodies would not fit through the doorway. They shouted and cursed as they attempted to wedge their way inside, until Rocky finally solved the problem by pulling Bill back to allow Jose entry. All the while they kept up a continuous chorus of pleas for Tex-Mex to answer them.

"Tex-Mex! Tex-Mex!"

"Tex-Mex! Where you at?"

"Tex-Mex! You all right?"

~~~~

The Texan was too busy trying to gain ground on the rock slinger to answer. He gave up any thoughts about shooting the suspect. There was no sign that he was armed, and besides, he just wanted to catch this asshole and give him a serious ass-whipping! But he had great difficulty climbing fences while holding his pistol. He thought about returning it to the small of his back or placing it in his pants pocket, but he worried about losing it as he competed in this ghetto decathlon. At about the fifth fence, Tex-Mex's fatigue caused him to grip the pistol tighter and neglect to index his trigger finger to prevent an accidental discharge.

BANG!

The resulting gunshot startled Tex-Mex so badly that he actually looked at the pistol as if he blamed the firearm for the discharge. And the suspect, believing that Tex-Mex shot at him, experienced such an adrenaline rush that he shifted gears into overdrive to escape. Tex-Mex watched in dismay as the suspect dove over the next fence head first without even touching it.

The fences and yards passed by in a blur. The rock slinger dashed across a street and into another yard, with the Texan laboring to match his strides. Tex-Mex gasped for air and his arms and legs felt spastic with fatigue. He clawed his way over the next Mount Everest of a fence and crashed on the other side too winded to rise to his feet. Then he heard welcome sounds. Deep barks, savage throaty growls, and screams of terror coming from the next yard over told him that the suspect wallowed up to his neck in deep shit.

Tex-Mex struggled to his feet, staggered to the fence and peered over the top. A hundred pound plus Rottweiler attacked the dope dealer with unmitigated fury. As Tex-Mex watched like a spectator at a modern era gladiator game, the huge mastiff lunged and tore at the human who dared invade its territory. The rock slinger tried arming himself with a flimsy plastic garden chair in a futile attempt to ward off the dog's charges. But this ineffectual defense was about as successful as a matador using the same chair to dispatch a bull at The Moment Of Truth. Tex-Mex beamed a broad smile of intense satisfaction as the Rottweiler's teeth found their mark time and time again, causing the suspect's cries of pain to resonate throughout the Campbell Village neighborhood. He recalled Robert Duval's famous line in the movie *Apocalypse Now* and modified it to reflect present circumstances.

"I love the sound of agony in the morning," Tex-Mex recited. "It sounds like. . .victory!"

The suspect accumulated an alarming number of bite wounds, and Tex-Mex briefly considered interceding on his behalf. While the battle raged on, Tex-Mex contemplated his options. He could not attempt to shoot the dog for fear of hitting the suspect in such close quarters. OPD regulations strictly forbade warning shots, so he could not use that option. And physical intervention might result in his becoming additional Rottweiler fodder. Tex-Mex was stumped. Since his rescuing the suspect would not be a viable alternative, the Texan happily abandoned the thought altogether and rabidly rooted for the carnivore to inflict as much carnage as he could. His conscience did not bother him, either. This dope dealer only got what he deserved after bringing so much pain and misery into other people's lives.

Seconds later, Jose, Rocky, and Bill joined him at the fence, and they formed an enthusiastic cheering section supporting the redoubtable canine. It became a war of attrition. The suspect jabbed the chair at his foe to keep him at bay, and the dog feinted and counter-attacked, digging his teeth into whichever of the suspect's limbs presented the most vulnerable target. This was no Marquis of Queensberry sanctioned match, no exhibition of the finer points of the "sweet science." This was a no holds barred, knock-down/drag-out, every man or dog for himself survival slug and bite fest, and this dope dealer was clearly out of his league. The bout soon degenerated into a massacre about to happen, and the OPD Rottweiler booster club began to lose interest.

"You know," Jose complained. "This rock slinger swine of a motherfucker is a disgrace to our species. Hell, with our superior intellect, we're at the top of the food chain. Surely he should be able to think of some tactic to give this dog more of a fight."

"Yeah," Rocky agreed. "Look at that rake leaning against that tool shed. Why doesn't he use that to hold the dog off? Maybe we should tell him about the rake."

"Noooo!" the other three vice officers gasped in unison.

"Let the asshole find it himself!" Tex-Mex shouted. "Shit, he invaded the dog's territory, the dog didn't invade his. All animals have a right to defend their territory. It's an instinct thing. Kind of like cops defending their city against slimeballs like this rock slinger."

The suspect let out a horrible shriek and Rocky frowned.

"Yeah, you're right," Rocky conceded. "But, you know, maybe we should do something pretty soon 'cause the Rottweiler might actually kill him."

The other three thought over Rocky's suggestion for a few

seconds.

"OK," said Bill. "But let the dog get one more good bite before we take any action. All, right?"

At precisely that moment, the Rottweiler lunged and snagged the suspect's left arm, causing him to scream in agony.

"Ooooooo!" the four officers moaned and winced.

"That's enough," Tex-Mex proclaimed, and the rest nodded in agreement.

Jose leaned over and patted the fence. "Here, boy! Here, boy!"

The dog immediately stopped his attack and turned toward the sound of Jose's voice. With his muzzle bathed in blood and slobber, the Rottweiler gave a look back at the suspect, who grimaced and held his wounded arm, and then playfully loped over to the fence with his tail wagging. He propped his huge front paws as high as he could on the wooden boards and accepted Jose's pats on his head.

"Good boy!" Jose praised the dog. "Thanks for taking our side."

~~~~

The saga ended with them taking the suspect into custody and transporting him to the hospital for extensive medical treatment. A search of the rock house turned up a large quantity of cocaine and a garden variety assortment of other drugs. They couldn't find or identify the second suspect who did the shooting, but Tex-Mex was satisfied. He settled an old score and got some additional payback compliments of a bad-to-the-bone Rottweiler defending his turf. His first operation in narcotics proved a memorable one. At least he didn't fuck up his cherry buy.

16

While Tex-Mex and the other narcotics officers busied themselves with Rottweiler obedience training in West Oakland, Bull patrolled the other end of the city near Carney Park in East Oakland. Bull often laughed when someone mentioned this "park," for it was little more than a geographical postage stamp close to the boundary line between Oakland and the City of San Leandro. It had only three features that remotely qualified it as a park: a basketball court, a swing set, and two picnic tables. For over two decades, the park really served as a major drug distribution point, and for the past few years Hollywood Hawkins based his operations there. At any given time, ten to twenty slingers dispensed their product and plied their trade. They lounged around playing cards, dominos, and basketball to wile away the hours between sales. OPD units made periodic sweeps to rid the park of the dealers and their clientele, but due to other priorities, police had to scale back their presence and the drug sales inevitably returned and thrived as before.

Bull made it part of his daily routine to stop and walk through the park to disrupt the dealers' business. Because the dealers were too street-wise to get caught holding their stash, Bull checked their favorite hiding spots and confiscated any

drugs he found. It developed into a cat-and-mouse game that pit-
ted the dealers' creative innovation against Bull's stubborn per-
severance. He also used direct law enforcement tactics to punish
the slingers. He issued citations to violators who littered, possessed open alcoholic beverage containers, jaywalked, or had the
temerity to urinate in public. If the violators had no identification, he arrested and shipped them off in the wagon along with
those who had outstanding warrants, were drunk in public or
under the influence of a controlled substance. Bull showed zero
tolerance for even the most trivial infraction.

But both sides understood the rules of the game, and except
for an occasional maverick that flouted Bull's authority and
thereby suffered the consequences, the park's denizens and Bull
tolerated one another and respected their contradictory roles.
The dealers had their job to do—sell dope and evade arrest—and
Bull had his—stop the sales and send them to prison. Bull maintained this mutual toleration by treating the dealers sternly, but
fairly, and using physical force only when necessary. There was
no love lost between them, but they coexisted on this tiny parcel
of land as long as no outside interference upset this informal
pact.

The détente ended on this particular day, when Bull happened on a strange scene. A white stretch limo stopped along the
Acalanes Street side of the park's periphery, and several black
males surrounded the vehicle. A slender man in his mid-thirties,
dressed in a flamboyant, three-piece, sparkling gold suit, with a
matching cape and wide-brimmed hat, took new basketballs out
of the limo's trunk and tossed them to several slingers shooting
hoops on the court. Bull recognized the man at once and a stream
of adrenaline pumped through his body: Hollywood Hawkins, in
all his majestic splendor. Bull correctly attributed the drug kingpin's unusual foray deep into his territory as a power play to
stake his claim for control of the park. To roll in with his posse,
in full regalia, Hollywood challenged OPD and threw down the
gauntlet to let everyone know *he* owned the park.

Well, Bull smiled and thought to himself, I'll just see about
that. As Bull neared the park, Hollywood threw the last of the
basketballs to his "employees," like a CEO contributing the cor-
poration's share to their 401K plan, and the slingers cavorted
around the court shooting baskets and putting on dribbling dis-

plays.

Bull and Hollywood had a short but eventful history, and Bull made Hollywood a guest at the OPD Hilton on two prior occasions, compliments of his aggressive police work. In their first encounter, Bull confiscated a kilo of heroin from Hollywood during a pat-down search for weapons, but the court ruled it an illegal search and dismissed the case. Another time, Bull conducted a security check at a popular Jack London Square nightclub, found a loaded handgun under Hollywood's chair, and arrested him, but the court dismissed that case, too, for lack of evidence.

But today Hollywood made a critical error in judgment, when he left the sanctuary of his mansion in the Oakland hills to visit his base of operations in the flatlands. His brazen blitzkrieg placed him at great risk, for he intruded on Bull's turf now and made himself as vulnerable as any other common gangster to the creative mind of a good beatcop. Bull raised his eyes upward and gave silent thanks to the celestial powers that governed the universe for allowing this chance encounter to take place. Then he committed himself to this High Noon showdown.

"2L31," Bull broadcast over his car radio. "Put me off on a car stop at Carney Park, 105th and Acalanes, a white stretch limo, personalized plate 1PLAYA. And start at least three cover units."

The dispatcher relayed the request for cover to other OPD units, but every officer in the district recognized Hollywood's limo, and they all swarmed toward the park to take part in the feeding frenzy.

When Bull first made the corner and came into view, Snuff Dog, one of Hollywood's top lieutenants, saw the black and white approaching and alerted his boss that the PO-PO arrived on the scene. Hollywood's response was unflappable. He didn't even glance in Bull's direction. To do so would have violated the sanctity of his gangster code of cool and created the impression that he gave a shit. Instead, he sauntered to the limo's passenger side, and his huge personal bodyguard, Antoine "Bear" Bevins, opened the door and he stepped leisurely inside. Then the rest of his men also entered the limo in preparation to leave.

Bull had other ideas. He stopped his cruiser immediately behind the limo and approached the driver's door. Hollywood's retainers emulated their boss's nonchalant attitude by looking as bored and unconcerned as possible, and Bear Bevins took his time to start the engine. Bull took a brief glance towards the park. All activity came to a standstill. The basketball game stopped as if a referee called a timeout. The domino and card games ceased. Every eye focused on this tense street drama. Bull flexed his huge arms for visual effect, withdrew his long baton from its O-ring, and rapped gently on the window to get the driver's attention. But Bear Bevins ignored him until Bull struck the window with his baton hard enough to make it vibrate. Snuff Dog and Tremane, another of Hollywood's lackeys, came to life and opened their doors to climb out, but Hollywood raised his hand, said something to the two men, and they eased their doors shut. Then Bear Bevins rolled down his window.

"What?!" he shouted.

Bull exaggerated his polite greeting. "Sir, I'm going to cite you for parking in a red zone. Also, your registration tab has expired, and the left rear tire of your vehicle does not have sufficient tread and needs to be replaced. I need to see your license and vehicle registration."

While the big man scowled and gathered the documents, the first of many OPD police cruisers screeched to a halt in front of the limo to block it from leaving. All the limo's occupants except Hollywood lost their detached sense of indifference now and twisted their heads in all directions as the rest of the OPD cover units arrived and surrounded the limo one after another. Hollywood merely gazed out the window as if this was a minor inconvenience that would soon disappear.

With the troops in place, Bull moved on to the detainment's next phase. He leaned down to look into the limo's interior and adopted a sham look of shock.

"Mr. Hawkins? Is that you back there? I didn't know you were in this vehicle. Now, I *know* you're *not* aware that this is a high narcotic sales area, or you wouldn't be here. And it's also an area of recorded acts of violence against police officers, so I'm going to have to ask you and your, ah, associates to exit your vehicle for a precautionary pat-down search for possible weapons. I realize that this will delay you from leaving, but it's a necessary part of police *procedure*."

For the first time Hollywood's cool demeanor suddenly turned red hot. "Motherfucker, you want to write your fuckin' ticket, go 'head! But we ain't gettin' out of this ride!" Looks of shock registered on his entourage's faces. Never before had they witnessed their boss lose his cool. "Bear, roll up your window!"

Bull watched the driver's automatic window roll up and felt another jolt of adrenaline tingle his nerve endings. If Francis Ford Copploa scripted and directed this melodrama, it couldn't have played out any better. Both he and Hollywood spoke their lines and worked their way through the script toward the inevitable denouement. Bull scanned the park. The slingers still waited for the action to unfold. Bull turned to the cover officers and flashed them a grin, and they instantly decoded what his smirk meant. Eve Lawson's eyes lit up when she realized the implications of the drug czar's refusal to exit his vehicle. Big Lester Michaels nodded to Bull and put on his black leather gloves like a boxer readying himself for the main event. Becky Farmer gave Bull a double thumbs-up, and the other five cover officers circled the limo, waiting for the gladiator games to begin.

Now, it was Bull's turn to affect an aura of nonchalance. He strolled to Hollywood's closed rear window and bent over at the waist, so that he dropped down to the drug czar's eye level.

"Mr. Hawkins? I've given you a lawful order to get out of your vehicle. If you don't unlock your door and get out, I'm going to force entry and drag you out. Now, you don't want that, do you?"

Hollywood gritted his teeth and let loose with a torrent of verbal abuse that again dismayed his retinue and caused them to sit rigid in their seats as if they were paralyzed by his outburst.

"Brewster, you damage my fuckin' car and I'm gonna sue the City of Oakland and you for all you're worth! Motherfuckin' PO-PO always fuckin' with niggas. Why don't you go fuck with some peckerwoods for a change, you fuckin' honky piece of shit!"

Bull looked toward the park and saw that Hollywood's tirade energized the slingers, who now edged closer toward the limo. Bull knew the slingers merely meant to show their boss their loyalty. They would only get involved in a major fracas with OPD as a last resort. But he wanted to draw a symbolic, "do not cross this line in the sand" warning, so he signaled for Becky and Eve to join him just outside the basketball court. Then he announced in a voice loud enough to be heard anywhere in the park.

"If any of these Carney Park NBA All Stars takes *one* step

forward, take out your .40 cals and blow their balls off!"

While Eve and Becky faced off against the slingers with their hands ready on their Glocks, Bull returned to the limo and beamed Hollywood his best counterfeit grin.

"Last chance," Bull said.

When Hollywood responded with another slew of curses, Bull recited an admonition that would legitimize his following actions. "Mr. Hawkins, I repeat my lawful command for you to exit your vehicle and submit to a pat-down search for weapons. If you don't comply with this order, I will place you under arrest for resisting a police officer in the proper performance of his duties, California Penal Code Section 148.1. Mr. Hawkins, will you get out of your vehicle?"

Hollywood's X-rated retort barely began, when Bull reared back and used his long baton to smash Hollywood's window into fragments that exploded like shrapnel into the limo's interior. Hollywood had just enough time to raise his cape to shield himself from the glass splinters.

"All, right, all, right! I'm gettin' out!" he screamed, as he opened the door.

But surrender was no longer an option. Bull's huge hands grabbed two fistfuls of Hollywood's suit in vise-like grips and snatched the drug czar from the limo. Then he held him at arm's length and thrashed him back and forth in mid-air like a rag doll, while he bellowed in a bullhorn voice that boomed over the entire neighborhood.

"You're under arrest, you punk-assed, drug-dealing pimp!"

Abject fear contorted Hollywood's face into a mass of quivering flesh. His lips trembled so rapidly that they were a blur of motion. As Bull flung and shook him, Hollywood's eyes bulged from their sockets, with the whites so large and luminous they looked like miniature moons. His gangster code of cool vanished in an instant. Hollywood's worst fear came to pass, for his fearsome reputation did not protect him when he needed it most. Then it happened. A small stain appeared near the zipper of Hollywood's pants. The stain grew to a few splotches that darkened the gold cloth like a few rain drops inexplicably fell from the cloudless sky. Once the trickle began, the deluge followed. The voiding mechanism gained momentum until the stain covered his entire groin. The rivulets continued down one pants leg until the urinary stream turned on all the way, and a torrent of golden fluid formed an increasingly larger puddle on the street.

And a strange thing happened. People from houses around the park gathered on their porches, on their front lawns, on the balconies of their apartments, and in front of a nearby liquor store to watch this latest episode of Cops and Dope Dealers. For years, the community lived under a continuous threat of violence from dealers involved in wars over the valuable drug turf, and the thugs held the neighborhood hostage in this warfare and the fear of reprisal if they reported the dealers' activities to the police. But now, the drug overlord himself, the Godfather of the drug trade, pissed his pants in public as a police officer scolded and shook him like an errant child whose bad behavior needed correcting.

And people began to laugh. Slowly at first, and then more boldly, until waves of laughter swept over the neighborhood. The community's laughter proved more effective in humiliating Hollywood Hawkins than all the police harassment in the world would do. The laughter reached its crescendo when Bull finally noticed Hollywood's bladder malfunction, lowered him to the ground, and shook his head in disgust.

"Anyone have a *diaper* handy?" Bull shouted. "Looks like Mr. Big Time Drug Dealer here had himself a little *accident.*"

The citizens roared their approval, and Bull put on a big show of obtaining a pair of plastic gloves from his vehicle trunk and then made distasteful faces for the crowd's benefit, while he patted Hollywood down. Such was Hollywood's complete embarrassment that he looked genuinely relieved when Bull placed him in the rear seat of his black and white and locked the door.

One by one, the District Five officers rousted Hollywood's posse from the limo, frisked, handcuffed, and placed them in separate police cars. For the most part, they were humbled, passive, and submissive. Their boss's behavior meltdown and infamous incontinence became their disgrace too. But one feisty henchman felt compelled to redeem their lost honor by exhibiting typical in-custody courage. He hurled the usual assortment of insults at officers, knowing full well that his entreaties to be released from physical restraint would not be granted.

"Fuckin' PO-PO!" the Woofer shouted for all to hear. "Just take these handcuffs off and I'll kick your fuckin' asses! Y'all ain't shit without those badges, clubs, and gats!"

But Becky shut him up. "You know, you're right. We aren't shit without the badges, clubs, and guns. But that's why the City of Oakland gave them to us. So we can handle miscreants like you."

The thug gave Becky a perplexed look as if to ask what the hell she meant. Becky recognized his intellectual dilemma and translated her comment.

"A miscreant is an evil person, a criminal."

The thug's face lit up with instant enlightenment, and he merely nodded in agreement at his self-description.

Bull "tossed" the limo, but found no weapons or other contraband. One of Hollywood's flunkies had a warrant for his arrest and made the trip to jail with his boss. Bull's final insult deprived the entourage of their wheels. He towed the limo and forced Bear, Snuff Dog, Tremane, and the rest to find some other way home. The OPD victors watched Hollywood's henchmen march disconsolately up 105th Avenue, glancing back with sullen looks as Bull and the rest of District Five waved goodbye.

Bull held no illusions about what would happen to this case. He knew the resisting charge would be dropped. Hollywood retained a number of high profile attorneys, who would file motion after motion for dismissal and eventually succeed. After all, they lived in America, where the guilty worked the legal system to their advantage, as long as they had enough money or political clout to buy or weasel their way out. But to Bull, the outcome didn't matter. With the help of Hollywood Hawkins' lack of intestinal fortitude and its effect on his delicate bladder, he demeaned and humiliated that bastard well beyond what he ever imagined possible.

17

Early September's summer heat made one last stand before bowing out to the first cool breezes of fall. Rondell and Larry White cruised Oakland's funky streets in the Camry, searching for their next victims. They made the circle around Lake Merritt, checking out the hootchymamas displaying their wares. They hid their guns, masks, gloves, and duct tape under the bolted down spare tire in the trunk. They had no concern about Save-A-Lot reporting the Camry stolen or listing it as an overdue rental. One of Rondell's ladies worked for Save-A-Lot Rentals and had access to the rental fleet. She gave Rondell the Camry, a fraudulent rental agreement that would pass muster if the police stopped them, and entered the Camry into their computer showing Rondell as the current renter.

Rondell brooded as he drove. Their last few jobs were carbon copies of each other. He wanted to try something different. Something that proved more of a challenge. A bank heist, maybe. Or an armored car. He wanted to experience the total criminal life and feel the rush of its euphoric high. But he also knew that their luck would one day run out. As much as he reassured Larry that they would never be caught, he knew their day of reckoning would arrive someday. But if he and Larry went down, he envi-

sioned them going out with their gats blazing like so many famous gangsters in the past. He even imagined them going down
in history as two of the most famous gangsters ever. Like Al Capone or Pretty Boy Floyd.

But Rondell conceded they should be cautious. They would
start out slow and work their way up to more complicated
crimes. More than anything else he wanted more drama involving lots of people. Where they could put on a show. Have people
shit their pants in fear. He loved the looks on people's faces when
they realized that the next moment might be their last. The feeling of power he got when he had their fates in his hands. A restaurant, he mused. He mulled it over and it fit their needs. Take
it down at closing time. Herd all the employees to the rear. Get
the safe opened. And if anyone gave them any shit. . .

"Larry, how 'bout doin' a restaurant tonight?"

Larry frowned. "A restaurant? Why?"

Rondell shrugged. "Just thought 'bout doin' somethin' different for a change, blood. Ain't no thang always robbin' bitches."

"Well, I kinda like robbin' bitches and takin' the pussy like
we been doin'."

Rondell gave Larry a look of disgust. "Won't hurt you to miss
the pussy now and then. Shit, go buy you some from that little
'ho you always see."

"She's all right but it ain't the same. I *like* takin' it," Larry
said and paused. "But, hey, whatever breeze is blowin' in the
trees. Don't matter to me. You got a place picked out?"

~~~~

Officer David Fong patrolled Lake Merritt scouting for bad
guys. He glanced at his Daily Bulletin and noted that the BOLO
for a newer, dark green Camry was still there. He took a second
look at the Camry in front of him and debated whether a stop
would be worth the effort. He already stopped and FC'd more
than half a dozen Camrys. He typed the Camry's license number
into his DIGICOM computer and the query showed it registered
to Save-A-Lot. Another rental. Rental cars were a colossal pain
in the ass. He decided that this would be his last stop for this DB
item. After giving the dispatcher the license number and location, he activated his red lights and siren for the stop.

~~~~

Rondell thought a while before he answered Larry's question about which restaurant they would take down. "Well, we need a place close to the freeway for the getaway bounce. How 'bout that Mexican place up by Montclair? Place is always packed. We could wait on a side street until—motherfucker! PO-PO's got his lights on us!"

Larry started to turn around and look back.

"Fuck you doin'!" Rondell said. "Just face forward and act cool. PO-POs always be stoppin' motherfuckers cruisin' the lake. So don't trip and let me do the talkin'."

Officer Fong slipped out of his black and white and approached the Camry's driver's side. "Afternoon, I stopped you for failing to signal for a lane change. I need to see your license and registration."

"Yeah, sure, Officer. No problem," Rondell replied. "I didn't realize I didn't signal. Sorry 'bout that."

Officer Fong scanned Rondell's license and the registration. "Is your rental agreement current?"

"Yeah, sure. You want to see it?"

Fong considered Rondell's response for a moment and then convinced himself that he didn't want to get bogged down in some convoluted mess over an overdue rental. He shook his head no and turned his attention to Larry.

"You have any ID?"

Larry handed over his license without answering.

Fong took the license and noted that the passenger's hand shook. This caused him to take a closer look at him, but Larry avoided eye contact and turned away sideways to look out the window. After over twenty years on the street, Fong's instincts were well-honed to read someone's body language for bad guy clues. This dude could be holding, have a warrant, or maybe he just had blue suit fever. More than a few times Fong had been fooled by a dude exhibiting nervous behavior only to toss the ride and come up empty. After a few seconds deliberation, Fong decided to check them for warrants and probation/parole status, and if the computer check revealed anything further, he'd reconsider his options.

Fong saw that the two men had the same last name. "You

two brothers?"

Rondell laughed. "Yeah, but I'm the better lookin' one."

"Be a few minutes," Officer Fong said and returned to his vehicle.

The White brothers were clear warrants and probation/ parole status. Fong thought again about tossing their ride, but they were cooperative and he didn't think it would be worthwhile, so he made out the FC's, had the driver sign the citation, and then returned to his vehicle and drove away.

Once the officer was gone, Rondell grinned at Larry. "One thing you got to remember 'bout the PO-PO, blood. They're people just like us. If you smile, be polite, and joke around, then they won't go out of their way to fuck with you. Lots of niggas don't understand that, and they start trippin', talkin' a lot of shit that gets them in trouble. Ain't no need for that. Now, let's go check out that Mexican joint."

~~~~

Becky and Bull studied their menus. Servers scurried through the packed restaurant taking orders and bringing drinks and meals. A hand clasped Bull's shoulder, and he turned into the smiling face of Mike Torres, the Cha Cha Cha manager.

"Where have you been keeping yourself lately, Bull?" Mike asked.

"Hi, Mike," Bull replied and returned the smile. "Yeah, it's been a while, hasn't it? Mike, this is OPD Officer Becky Farmer. Becky, this is Mike Torres, the restaurant manager."

"Nice to meet you, Becky," Mike said. "Any OPD officer is welcome at Cha Cha Cha. So, Bull, are you going to start off with your usual margarita?"

"Please, Mike, and one for the lady."

"Two margaritas coming up, and I'll make certain the bartender doesn't spare the tequila. Please enjoy your meal."

Becky watched Mike walk away. "Seems like a nice guy."

"The best," Bull replied. "I've been coming here since the place opened nine or ten years ago. They treat OPD real good."

Their server brought two gigantic margaritas to their table. "Compliments of Mike, Bull. Let me know when you're ready to order."

Becky took a sip of her drink and pursed her lips. "Well, you weren't exaggerating. This margarita is *strong*."

"Yeah," Bull agreed. "Makes hair grow on your teeth."

Becky laughed and took another sip. "I couldn't believe the other day at Carney Park. I'd always heard of Hollywood Hawkins, but I'd never seen him until that afternoon. The limo, his clothes, the entourage, it was like something out of a movie. And he was acting so cool until you smashed out his window and he screamed like a little girl. Then you shook him and he peed all over himself. . ."

Bull grinned. "That had to be one of the highlights of my career. I wanted to humiliate that asshole, and it worked better than I thought possible."

"Especially when you asked if someone had a diaper."

Bull's grin broadened. "*That* was a little bit of genius, even if I do say so myself."

"Another legend in your dossier, Bull?"

Bull dipped a tortilla chip in salsa and took a bite. "I guess. I live for moments like that. It makes all the other bullshit we have to put up with at least somewhat bearable."

Their server arrived to take their order, and Bull forced another margarita on Becky.

"Just remember, Bull, I warned you."

Bull responded in courtroom jargon. "I have been warned and let it be so stipulated and made a matter of record."

Becky caught his eye for a second and then changed the subject. "So, are Tex-Mex and Eve still an *item*, or have they split the sheets and gone their separate ways?"

"Hard to tell with the Texan. His romances are always waxing and waning. What seems like yesterday's love drama may be resurrected tomorrow. She hit him with a pretty good shot of pepper spray, but hell, that might be thought of as a kind of foreplay between brother and sister officers."

Becky laughed so hard that some of her margarita dribbled out the side of her mouth. When she recovered her composure, she used Tex-Mex's troubled relationship history as a transition question to pry open Bull's past, present, and future. They traded personal information about their relationships and family history, and their conversation flew effortlessly from topic to topic. Only when the employees started stacking chairs on top of tables to prepare for clean up, did they realize that the restaurant was about to close.

Bull paid the bill, waved good night to Mike Torres, and they stepped out into the balmy night air. Bull slipped his arm around Becky's waist and guided her to his truck. Then he saw a dark colored sedan parked in the shadows a few houses away on a side street. There were two occupants in the vehicle, but it was too dark to tell anything about their description. Bull felt a vague premonition creep over him. That *something* was not right. But then he shook his head and dismissed it as paranoia. He'd been a cop so long that he had his bad guy radar turned on even when he was off-duty.

Becky noticed the sudden change in his demeanor. "What is it, Bull?"

Bull took a quick glance back over his shoulder as they walked away from the restaurant. "I don't know. Thought I saw a car that. . .nothin'. It's nothin'. Want to rent a video on the way to your place?"

"Sure. Any ideas?"

"Nah. You pick it out. Anything's fine with me."

Rondell and Larry White watched from the shadows as Becky and Bull drove away. Then they waited until the last patrons left.

~~~~

Becky and Bull didn't watch much of the video. They spent the next few hours in passionate lovemaking. He left Becky's condominium an hour before lineup and rushed home to shower, shave, and change clothes. As he made his way through the early morning traffic, it occurred to him that this was the first time in quite a while that his thoughts at the start of the day did not center almost entirely on police work. Instead, he focused on Becky and the magical night they spent together. Just one night with her and his world view expanded beyond his life in uniform. Already, he imagined sharing his interests with her that would transcend police work.

Bull sat in front of his locker brushing the smudges off his boots, when big Lester Michaels paused before exiting the locker room.

"You hear what happened at Cha Cha Cha last night?" Lester asked.

In an instant Bull knew what would follow. He turned to Lester and waited for his premonition to come true.

"Two dudes robbed the place and then shot and killed the manager and dishwasher. Suspects entered right after the last customers left. They took all the employees to the rear, and when the manager wasn't fast enough opening the safe, they shot the dishwasher and told him he was next if he didn't hurry up. Then after the manager opened the safe, they shot him anyway. Some cold ass motherfuckers!"

Lester stopped and waited for a reply. When Bull dropped his eyes to the floor and remained silent, Lester's confusion mounted until he stood mute and uncertain how to react. He took a few steps toward the line-up room, but then stopped and faced Bull.

"Bull?" Lester said. "Bull, you OK?" When Bull still did not respond, Lester continued on and took a last bewildered glance back over his shoulder.

Captain Ernie conducted roll call over a somber lineup. All of them were aware of the Cha Cha Cha murders by now, and most of them dined there regularly. Mike Torres was a favorite of theirs and his and the dishwasher's senseless, merciless slayings shocked even the most jaded, cynical officers. Captain Ernie briefed them all on the case's salient facts, but he added that they didn't have much of a case at the present time. Captain Ernie asked all officers whose beats were close to the restaurant to do some knock and talks with residents in the area for possible leads. After line-up ended, Bull made his way to the homicide office.

Mary and Duke were alone in the office when Bull quietly opened the door and entered. Duke glanced up from the mountain of paperwork piled on his desk and nodded hello. He knew why Bull was there and waited for him to bring up the topic. When seconds crawled by and Bull still didn't speak, Duke brought it up himself.

"Captain Ernie brief lineup on the Cha Cha Cha murders?"

After a short pause, Bull said, "I was there last night."

Duke furrowed his brow, puzzled. "You were where, Bull?"

"Cha Cha Cha."

Mary immediately raised her eyes from a report she read, leaned back in her chair, and crossed her arms over her chest. Waiting. Duke flicked the button on his ballpoint pen open and closed several times. It made a rhythmic clicking sound that punctuated the silence.

Bull began in a subdued, toneless voice. "Becky Farmer and I went there for dinner. It was our first time out together. Mike Torres bought us our first round of margaritas. You know how he is. . .was, Duke. Loved OPD." Bull paused before continuing. "I saw a dark sedan with two occupants parked in the shadows on a side street. It was too dark to see much about the car or the occupants, but I just had this feelin' about it. A feelin' that something wasn't right. But then I thought that I was imaginin' things, so I let it go. Now, of course, I know I should have—"

"Bull—" Duke tried to break in.

Bull went on. "I should have let my instinct take over. I should have relied on my gut feelin'. If I had, maybe Mike and the dishwasher would still be alive. But I didn't and now two people are dead. If only I'd checked a little further, phoned it in to the PD. . ."

Duke tried again. "You can't know everything, Bull. Yeah, you had a *feeling*. But how many times over the years have you had a feeling and it turned out to be nothing? You were off-duty for Christ's sake! You're not a cop twenty-four hours a day."

"Yeah, but. . ." Bull began and faltered.

"Yeah, but *what*, Bull?" Mary asked. "Are you going to stand there with a straight face and tell us that you're going to call in every suspicious vehicle you see? Get real, Bull. You can't blame yourself for what happened. You've got to stop beating yourself up over this."

The three of them remained silent for a time.

"OK," Bull said at last. "What do you have?"

Mary cast Duke a quick glance before answering. "Looks like our serial killers have switched from doing home invasions to restaurants."

Shock drained the color from Bull's face. "The Camry? The sedan I saw was the Camry?!"

Mary and Duke did not reply. They let the ensuing silence answer for them. Bull's shock turned to rage, and he kicked a wastebasket that flew across the office and struck a desk with a loud, metallic bang. Bull stood with his hands on his hips, breathing hard, staring down at the overturned container and its contents strewn on the floor. Then he bent down, methodically picked up the mess piece by piece, and returned the wastebasket where it belonged.

Bull took a deep breath and exhaled. "How do you know it was them?"

"We're not absolutely certain, but what info we have points to them," Duke said. "We have a witness who just phoned before you walked in. This witness said he arrived home last night and found a dark green Camry blocking his driveway. He was about to phone OPD to have it towed, but two male blacks got in the Camry and drove away. Since the vehicle was gone, he ignored it and went to bed. This morning he saw all the police activity, found out what happened, and contacted officers on the scene and told them about the Camry."

Mary spoke for all of them. "Something has got to turn our way soon." She paused and looked down at her desk. "But how soon?"

~~~~

Duke sat at his desk sifting through a stack of FC's generated by patrol officers in response to the BOLO request in the Daily Bulletin. He examined each FC to determine if the persons stopped in a dark green, newer Camry might have some connection to their cases. It was an exhausting process that took a great deal of time to complete. Most of the FC's were so generic that the only ones that stood out were for those whose prior arrests included violent crimes that fit the serial killers' MO—murder, rape, robbery, and home invasions. Mary and Duke desperately needed the Camry's license plate number. Even a partial plate number would be invaluable. But without a plate number. . .

Duke picked up the next FC's. Rondell and Larry White, male blacks, 25 and 23 years old, stopped by Officer David Fong on September 3rd, 1450 hours, in the 3000 block of Lakeshore. At least these two fit the suspects' general physical descriptions, Duke thought. The Camry was registered to Save-A-Lot Rentals. Shit. Another rental clusterfuck. But he had to go through the motions anyway. A quick phone call to the rental agency revealed their records showed the Camry rented to Rondell White, with an address at a North Oakland motel, and not due for return for another two weeks. The motel address was the same as the address on their driver licenses. A call to the motel had negative results. The clerk advised Duke that they had no registration listing for either Rondell or Larry White during the past several weeks.

With the motel out of the picture as an information source, Duke turned to other information avenues trying to establish a paper trail. Duke forged ahead and one by one exhausted the traditional means to track a person down: DMV, IRS, SSI, OHA, CORPUS arrest records, Oakland Public Schools, phone company, birth certificates, and a host of other public and private agencies drew blanks. Duke marveled at how these two men existed in today's modern world without establishing any ties to any major institutions in mainstream society. He was stymied but because the two men seemed to vanish without leaving a trace of information, he placed the FC's with others that needed further checking. Then Duke yawned, stretched, and picked up the next FC.

18

The murders of Mike Torres and the dishwasher affected Bull more than he would admit to himself. Although he did not discuss it openly, the crime weighed heavily on his mind and the people closest to him, particularly Becky, took notice. His once caustic, cynical wit lost its sting, and he became uncharacteristically quiet and reserved. Becky tried to draw him out of his depression, but he mildly rebuffed her and stated that he would work it out on his own. Bull's reclusive behavior finally prompted Becky to take a more forceful stand and confront him with his brooding introspection. After a heated exchange of viewpoints, Bull yielded to Becky's arguments and emerged from his protective shell. Becky proposed that they get away for the weekend to unwind and push police work to a back burner for a much needed change. Bull agreed and they made plans for Eve and Tex-Mex to accompany them to Las Vegas for a three day holiday.

~~~~

A blast of oven-like heat enveloped Becky, Bull, Eve, and Tex-Mex as they joined the other passengers filing off their plane into the connector corridor at the Las Vegas International Airport.

"Jesus!" Tex-Mex exclaimed. "Don't they have an autumn down here? Hell, it's gotta be 110 in the shade!"

"The A/C and an ice-cold brewski are only a few steps away, baby," Eve said.

Once they were in the connector corridor, the A/C gradually cooled them as they walked into the terminal. Then the foursome wound their way through the crowd until they were outside and filed aboard a complimentary van for the short ride to the MGM Grand Hotel. This was Becky's first visit to Sin City, and she gazed out the window in wonder as the van made its way along the boulevards leading to the legendary Las Vegas Strip. When they reached this glitzy road to perdition, it teemed with hordes of tourists clogging the sidewalks and scurrying in and out of the hotels and casinos. Becky was enthralled with the Strip's frenetic energy, and her eyes lit up as she pointed out the window.

"Hey, you future members of gamblers anonymous," Becky said. "Look at that billboard. Corvettes for rent. Now, there's one hell of an idea. I've never driven a Corvette. How about you, Eve?"

Eve read the advertisement. "No, never. Wonder how much it costs?"

"Let's do it!" Becky said. "It'll be worth whatever they charge!"

"Yeah!" Eve seconded the motion. "We could rent two of them, find some deserted road out in the desert, wind those suckers up, and let 'em rip! Let's check it out when we get to the hotel."

The Texan looked concerned and leaned close to whisper to Bull. "I don't know about this Corvette rental shit, Bull. It has that déjà vu thing written all over it. Remember Chi Chi, Ebony, the golf carts, the naked guy, and the Water Meter Bandits? We could be askin' for trouble if we get involved with this Corvette caper. I see a massive dark cloud of doom headed toward us."

Bull looked at the Texan as if he'd committed an unpardonable sin, such as backing off from a felony car chase or refusing a free drink. "Ahh, don't be a wuss. Come on, let's have some fun and let it all hang out!"

The Texan grimaced and shook his head. "All right, but just

remember I tried to warn you."

Becky jumped into the conversation. "Warn who about what?"

Bull gave her a hug. "Nothin', babe. We'll call the Vette place at the hotel."

~~~~

After checking into the hotel, the two female neophyte Indy 500 qualifiers and their trusty sidekicks made their way to the Rent-A-Vette rental agency. Due to Tex-Mex's expert knowledge of racing cars, they elected him as their designated negotiator. Despite his initial reservations, Tex-Mex decided to go with the flow and endorse the risky caper, but he still took furtive glances at the azure blue sky to see if that dark cloud of doom loomed on the horizon.

The Texan sought out a salesman to begin the bargaining powwow, and Rent-A-Vette's top Willy Loman impersonator, Jim Teller, marched confidently toward the tall man wearing the ten gallon black Stetson. At first, Jim launched into his well-rehearsed Machiavellian sales spiel, and Tex-Mex countered with the customer's obligatory demands for price reductions. They performed this perfunctory dickering dance until Jim took nervous glances at the tall man's three companions, who cavorted through the lot like crazed teenagers, hopping in and out of the Vettes with wild abandon.

Jim had good reason to be concerned. Over the past few weeks, Rent-A-Vette experienced a significant increase in customer collisions that caused its insurance premiums to spike at an alarming rate. Now, he had to contend with this group, who obviously experienced some kind of collective adolescent flashback, about to rent two more vehicles and place the agency's rental fleet at risk. The wary salesman licked his lips, hem and hawed, and sought to avoid this imminent disaster.

Tex-Mex noticed that something troubled the diminutive salesman. His initial cocky sales harangue changed dramatically. Now, Tex-Mex sensed that the *last* thing he wanted to do was rent Corvettes to them. Tex-Mex puzzled over this fundamental turnabout to the American business ethos, but then he correctly intuited that perhaps his three *amigos'* madcap behavior might have something to do with the salesman's change in attitude. Tex-Mex sought to put the man at ease and assure him that there was no need for concern about the safety of his vehicles. He tipped back his Stetson and leaned down to read the salesman's nametag.

"Now, ah, Jim, don't you worry about a thing. We'll treat these Vettes like they're our own. Hell, we're off-duty police officers from Oakland, California, and we have the utmost respect for other people's property." Tex-Mex expected this revelation to have a calming effect on Jim, but instead it caused the opposite reaction.

Jim's face lost color. "Police officers?!"

Once again, Jim's reaction confused the Texan. "Uh, yeah, all four of us are police officers. Ah, something wrong, Jim?"

Jim's stammers morphed into full-blown stutters. He relived the last time he rented to a group of police officers. Ten of them rented five cars and totaled all of them in a race across the desert. The tow trucks brought the Vettes back in pieces. He stared out at the neat rows of Corvettes sparkling in the sun and imagined two of them returned mangled and torn apart. Ripped to shreds by these maniacal cops! He saw how they drove their squad cars. Lights and sirens blazing away. Blowing through stop signs and signal lights. Taking corners on two wheels. No way would he rent his treasured Vettes to these lunatics! No way!

Jim wrung his hands and shuffled his feet. "Ah, sir, I hate to say this, but I can't rent to you and your, ah, friends."

Tex-Mex looked down and frowned at the mousy little man and watched him fidget and tremble. "That so? Why not?"

Jim averted his eyes and studied the ground. "Well, you see, it's like this. Our, ah, insurance company won't cover, you know, our renting to, ah, high risk type of customers, and ah. . ."

The Texan crossed his arms over his chest and waited patiently, but the salesman's words just trailed off and then stopped. So they stood there. And Tex-Mex waited some more. But at last the salesman's steely resolve wilted under the tall man's uncompromising scrutiny. Tex-Mex noticed Jim's will power steadily crumbling, so he decided to bring in reinforcements to reduce the timetable to the salesman's unconditional surrender.

"Hey, Bull!" Tex-Mex roared so loud that the salesman visibly jumped. "Our salesman here, Jim, says he can't rent to us 'cause we're *high risk customers!*"

Bull turned to where Tex-Mex and Jim stood and tried to figure out what the hell high risk customers meant, but this glitch holding up the rental process baffled and annoyed him. He reasoned that the solution to this mini-crisis called for them to take a forceful stance that left the salesman no alternative but to do business with them. So, he flexed his massive arms and lumbered over to where the stalled negotiations faced an impasse.

Tex-Mex put on a beatific smile. "Bull, I'd like you to meet *Jim.*"

Bull matched Tex-Mex's smile and grasped Jim's child-like hand in his huge paw. "Well, Jim, it's a pleasure to meet you. Now, what's this about you not bein' able to rent to us 'cause we're, how'd you put it, high risk customers?"

Jim swiveled his head from the tall Texan to the man whose mammoth chest muscles rippled under his blue tank-top. Then he merely pointed to the trailer that served as an office and spoke his first words since being struck temporarily mute.

"The contract forms are in the office."

In ten short minutes, Bull and Tex-Mex sat in the passenger seats of two matching candy-apple-red Corvettes driven by Becky and Eve, who revved the engines prior to making their way out to the desert, which would serve as their NASCAR training site. The two Vettes stopped side by side at a traffic signal waiting for the light to change to green—or someone to wave a checkered flag, whichever came first—when Becky gasped and pointed halfway down the block.

"That asshole just snatched that woman's purse!"

The other three musketeers jerked their heads in a Pavlovian response toward where Becky pointed and saw a slim male white holding a purse by its straps sprint to an older blue Ford Mustang, driven by a female white accomplice, and launch himself inside. Then the Mustang burned rubber and wove its way through the heavy Strip traffic, leaving the victim sprawled face down on the broiling sidewalk. The robbery triggered Becky's pursuit instinct and she ground the accelerator into the floorboard, burst through a narrow gap in the endless line of cars, and soon only a few vehicle lengths separated her from the

Mustang. Eve followed suit and Tex-Mex shook his head in dismay as the dark cloud of doom he foresaw descended on them like a mile-wide F-5 tornado.

Most people would consider two bright red Corvettes pursuing another car on the Las Vegas Strip unusual even by Vegas' bizarre standards, and the horde of tourists gawked in wonder as the chase unfolded before them. Becky blew the Vette's horn to clear traffic ahead of them, and vehicles swerved left and right to yield the right of way to the two maniacs. The felony purse-snatch in progress thrust Bull and Tex-Mex back into the gritty world of police work, and they held their wallets out the windows to display their police identification cards and shouted, "Police! Police!" whenever vehicles blocked their paths. The large crowd of tourists lined the sidewalks like spectators at a Grand Prix road race and speculated if the wild pursuit was actually a publicity stunt to advertise an upcoming attraction.

At the next intersection, a bus stopped and completely blocked forward progress on the roadway. The Mustang had only one way to go and turned right, with Becky and Eve hot on its tail. The next two intersections were also blocked, forcing the three vehicles to make two more right turns. Now, they headed in a full circle, returning to Rent-A-Vette's location. Becky blared her horn continuously to clear traffic, and harsh, non-stop honks filled the air.

Back at Rent-A-Vette Jim Teller waited in a funk. He *knew* those police officers would return the two Vettes so badly damaged that they would require significant repair to make them drivable again. Perhaps they would return them totaled and beyond repair. Or, so badly damaged that the four cops would just leave them in the desert to rust and decompose over the centuries. What would the general manager say? He warned Jim to be more selective in renting the Vettes, and he would hold him responsible for this debacle. But Jim recognized his primary problem. Confrontation did not suit him. And when those two huge policemen loomed over him, well, he couldn't say no.

The continuous sound of vehicle horns blaring in the near vicinity disrupted Jim's meditation on his psychological profile. Ah, he thought, it's probably a wedding procession, and he looked in the direction from which the clamorous horns emanated. Jim enjoyed watching wedding processions. The bride and groom smiling gaily. Their cars festooned with balloons and chalked inscriptions on the doors and fenders wishing them a happy marriage. Their whole lives ahead of them filled with the wonder and joy of matrimony. The blessed start of marital bliss. Ahh, just wonderful!

Jim smiled as the horns drew closer. He craned his neck to get a better look at the procession and. . .he stared in shocked disbelief. It was *his* two Corvettes! My God! Those deranged cops did not even wait to get out to the desert before they destroyed the Vettes. In fact, they intentionally drove past the agency just to ridicule him and pour salt in his psychic wounds! As Jim watched, horror stricken, a man walking on stilts advertising a casino's coming attractions had to take two hurried *long* steps to get out of the way of one Corvette hurtling toward him. Eve trailed Becky and the man on stilts had to take another two *long* steps in the other direction to avoid her. Jim now wavered on the verge of hysteria.

The same crowd that watched the pursuit the first time around remained for the second lap, and now they were certain that this had to be some kind of stunt and started cheering them on. The second lap turned into a third, and people eagerly waited for the insane spectacle to return. Then a familiar sound captured Eve's attention. Sirens. She looked in her rear view mirror and nudged Tex-Mex, who turned and waved his wallet and ID card back at the pursuing police car to identify themselves as police officers. But the pursuing officer seemed oblivious to Tex-Mex's intent and concentrated on *them* as the suspects in this felony evasion caper. More police cars joined in this mad dash through the heartland of America's gambling Mecca, and the pursuit began to resemble a parade.

Around the chase went for a fourth time and Jim covered his eyes to prevent him from witnessing the inevitable carnage. But at least the police now chased these heinous criminals, who belonged on the FBI's ten most wanted list. And when the police eventually caught them, no punishment would be too severe. Hanging! Death by stoning! A firing squad! All Jim wanted was a ticket to their execution and a seat in the first row!

When the fourth lap turned into a fifth, the fiasco took on a new twist. While the Mustang's female driver suddenly lost heart and stopped in the center of the intersection and passively waited her arrest, her male counterpart leapt from the vehicle and continued his desperate bid for freedom on foot. He fled into the herd of tourists and had to run half-bent over through the widespread legs of the man on stilts. When he finally broke free from this mob, he galloped across the Strip's broad boulevard, zigzagging between cars and vaulting and rolling over their hoods.

While Becky and Eve stayed with the Mustang and took the female suspect into custody, Bull and Tex-Mex sprinted after the male suspect, shouting that they were police officers and waving their wallets and ID cards for all to see. The LVPD officers, however, milled about in disarray and confusion. They stayed with Becky, Eve, and the female suspect and at first tried to take all three of them into custody, until Becky and Eve showed them their ID cards and told them what happened. Then most of the LVPD officers dashed after the male suspect and the two OPD stalwarts. And all of them crouched over as they ran through the widespread legs of the man on stilts, who suddenly developed symptoms of acrophobia and ochlophobia, causing him to quit his job and end a promising career as Las Vegas' only gainfully employed stilt man.

Phase three of the Great Strip Chase began when the male suspect chose the MGM Grand, gambling's Vatican City, as his refuge to avoid a return to Nevada State Penitentiary. Hugh Bromley was on parole for armed robbery, and he served as a classic, textbook case failure in rehabilitation. The only thing Hugh learned during his six years behind bars was not to use a firearm in future robberies because the firearm enhancement clause tacked on two additional years to his prison sentence. So the erudite, intellectual Hugh decided to change his MO to purse-snatching rather than armed robbery, and if the police captured him, he would do only *four* years in prison instead of *six*. And Hugh congratulated himself on his shrewd move to thwart the criminal justice system. In short, Hugh Bromley deserved an *honorable mention* inclusion in the Darwin Awards for doing a service for humanity by voluntarily removing himself from the gene pool during his years spent in prison.

Hugh was fifty yards ahead of his pursuers when he entered the huge hotel, and he immediately stopped running to keep from attracting attention. Winding his way through the cavernous casino lobby, he tried to blend in with the horde of wagering devotees, who sat hunched over their machines, mechanically feeding the voracious beasts like robots. Hugh planned to keep moving further and further into the hotel's vast interior until he could either find a remote place to hide or slip out unnoticed. In carrying out his simple plan, Hugh made two critical errors.

He made his first mistake when he entered the gambling domain of longtime Las Vegas denizen, Gertrude Swartz. Gertrude was a long-time Strip survivor who exemplified the basic tenets of the territorial imperative. Once she staked out her machines, she guarded them like a junk-yard dog and showed no mercy to anyone who attempted to swindle her out of her hard gambled booty. Unfortunately for Hugh, he decided to gamble at a nickel slot to mingle in with the other bettors, and he chose an empty stool and started playing the machine, taking cautious glances all around to determine if that huge Mr. Universe in the blue tank-top or the tall guy wearing the black cowboy hat still chased him. Unknown to Hugh, however, he'd violated a cardinal rule among slot zealots: never *assume* that a slot is not being played simply because someone is not sitting in front of the machine, for bettors are traditionally allowed to play two slots simultaneously.

Enter Gertrude. On the next stool over, the seventy-five year old Queen Of The One-armed Bandits systematically inserted nickels into her primary slot with such determined concentration that she failed to notice Hugh start playing her second slot. To describe Gertrude as *feisty* would be an understatement of the greatest magnitude. She had the temperament of a Tasmanian devil and a razor sharp tongue to match. Then the Prince of Purse-snatcher's made his second mistake. He hit a jackpot. When the bells rang and lights flashed, Gertrude turned and pierced Hugh with her stiletto eyes and let him know in no uncertain terms that the jackpot belonged to her. Gertrude's raspy voice rose above the casino's clamor.

"Hey, asshole! You're playing my fuckin' machine!"

Hugh glanced around furtively and attempted to placate the elderly woman. "Don't get excited, old lady. The jackpot is yours. I didn't know you were playing this machine."

But Gertrude was an old hand at playing the slots, and because this interloper *seemed* so willing to give up the jackpot, she immediately smelled a big, fat rat. No one voluntarily surrendered a jackpot. No one! Gertrude eased off her stool and took firm hold of her walking cane. Hugh saw the fury in her eyes and managed only a clumsy half step retreat before Gertrude's cane found its mark on top of his head.

Thwack!

With the jackpot's bells ringing and its lights blinking on and off as a fantasy background, Hugh collapsed to the floor and watched in a kind of dazed, slow motion as Gertrude's cane rose and fell twice more. Self-preservation now superseded Hugh's flight to freedom as his major objective, and he scrambled to his feet to escape the dowager's wrath. He staggered away with Gertrude limping after him in hot pursuit. Hugh thought he was in the middle of a hideous nightmare. First, two wild amazons chased him in red Corvettes. Then an Arnold Schwarzenegger clone and a tall Pancho Villa look-alike ran after him. And now this old lady from the depths of hell chased after him. Her smoky, cigarette mutated caws rose to the rafters.

"That asshole stole my jackpot! Stop that fucker!"

Hugh partially regained his senses and broke into a sprint. Like a wide receiver concentrating on catching the winning touchdown pass in the Super Bowl, Hugh developed tunnel vision on the escape path before him. He never saw the hit coming. Bull's 255 pounds smashed into the fleeing felon in a tackle that would have certainly aired on NFL highlights as the "hit of the week." Hugh Bromley, failed armed robber and failed purse-snatcher, remained unconscious for a good two minutes. When he came to, Bull, Tex-Mex, Gertrude Swartz, and half a dozen LVPD officers stood over him. Hugh's glazed eyes finally came into focus.

Tex-Mex adopted a look of mock concern as he stared down at Hugh. "Think we should get a priest to administer the last rites, Bull?"

Gertrude answered instead. "I'll give the asshole his last rites," she said and raised her cane over her head.

Bull laughed and took hold of her arm. "Whoa, there! I think the police can handle this."

While OPD's deputized twosome assisted the LVPD officers with Hugh "The Loser" Bromley's arrest, Becky and Eve remained back at the intersection where a massive traffic jam had vehicles backed up for blocks. Two LVPD officers worked with Becky and Eve to sort out the logistics of the situation and start the paperwork. After the tumult subsided, Rent-A-Vette sales-man Jim Teller made his way through the crush of onlookers to reclaim his two vehicles. Due to the confusion at the scene, peo-ple swarmed past the yellow caution tape strung up to bar their entry. One of these onlookers was an opportunistic thief, who de-cided to seize his chance to score a shiny Corvette and take it for a joy ride. Seeing that the key to one of the Vettes was still in-serted in the ignition, this conniving car booster waited for the traffic congestion to thin out, informed one of the LVPD officers that he worked for Rent-A-Vette, and then got behind the wheel and drove off. As the Vette disappeared in traffic, Jim ap-proached the officer and in his diffident manner inquired who drove his Vette away.

The officer turned to Jim with a puzzled look. "He said he was one of your employees."

Jim's despair reached the end of its tether. A look of total defeat registered on his face. As he watched the red spot in the roadway fade from view, what remained of his self-esteem hit rock-bottom. His afflictions and tribulations now exceeded those of the Biblical Job.

Becky tried to console the distraught salesman. "Just not your day, huh? Sorry about what happened today, Jim. But when we saw that asshole snatch that woman's purse, we just had to do something. You understand, don't you?"

Jim gave Becky a dazed nod and made his way back to the rental agency. He shuffled away slump-shouldered, a rumpled salesman slouching toward Rent-A-Vette and an uncertain fu-ture. But he made a solemn vow. He would never again, under any circumstances, rent another vehicle to a police officer. Any group of people who would interrupt a *vacation* in Las Vegas to apprehend two crooks were entirely too dedicated to their jobs to be trusted.

~~~~

They couldn't buy a drink. The LVPD officers who conducted the robbery investigation invited OPD's finest to their equivalent of the Hit 'N Run, the Lucky Seven Bar and Grill, and the drinks were on them. It turned out that Hurrying Hugh and his female accomplice were responsible for a string of purse-snatches dating back weeks, and their arrests cleared a cabinet drawer full of cases and removed a proverbial huge thorn from LVPD's side. And when Sergeant Steve Heston, the robbery scene supervisor, recognized Bull and Tex-Mex as the officers who rescued the children in the bus fire caper, the OPD foursome's status rose to a level where they could have asked for the key to the city and LVPD would have gladly given it to them.

"So, what are you going to do next?" Sergeant Heston asked. "Give a demonstration on how to walk on water?"

The crowded tables rocked with laughter.

Another LVPD officer added. "Or you can trade in those Corvettes and rent hot air balloons and race across the desert."

Bull looked intrigued. "You know, I've heard about that. Are there places in Las Vegas that rent hot air balloons?"

"Absolutely," Sergeant Heston said. "You guys interested in doing that? If so, I know the manager of Vegas Balloon Trips, and I can hook you up."

Bull looked at Becky. Becky turned to Eve. Eve glanced at Tex-Mex, and the Texan completed the round robin silent inquiry by fixing Bull with an arched eyebrow. And the four of them grinned and nodded their approval.

19

Sunrise the next morning brought with it a startling blue, cloudless sky and a gentle breeze that the manager of Vegas Balloon Trips proclaimed perfect for ballooning. The manager scheduled the flight to last two hours, followed by a champagne brunch immediately after landing. Their balloon was a massive, multi-colored oval that swayed slightly where several ropes anchored it to the ground. Their pilot, Frank Grimsley, greeted them warmly and described what they would experience during their flight. The four rookie balloonists brimmed over with excitement. After receiving a mandatory lecture on safety procedure, they made preparations for liftoff. Frank tried to alleviate their pre-flight jitters.

"I've been doing this for over thirty years and had thousands of passengers, and I haven't lost one of them yet. So, just relax and enjoy the flight."

Amidst a chorus of cheers from a few of the Lucky-Seven Bar and Grill faithful, who turned out to wish the four wayfarers a hearty bon voyage, the flight crew released the balloon's anchor lines to set them adrift. With each second that passed, the stunning beauty of balloon flight overwhelmed the four of them. They soared over a vast panorama that extended for as far as the eye could see. In the distance, Las Vegas' countless plate glass windows on The Strip reflected the sun's light and sparkled like diamonds. Frank brought their attention to the mountain shadows receding as the sun climbed majestically in the sky. The shadows seemed alive as they lumbered across the landscape. The countryside drifted slowly past, and they were so captivated by their floating like a cloud over the flat brown terrain that they almost missed Frank's murmur of concern about half an hour into the flight.

"Hmmm."

The four of them turned to him for a translation of what, "Hmmm," meant.

In a calm voice that belied the circumstances, Frank deciphered his throaty exclamation.

"We might have a bit of a problem. A valve malfunction with the propane tank. No need for alarm. What this means is that we might not make it to our scheduled landing point. We may have to put down elsewhere. This kind of thing happens now and then. Again, there's no need for concern. Just an inconvenience."

The four Jules Verne, *Around The World In Eighty Days*, adventurers concentrated on the ground below. Perhaps it was their imagination, but it did seem that they were losing altitude at a rapidly increasing rate. This observation coupled with Frank's explanation of his, "Hmmm," caused them to reconsider their former wholehearted endorsement of a balloon ride as a mandatory recreational experience. Off in the distance, Bull focused on a structure of some type, and he pointed it out to his fellow, incipient crash-landers. As they drifted inexorably in its direction, the structure took the form of a huge canvas tent. There was no doubt. They headed directly for this tent and its occupants inside.

~~~~

The huge revival tent looked out of place where it rose out of a barren patch of desert miles away from its formal parent church located on the outskirts of Las Vegas. Today, the First Church of God in Christ scheduled the second of three Revival services, and Reverend Joshua Freeman, its forty year old pastor, looked forward to another outstanding turnout. A man of great vision, Reverend Freeman had three major objectives in guiding his laity: show his parishioners the path to eternal salvation; personally lead them along this path to avoid the temptations of evil; and increase the size and wealth of his church to provide him and his family with a good living. Though he ostensibly held the first two goals as the bedrock of his ministry, the third frequently eclipsed them in terms of where he expended the majority of his efforts and resources.

Above all, Reverend Freeman preached fire and brimstone scripture, and his hypnotic sermons proved capable of moving his flock *close* to religious hysteria. His flamboyant style made him a charismatic, latter-day reincarnation of Elmer Gantry, and he prided himself in his ability to make ordinary people become so entranced with his sermons that they abandoned all rational thought and tithed accordingly. His intent was, quite simply, to put on a good show and have his flock return to the next week's performance. And tithe again.

His sermon this morning dealt with the Resurrection and modern man's responsibility to accept the Biblical version of Christ's return as the Gospel Truth. The congregation hushed as Reverend Freeman took his place in the pulpit. Starting slow to build momentum, his voice had a lyrical quality that rose from a near whisper to a bellow that shook the tent. The flock strained to hear every word and the Reverend mesmerized them with every inflection of his voice. He led them along expertly and let the tension build for the grand finale, holding them spellbound while they periodically punctuated his delivery with multiple cries of "Amen!" whenever the Holy Ghost Spirit moved their souls. After laying the groundwork, Reverend Freeman had the congregation enthralled with his oratorical powers, and he raised his arms and beseeched the Heavens.

"Lord, Almighty! We humbly ask that You show us the way to Salvation and give Your servants a sign of Your Eternal Power."

And God complied.

The gondola carrying the four intrepid balloonists and *their* spiritual sky pilot crashed into the top of the tent like a wrecking ball. The stunning blow dislodged the tent's center pole and the interconnecting guidelines tangled with the gondola's own ropes. For a second or two the tent stood inert, but then a strong gust of wind caught hold of the balloon and subjected it to the effects of Newton's Second Law of Motion. The balloon tore the tent stakes from the ground and ripped the canvas from its moorings, exposing the entire congregation cowering below. A collective shriek of both terror and a sense of an impending miracle about to take place erupted from the congregation.

~~~~

Beatrice Flemming was a particularly devout woman who *never* missed a church service. Through sickness and all types of natural calamities, she ensconced herself in the front pew to receive the Word from Reverend Freeman. When the gondola struck, she raised her bowed head and a blinding flash of direct sunlight caused her to believe that she entered the Kingdom of Heaven. With her eyes closed, she imagined that she neared the Pearly Gates and began talking in tongues, reverting to her scandalous practices as a previous member of an ultra-evangelical denomination, whom her present day church members condescendingly called "holy rollers."

"Lord, abba chanit combertin doobimpoi soewarin!" Beatrice prayed fervently.

Since she felt no physical pain or any other discomfort, the shrieks and lamentations of others in the tent convinced Beatrice that she joined the preordained the Lord chose to be saved, and the screams from the rest meant that God cast them into the fiery pit of Hell. Like a slot player who loyally and passionately fed her machine in hopes that it would eventually pay off, Beatrice felt vindicated that all her time spent in the House Of The Lord finally produced dividends.

"I've hit the Motherload of all jackpots!" Beatrice cried out. "Heaven, golden streets and all! Hallelujah!"

Only after she became aware of people moving around her did she open her eyes and see the balloon soaring away in the distance and realize what actually happened. She took furtive glances around the collapsed tent to determine if anyone witnessed her shameful lapse into tongue-talking and her boastful comparison that linked gambling to an ascent into Heaven.

~~~~

Wilson Sandusky suffered from a pronounced loss of libido, and he joined other members of Reverend Freeman's flock about to undergo delusional out-of-body experiences. At the time the gondola struck the tent, fifty year old Wilson attempted to interpret the Reverend's message within the context of his own particular *problem*. Reverend Freeman preached about the Resurrection, but Wilson noticed how close the word *resurrection* resembled the word *erection* and conjectured if this linguistic similarity could help him get a hard-on.

Wilson's prayers evolved into frantic entreaties to the Lord to restore his ever-diminishing manhood, and phallic images increasingly dominated his dreams. The Empire State Building, with its extraordinary dimensions was a recurring image in his dreams, which he subconsciously revered as the ultimate phallic symbol. After watching the movie *King Kong* on TV late one night, he thrashed in his sleep and gasped in horror during a nightmare, as the giant ape climbed and conquered the mighty structure, startling his wife awake babbling about gorillas and clutching his limp appendage to protect it from a simian assault.

When the gondola demolished the tent, the massive blow knocked Wilson and others from their chairs and sprawled them on the ground. During the chaos that followed, Wilson glanced to his right and came up close and face-to-pubic-area-personal with a sweet young thing, whose dress hiked up past her hips, revealing her panty-less bush in all its luscious, dewy, pink-lipped splendor. He even detected the bush's slightly pungent aroma. And suddenly God answered Wilson's prayers! As he stared in a trance at the vaginal opening to God's ultimate gift to man, a torrent of pulsating blood flooded his groin and his erection grew. He stood and watched in ecstasy as the bulge in his pants dramatically increased in size, straining to be liberated from its confines and set free to boldly go where multitudes of men before him went. His one and only thought was to rocket home to have sex with his wife before God had second thoughts and cast him back into impotence purgatory.

~~~~

Reverend Freeman was not immune to the spiritual special effects the gondola's destruction created. When the light nearly as bright as an atomic blast flashed above and blinded him, the Reverend first thought his beseeching the Almighty for a sign of his Eternal Power had *actually worked,* and The Second Coming would follow. For a brief instant, unmitigated joy surged through him as he celebrated Christ's return. But then a sudden shadow of doubt erased this momentary euphoria. If Christ was as omniscient as the Bible maintained, then perhaps He would not look too kindly upon the Reverend's intense preoccupation with the accumulation of wealth and power. For a fraction of a second, this insight caused him a guilt induced anxiety attack until reality reasserted itself, and he became aware that the present phenomenon had nothing to do with the Second Coming of Christ, but instead it was the First Coming of a hot-air balloon that crash-landed into their tent. He breathed a sigh of relief that his chicanery went undiscovered, yet like Beatrice Flemming, he still took covert looks around the tent to determine if anyone saw beyond the piety façade he constructed.

~~~~

After another 100 yards dragging the huge tent, the gondola jolted to a landing and Frank and his four survivors secured the balloon in place. Using the gondola's radio, Frank gave the Vegas Balloon Trips ground crew their location, and within minutes the rescue team arrived to deal with the carnage that occurred. Except for some bruised egos suffered by those whose hyperactive imaginations swept them up in excessive religious fervor, the congregation suffered no serious injuries. In fact, the mishap had one positive aspect associated with it: Wilson Sandusky's libido was fully restored, and he no longer suffered torturous nightmares imagining gigantic apes attacking his Johnson.

~~~~

Two self-induced insomnia days later, the four proactive purse-snatcher catchers/balloon crash survivors waited at the airport to board their flight back to the workday world. Their sloppy appearance and colossal hangovers let them know what a great time they had. Now, it was time to return to Oakland and deal with the murders, robberies, and general mayhem that awaited them.

Tex-Mex and Bull stared dully out the lobby's large plate glass window, watching planes take off and land. Both of them slurped high-octane espresso to keep from falling asleep on their feet. Becky and Eve crashed in their waiting room seats, their heads lolling off their shoulders as they sought more comfortable sleeping positions. Tex-Mex took a big gulp of his fiery brew, and focused on the runways. A chorus of loud voices and raucous laughter caused Tex-Mex to shift his attention to a number of passengers making their way from the connector corridor into the terminal. A huge man led an entourage that surrounded a slender man dressed in a bright pink suit, with a matching fedora and cape. Tex-Mex nudged Bull and pointed to Hollywood Hawkins, Bear Beavins, Snuff Dog, Tremane, and others making their way through the throng of people in the crowded terminal. Bull and Tex-Mex were in a secluded corner out of their view.

"Shit," Bull said. "We can't get away from that asshole."

Tex-Mex laughed. "Hey, dope dealers have a right to take holidays too."

Then Bull happened to glance back to that same connector corridor and stared as a man wearing a Yankees baseball cap and mirrored sunglasses entered the terminal at discrete distance behind Hollywood and his retinue. Now, it was Bull's turn to nudge the Texan.

"Well, well, look who we have here," Bull said.

The Texan smirked. "You think there's a chance he just *happened* to be on the same flight as Hollywood and his assholes?"

Bull pondered the Texan's question for a moment. "Well, if you buy that possibility, then I've got a bridge that stretches from Oakland to 'Frisco I'd like to sell you."

Tex-Mex shrugged. "Yeah, I get your drift. Well, it looks like we now know why we've never been able to put any cases on Hollywood Hawkins."

Bull grunted an affirmation to Tex-Mex's astute observation, and both of them watched OPD Narcotics Officer Sean Morris disappear in the crowd.

20

Lieutenant Hal Allen listened in incredulous disbelief to what Tex-Mex told him over the phone from the Las Vegas International Airport. The lieutenant rose from behind his desk and closed his office door. Then he spoke in a hushed voice even though there was no need to do so.

"And you're absolutely certain Hawkins and Morris were together on that plane?"

"Absolutely, LT," Tex-Mex replied. "Oh, Sean had on a Yankees cap and dark glasses in a half-assed attempt to conceal his identity, but it was him. And Hollywood? Shit, he was dressed in his usual pimp attire, so even a blind man wouldn't have any trouble recognizing him. And of course Hollywood had his gangster entourage with him too."

"All right, but all we have, unfortunately, is Sean on a plane with Hawkins. Nothing else. No crime. But at least we know who our mole is. Now, we have to establish further connections between the two of them. Once we accomplish that, the Feds can get a court order for wiretaps."

"What about Aaron Cook, LT? My bet is that he's as dirty as Sean."

"Yeah, probably, so we'll treat him as such," the LT replied.

He paused as he organized his thoughts. "OK, this is the course of action. I want absolute secrecy. Tell no one. Anyone there with you? Becky Farmer and Eve Lawson? Did they see Hawkins and Morris? No? Well, don't mention it to them. We've got to keep this under tight control. I'll brief the Chief, and as soon as you get back into town, contact me immediately so we can coordinate our response."

When Tex-Mex reported to work the next day, Lieutenant Allen assigned him and Rocky to check and double-check every known document pertaining to Hollywood Hawkins and Sean Morris. Sifting through the reams and reams of paperwork proved an exhausting ordeal, but it was necessary to uncover any link between Morris and Hawkins. Surveillance on Morris and Cook started the next day. Using agents and officers from other agencies with whom Sean and Aaron had no previous contact, they began the tedious task of following their every movement, on-duty and off.

They audited Sean's flamboyant lifestyle and the mystery surrounding his finances began to clear up. The other narcotics officers always speculated how Sean was able to afford the many luxuries he enjoyed. They tallied up his expenses for his home, cars, holiday trips, and expensive jewelry, and the numbers crunch revealed conclusively that either he was the thriftiest man on the planet, or he hit the Lottery on a consistent basis. His police salary did not come remotely close to covering his expenditures.

Tex-Mex and Rocky waded through stacks of paperwork, searching for any incriminating evidence that would link Sean Morris and Aaron Cook with Hollywood Hawkins. Court orders authorized them access to Hollywood's personal business records, and the hours turned into days as they poured over a plethora of documents that all began to look the same. The repetitive, boring work exhausted them, making it difficult to maintain their concentration. Box after box, thousands of notes, bills, bank statements, credit card histories, and police documents taxed their endurance to the utmost. It was Friday, the fifth day since the lieutenant assigned them to their Sisyphean-like task. Tex-Mex looked at the wall clock. Ten minutes until quitting time.

"Needle in a haystack," Tex-Mex quipped.

"*Big* fuckin' haystack," Rocky said.

"You think we'll find it?" Tex-Mex asked.

Rocky glanced back at the stacks of boxes full of documents and shrugged wearily. Officer Harold Osgood entered the office and tidied up his desk in preparation to leave for the day. He was not privy to Sean and Aaron's investigation. For the present time, Lieutenant Allen decided to keep him and the other narcotics officers out of the information loop for security reasons. Harold thought Tex-Mex and Rocky combed through Hawkins' business documents to extract enough evidence for another search warrant. He opened and closed his desk drawers in rapid succession until he found the tickets he sought.

"What's your hurry, Harold?" Tex-Mex asked.

Harold looked back over his shoulder as he headed for the door and waved the two tickets he held. "Goin' to see my alma mater play tonight. Supposedly have a hell of a football team this year."

"Oh yeah?" Rocky said. "Where'd you go to school, Harold?"

"McClymonds. The Warriors! Lots of great athletes came out of there. Bill Russell. Paul Silas. Frank Robinson. Even Hollywood Hawkins went there and was a pretty good athlete. Played football and basketball with Sean Morris. Funny how dudes turn out. One goes in one direction, the other in the opposite direction." Harold stopped when he saw the perplexed looks on Tex-Mex and Rocky's faces. "You two didn't know that? Common knowledge among us Oakland bred and raised boys. Well, I got to get movin' or I'm gonna miss the first quarter. See you in the A.M."

Rocky grinned as Harold shut the door behind him. "It's here, Tex-Mex. Let's keep lookin' for that demonic Holy Grail, man. I'll authorize the overtime."

They found it an hour later. Tex-Mex held up a telephone bill that listed dozens of calls Hollywood made a few months before the Feds obtained a court order for the wiretap. He scanned the long list and was about to put it aside in the already checked pile, when one entry caught his eye. The area code differed markedly from the rest of the calls, and he brought it to Rocky's attention. Rocky checked the list of area codes and frowned.

"Who the hell does Hollywood know in San Ramon?" Rocky asked.

In an instant, Rocky and Tex-Mex traded wide-eyed looks.

Then they blurted out simultaneously. "Sean Morris lives in San Ramon!"

Rocky fumbled through Sean's personnel folder and used his forefinger to scroll down the page until he came to the proper entry line.

"It can't be. . ." Tex-Mex whispered.

"He can't be *that* stupid. . ." Rocky added.

They both glanced back and forth from Hollywood's phone bill to Sean's home phone number. It was a match.

21

The large, two-story home overlooked an expansive view on a secluded cul-de-sac in an upper income neighborhood in the city of San Ramon. The tastefully landscaped home had a rear yard with a large pool, built-in spa, gazebo, and brick barbeque, which made it a model for entertaining. In the circular driveway, a new Mercedes Benz and a late model Toyota Land Cruiser parked there added to the well-to-do ambience. In the five-bedroom, three bath interior, the homeowner converted one of the bedrooms into a game room, with a pool table, full service bar, and a surround sound system for the 56 inch television prominently displayed in one corner. The stainless steel kitchen had an island equipped with its own grill and rotisserie. The mortgage payment was an eyebrow raiser, but Sean Morris had supplemental income to help tote the note.

Aaron Cook cradled his glass of Hennessey and looked across the kitchen table at Sean Morris. How in hell did he ever let Sean talk him into this mess? Dollar signs blinded him, he admitted to himself. Now, he was close to a mental breakdown. He couldn't sleep. He had no appetite and he lost weight. He stayed constantly on the alert for other officers' changes in behavior toward him. Their innocuous jests made him wary and look for hidden meanings behind their words. He imagined people stared at him, trying to look behind the façade he built to cover up the truth. Worst of all, he recognized his own paranoia, yet he could not relieve his anxiety. He teetered on the edge. He glanced at Sean again, and what he saw enraged him. Sean had a twinkle in his eyes that revealed his amusement at Aaron's obvious distress. Everything was a joke to Sean. He could not make Sean see the gravity of their situation. Aaron shook these thoughts from his mind and plunged ahead.

"I want out, man."

Sean took a sip of his drink and studied Aaron. He still had the glint of amusement in his eyes, but it mutated into a more virulent form. "That so? Where you comin' from with this shit?"

Sean's game-playing angered Aaron. "You know exactly what the fuck I mean, Sean. Out. O-U-T!"

Sean's broad smile broke through. "Well, that presents a problem, bro. Just how are you gonna get *out*? We have a business agreement with Mr. Hollywood Hawkins. I'm certain you *remember* our business agreement with him, don't you? What do you think he's gonna say about you wanting *out*? You think he's gonna just shake hands and say, 'Hey, thanks for signing on with my narcotics trafficking organization, and I wish you the best of luck with the rest of your OPD career.' Is that how you think he'll react?"

Aaron felt his anger rise. "I don't care what the fuck he'll say! I'm sick of all this cloak and dagger shit. Havin' to sneak around and find out when the task force is gonna move on him. Letting him know far enough in advance when a search warrant is goin' down, so he can move the dope, money and guns to another location. I'm tired of always lookin' over my shoulder to see if the LT or any of the guys are on to us. This shit is driving me crazy!"

Sean changed his facial expression like a chameleon to exploit an advantage. "What? Is this a money thing? You want more money? Want me to hit him up for more cash? Come on, Aaron, talk to me! You and me go way back. Ain't no secrets 'tween us." Sean let that hang in the air before continuing. "But, you see, Aaron, I've gotten used to the cash. Bought me this home and my rides. Pays for my trips to Hawaii. Cruises to Mexico. I go to Vegas anytime I want. So, if it's a money thing, don't be bashful. Just let me know and I'll renegotiate our *contract* with ah, *Mr. Hawkins.*"

Aaron scowled. "It ain't about the money, Sean. You *know* that. You see where we're headin'. I've been a cop long enough to know that sooner or later, the shit's gonna come down on us. Only a matter of time. And you know it too. And then we're gonna end up in the joint gettin' butt-fucked by some dudes who we put cases on in the past!"

Sean laughed. "Damn, dude, you got no faith in my abilities. I can manage this shit. Nobody in the squad knows anything. They're all wanderin' around in the dark tryin' to figure out what's goin' on. All we have to do is be cool, don't make no stupid mistakes, and everything is gonna be fine." Sean tried to read Aaron's response. "But like I told you, it's not like we can walk away from this. All Hollywood has to do is drop a dime on us and we're fucked. Just an anonymous call and gettin' terminated by OPD would be the least of our worries. But don't think he hasn't thought about us goin' to him one day and sayin' that we want out. I'm absolutely sure he's already thought that out and has a reply waitin' on our asses. Not to mention, of course, that if he feels we're gettin' weak, he could arrange for our *disappearance* without any trouble at all."

Sean watched Aaron's anger escalate even higher.

"Fuck!" Aaron said. "Why did I ever let you talk me into this? Yeah, the money's good, but money ain't gonna help me when I'm staring out of bars in prison. So, we're just gonna keep on bein' Hollywood's snitches? Is that what you're tellin' me? Well, I'm tellin' you, Sean, sooner or later we're gonna get caught. Only a matter of time."

Sean's high-pitched laughter belittled Aaron. "Stop bein' a little bitch. Damn, you whine more than a sniveling little ho' doin' the stroll on West Mac. You just let me do the thinkin' and all you have to do is keep your eyes and ears open and keep me informed. I'll take care of the rest. Oh, and I'll get us a raise too."

Aaron stared out the kitchen window with a blank expression.

Sean eyed him carefully. "You want me to freshen up that Hennessey?"

Aaron's anger smoldered. "Nah, I gotta split."

Sean watched Aaron circle the driveway and drive out of the

cul-de-sac. He didn't like the looks of this. Aaron's starting to punk out. Talking scary. All it would take would be one mistake. Just one. He wrestled with the thought of telling Hollywood, but he knew that doing so would sign Aaron's death warrant. Hollywood Hawkins had a multi-million dollar enterprise working, and he wouldn't allow one punk-ass OPD narcotics cop to fuck it all up. Aaron knew too much for Hollywood to allow him to *retire*. So, if he snitched off Aaron, and Hollywood whacked him, he'd be involved in premeditated murder. Not a good thing since that made it a death penalty bounce. Sean knew that people facing a few years in the joint often ratted out others to escape or reduce their incarceration time. That's how the criminal justice system worked. Sean sensed Aaron's desperation, and desperate men do desperate things. For now, he'd watch Aaron and evaluate the level of danger he posed. But if Aaron continued to trip, he'd have to make a decision. A decision that would either place him in greater jeopardy, or free him from the *problem* Aaron represented.

22

Rondell seethed with rage. He scanned the front pages of all the major Bay Area newspapers, but there was no mention of the Cha Cha Cha robbery/murders. A crime like that and it didn't even rate a front page story? Rondell fumed as he thumbed through the papers searching for the report. He found it on page two of one paper, page five in another, and in the second section in yet a third. He picked up the pile of newspapers and flung them across the room. The TV channels were no different. Only one newscast gave an account of what Rondell thought should have been headline news. Shit, he should have popped a couple more of those restaurant employees to make certain he got the media's attention!

Rondell lit a joint to mellow out. What the fuck would he have to do to rate the news coverage he deserved? He inhaled deeply and let his imagination soar. Had to be something original. Something that would make even the FBI sit up, take notice, and place him on their Ten Most Wanted List. He toked the joint down to a roach, and the perfect crime came to him as he watched a movie rerun on TV, *Butch Cassidy and the Sundance Kid.*

A train robbery.

Now, that crime would capture the attention of *all* America. As the weed took hold, Rondell let his creative gears mesh. How long had it been since a train robbery took place, he wondered? Probably a hundred years. He and Larry would be like a modern day Jesse and Frank James. In order to blaze their way to the top of the criminal world, they needed a gimmick, something that would set them apart from the average gangster. A train robbery offered them a golden opportunity to cement their reputation.

And following the Great Train Robbery, they would do a re-enactment of a crime from another time period, like the Roaring Twenties. They could get AK-47s and become Machine Gun Kellys. Rob a bank and conceal AK-47s in violin cases, like in the movies. Totally off the wall shit. Rondell's mind reeled with the possibilities. He had no idea what megalomania meant, but with each additional daring crime he perpetrated, his delusional obsessions personified this psychopathological concept more and more.

Two days after the Cha Cha Cha caper, Rondell proposed a takeover robbery of a Bay Area Rapid Transit, or BART, train. At first, Larry vehemently opposed the proposal, and Rondell had to sell the idea to him.

Larry looked at Rondell like he lost his mind. "Train robbery? The BART train? Blood, you been smokin' too much shit. You trippin'! You been comin' up with more and more crazy shit, but this is the craziest yet!"

"Trippin' my ass," Rondell scoffed. "I'm tellin' you, nigga, a job like this will put us on the criminal map. And after the train robbery, we could rob an armored car or a casino in Reno or Vegas, like in the movie *Ocean's Eleven*. I got loads of ideas, blood."

Larry waved his hand dismissively at Rondell and turned away. "You know, Rondell, you lettin' this criminal shit go to your head. We ain't nobody but Larry and Rondell White, two niggas from Oaktown. Tryin' to make us anything different is just gonna get our black asses put on death row."

Rondell saw the doubt on Larry's face and took a more persuasive approach. "Look, blood, think of all the famous gangsters from the past. Pretty Boy Floyd, Al Capone, Bugsy Siegel, the Mafia, and a whole lot more. If we use our heads and take care of business, someday our names will be on that motherfuckin' list."

"Fuck, Rondell, why are you so fuckin' hyped 'bout gettin' to be famous? Gettin' famous only makes the PO-PO want to catch us more and. . ."

"That's the trouble with you, Larry!" Rondell shouted him down. "You got no sense of self-respect. No pride in bein' the best in what we do. And what we do best is rob, rape, and murder people! We got a chance to go down in history as two of the wildest, baddest motherfuckers who ever lived. Shit, people be talkin' 'bout us a hundred years from now!"

Rondell knew Larry. He knew Larry would put up a weak front and then cave in and do what he wanted. But Rondell also knew that he would gain greater compliance from his baby 'bro if he put a positive spin on the caper. So, the more he built it up and described how it would go down, the more Larry began to reluctantly accept and finally endorse the BART robbery.

Rondell also knew that the heist would take a great deal of casing to make certain all the bases were covered to insure success. To this end, he and Larry became regular riders on the train to determine when the train would be ripe for the taking. They monitored the trains and stations for police presence, and a clear pattern emerged. Police staffing was lowest in the early morning commute hours.

~~~~

It was the start of another work week, and OPD Officer Rita Sims joined the rest of the commuters aboard the BART train heading to Oakland. Rita settled into her seat and worked on a crossword puzzle. She commuted by BART for years, and she overwhelmingly preferred the train to driving her car in the daily traffic jam that plagued Highway 24 and the Caldecott tunnels. The fact that as a police officer she rode free of charge also influenced her decision to ride the rails. It was BART's way of increasing police presence on its trains, even if the majority of officers, like Rita, dressed in casual civilian clothing. As a matter of habit, Rita rode the train unarmed to and from work. Although the California Penal Code authorized off-duty officers to carry concealed firearms, Rita, like many police veterans, regarded this firearms obsession as a rookie ritual practiced by young officers entranced with their power to be armed wherever they went.

It was a little after 6:00 A.M., when the train left the Lafayette station and entered the tunnel that bored through the hills into Oakland. Rita heard faint shouts coming from the car immediately to the rear. She noted that a few passengers in her car also heard the commotion and craned their necks toward the two cars' separation doors to determine its cause. Rita left her seat and started down the aisle toward the rear car to identify the problem. As she approached the double accordion style doors, the shouts grew louder and more distinct. Then she looked through the door windows, and what she saw froze her in place. Two men wearing ski masks and gloves waved handguns and forced people to remove their wallets and jewelry and deposit the valuables into a small carry-bag. She focused her attention on a male passenger lying on the floor with blood streaming from a cut to his head. One of the gunmen stood over the injured man, holding his pistol in a threatening manner as if to pistol-whip the man again.

Initially, Rita felt a pang of regret for not being armed and able to take action. But then her common sense screamed at her that being armed would only make matters worse. A gunfight in a crowded train car or railway station with dozens of people milling around the platform? That would be insane. Her only option was to return to her seat and concentrate on being a good witness. Then a sudden, sickening thought came to her. What if these two men were the serial killers? The masks, gloves, 9mm pistols, and the violent, brazen crime matched their MO.

Rita started to return to her seat, but she was not quick enough. The suspect who pistol-whipped the passenger swiveled his head in her direction and their eyes locked. Rita saw the rage in those eyes and felt a paralyzing fear spread from the pit of her stomach to her limbs. The man's penetrating stare held her captive. She could not look away. His unwavering glare showed no clemency. They were the eyes of an executioner about to carry out a death sentence. Rita stood rooted in place while he raised his pistol, aimed through the door window, and the muzzle flash was the last thing she ever saw.

~~~~

Rita Sims' funeral took place five days later. Since her death occurred during an off-duty incident and she was not engaged in an official police action, the memorial organizers did not plan the usual massive police funeral attended by officers from all over the state. But Rita was a well-liked, popular officer, and the OPD family turned out in the hundreds to pay their respects and honor her passing. The intensity of the serial killers' investigation rose several degrees, and apprehending them took on the aura of a vendetta. Now, the OPD rank and file looked upon their capture as personal.

And to no one was it more personal than Duke. When Duke served as a newly promoted sergeant and Rita became a member of his squad, she helped him navigate the many pitfalls virtually all rookie supervisors had to overcome until their stripes lost their gloss and they settled into making competent decisions. Though Rita had only three years on OPD when Duke acquired his new rank, she had the savvy of a far more experienced officer, and she successfully treaded the quagmire of difficult situations police officers faced on a daily basis. Duke recognized her unique ability and routinely sought out Rita's advice on particularly thorny issues, and she discreetly served as a quasi-mentor or sounding board without revealing their association to other officers, or assuming haughty airs for assisting her supervisor. Moreover, Duke felt genuinely fond of Rita, though their relationship never crossed the line to a romantic one. When Rita joined the serial killers' victim list, Duke's hunger for retribution and his dedication to their capture became as intense as Mary's. Together, they formed a formidable team on a quest for justice that transcended their jobs.

~~~~

The publicity Rondell White coveted was unprecedented in its scope and magnitude. He glowed with pride, when the national news media made the train robbery and murder of a police officer front page news. The bold, ruthless crime sent shock waves through mass transit systems nationwide and generated immediate inquiries to assess their safety. Even though law enforcement officials viewed it as a crime of financial gain, anti-terrorist agencies felt its impact as well. Rondell knew he pricked a sensitive nerve that earned him and Larry the notoriety for which he yearned.

Now, the law enforcement community anxiously waited for the serial killers' next strike like a condemned collectivity under a sword of Damocles poised above them.

23

A week later, Mary and Duke labored away in the office, trying to break open their stagnant cases. Since Rita Sims' murder occurred aboard a BART train, BART PD was the principal agency probing the crime. But due to Rita's OPD affiliation, both departments agreed to share jurisdiction in the investigation.

Mary closed her eyes, kneaded her temples, and thought outloud. "Duke, I wonder why only one of the suspects is doing all the killing. What's going on between those two assholes? One is aggressive and the other is passive. And what's with the changing MO? From home invasions, to a restaurant, and now a train. Where did *that* come from? Hell, they'll probably hijack a plane next! Is this some kind of game to them? Jesus, we've got to figure them out."

Duke didn't respond until Mary met his eyes. "Things will fall into place, Mary. They'll eventually make a mistake and pay the price. I just hope we're there to insure that justice is carried out."

Mary and Duke maintained eye contact, and it was as if an intrinsic understanding bound them together in an unspoken pact. Then the shrill ringing of Mary's phone broke the spell.

Mary's rote answer revealed her fatigue and irritability.

"Sergeant Sanders, homicide."

"Sergeant Sanders?" a familiar voice asked. "This is Angel Bennings, the 'ho, I mean workin' girl, you told to call you if I ever came up with somethin' on that dude who gave me that ring. Remember?"

Mary felt the hairs on the back of her neck stand up. "Yes, Angel, of course I remember. You say you have something for me?"

"Yeah," Angel replied. "That same dude came back and wanted a date, so after we finished our business, I got the license number of that dark green car. You want it?"

Mary recorded all the information Angel could provide. "All right, Angel, be certain to phone me or Sergeant Washington immediately if you have any further contact with your, ah, client again. Later on, we'll arrange for you to come to homicide to give a tape-recorded statement. OK? All right, talk to you later."

Mary dropped the piece of paper with the Camry's license number on Duke's desk.

"She certain?" Duke asked.

When Mary nodded, Duke went to the computer and entered the license number. Mary saw the dejection on Duke's face as the computer printed out the response. Duke gave her the printout.

Mary sighed and shook her head when she read it. "A Save-A-Lot rental vehicle."

Duke picked up the phone and dialed. "I'll call Save-A-Lot to get the latest rental information. Maybe we'll get lucky and they'll actually have recent rental history."

Mary smiled and gave him a doubtful head shake. "You're a dreamer, Duke. You know the saying: if it wasn't for bad luck we wouldn't have any luck at all."

A short conversation with the Save-A-Lot clerk caused Duke's downcast visage to suddenly brighten. He jotted down the information the clerk provided, and after hanging up he leafed through a stack of FC's until he held up the prize. "Rondell and Larry White, stopped by Officer David Fong on September 2nd, 1450 hours, in the 3000 block of Lakeshore! We got 'em, Mary! We got those assholes!"

While Duke recorded the information, Mary went to the Homicide Division Commander, Lieutenant Vic Kelso, informed him about their finding, and requested two additional homicide teams be assigned to assist them. When she emerged from the LT's office, Mary's tired, irritable demeanor changed to an energized optimism. She marched to Duke's desk and Duke grinned and waited for her obligatory summation why the White brothers made their fatal mistake.

"What did I tell you, Duke? Our *hero* couldn't resist the temptation. The power of poon-tang cannot be denied!"

~~~~

Mary, Duke, and the other two homicide teams returned to the investigation with renewed vigor and determination. The office swarmed with activity. Every dead-end Duke originally encountered, when he initially delved into the White brothers' lives, the teams reexamined until each facet was totally exhausted. Where before Duke made phone calls to garner information, now the teams conducted interviews in person. They utilized the Daily Bulletin again to request a felony car stop BOLO on the Camry, and officers received the suspects' mug photos. They thoroughly examined every investigative avenue imaginable, but it was if the White brothers dropped off the face of the earth and the investigation ground to a halt.

~~~~

Duke stood outside the homicide office watching the first rain of autumn. He sought cover under the vestibule and the overhang kept him dry. It was an intense thunderstorm by Bay Area standards, and he could smell the rain's fresh, earthy odor. He cradled a scalding cup of coffee and took cautious sips as he listened to the rumbling thunder and watched people scurry for cover as the wall of water poured down. The door to homicide's private entrance opened and Sergeant Cecil Baxter poked his head out.

"Duke, you've got a call on line two."

Duke nodded and reentered the office. "Sergeant Washington speaking."

"Sergeant," a woman's voice began. "I work at Save-A-Lot Rentals out on Airport Drive. You and a female sergeant came by yesterday to show us photos of two men you were interested in talking to."

"Yes, ma'am, what can I do for you?"

"Well, I don't want to identify myself because I'm afraid of, you know, repercussions. But I did recognize one of the men in those photos."

"OK," Duke said. "I understand about not wanting to ID yourself, believe me. But I can assure you that anything you tell us will be held strictly confidential, and we will protect your identity at all costs."

"Look, sergeant, I. . ." the woman stopped.

Duke was concerned he would lose her. "Ma'am, that's OK. You don't have to ID yourself. You can remain anonymous."

The woman let out a deep breath. "I hate to be such a worry-wart, but you know how sticky things can get between fellow employees."

Duke's adrenaline raced. "Employee? One of those men is a Save-A-Lot employee?"

"No, not quite," the woman explained. "I saw him once a few days ago in one of our rental cars with Nyisha Clemmons, who works our sales counter."

"Are you certain that the man Nyisha was with is the same man in the photo?"

"Oh, yes, he had the same distinctive corn row hairstyle."

"All right, ma'am, my partner and I will be right out to talk with Nyisha. And don't worry, we won't mention a word about what you've said."

Mary was out of the office at the time of the call, and she returned just as Duke finished a DMV and CORPUS check on Nyisha Clemmons. Duke briefed Mary on the call and they discussed how they should respond.

"Well," Mary said, "at least we know how they obtained the Camry and how they've been able to keep under our radar."

"Embezzled vehicle," Duke said. "Nyisha prints out a fraudulent rental agreement, enters Rondell into their computer as the renter, gives Rondell the keys, and away he goes."

Mary nodded and added. "And, she updates the rental agreement and the computer entry every few weeks to keep it current in case he's stopped. What kind of girl are we dealing with here, Duke?"

Duke read the DMV printout. "Nineteen years old. Lives in

North Oakland. Never been arrested. Not even any traffic citation history."

Mary wrinkled her forehead. "How the hell did she ever get involved with Rondell White? And, does she know about his alter ego?" She thought for a while and then offered her opinion. "I'll bet that she's no ghetto queen and has no knowledge about Rondell's dark side. I'll lay odds that if we do it right, she'll give us what we want to know. But we don't have time to conduct surveillance. We've got to act now."

"Agreed," Duke said. "Let's bring her in and give her the embezzled vehicle 10855 VC statute to get her thinking how much time she'll do as a principal to a felony. If she cooperates, fine. If not, we'll lay out the serial murder spree and bluff her into believing she could be charged as an accessory to multiple homicides. Of course, if we're wrong and she doesn't roll over, then. . ."

"A chance we'll have to take, Duke. Are you driving or am I?"

~ ~ ~ ~

Nyisha Clemmons met Rondell White when he arrived at Save-A-Lot Rentals to rent a vehicle. A pretty girl, with a light brown complexion and a slim figure, she was instantly smitten with his boyish good looks and confident charm. They began dating and he pressured her into accepting a *gift* of $250.00 to get him a vehicle and a fraudulent rental agreement. He convinced her that the police regarded vehicle embezzlement as such a minor crime and so common that they rarely prosecuted it, and if she remained careful her chances of ever being arrested were slim to none.

But Nyisha was startled when the police arrived the day before and showed Rondell's photo around the office. She hid her nervous behavior from the male and female plainclothes officers, but she realized that Rondell duped her into believing that the police did not take embezzled vehicle theft seriously. She had no way to contact him because he always refused to give her his phone number. He told her that he lived with a jealous woman who might find out about their dating and cause trouble. All she could do was wait for one of his infrequent calls to tell him about the police showing his photo around the office.

The next day Nyisha's stomach turned when she saw the

same two police officers again enter the office and walk directly toward her. Her hands shook and her mouth went dry.

"Hi, Nyisha," Mary said and displayed her badge and ID card. "You remember us from yesterday? Sergeant Sanders and Sergeant Washington?"

Nyisha nodded weakly and kept her hands flat on the counter to keep them still. She started to speak but the words would not form.

Mary saw the strain plainly visible on the girl's face, and her voice took on a more strident tone, when she sensed Nyisha's fear. "Nyisha, we're investigating an embezzled vehicle theft and you'll have to accompany us downtown to discuss the matter."

While Duke drove, Mary sat with the girl in the rear seat. During the entire time at Save-A-Lot and the ride to homicide, Nyisha never said a word. They placed Nyisha in the interrogation room for a few minutes and then entered with the tape recorder and read her the *Miranda* admonition. Within minutes Nyisha Clemmons admitted to the embezzlement, and Duke and Mary concentrated on Rondell White.

"Nyisha, do you know where Rondell stays?" Duke asked.

Nyisha was close to tears. "No, sir, he never said."

"Does he stay in Oakland?" Mary asked.

"I don't think so, 'cause when he and I would be at the motel, he'd say he had to leave early 'cause he had a long way to drive. But he never said where."

"Which motel?" Duke asked.

"The Motel Six across from that restaurant on Edes. We spent the night there a few days ago. Last Saturday, I think."

Mary and Duke arrested Nyisha and booked her into jail for vehicle embezzlement. Mary contacted the court and requested a higher bail to keep her incarcerated for as long as possible. They both knew that if Rondell contacted her, then he and Larry would abandon the Camry and vanish.

Mary and Duke went to Motel Six to conduct a follow-up investigation. They hoped to discover some type of information Rondell inadvertently left behind.

As Duke drove, he glanced over at Mary. "You know, we're probably spinning our wheels going to the motel."

"Yeah, probably," Mary answered. "But you know as well as I that we have to do it."

The Motel Six desk clerk dug through reservation slips until she held up one for closer examination. "This what you're looking for?"

Duke took the registration slip and saw the same motel address Rondell listed on his driver license. With one exception. In the spot reserved for city, there were a few letters written down and then heavily scribbled over to obscure them. To the right of the scribbled out letters Rondell printed "Oakland." Duke held the slip up to the office's overhead light to better make out what letters were blocked out. Then he passed the slip to Mary and she repeated the procedure. The letters "Vall" were just barely legible.

Mary smiled. "Our two assholes have a safe house somewhere in Vallejo. Rondell fucked up big-time."

24

It was 9:00 A.M. on the morning following their discovery of the motel registration slip, and Mary and Duke drove on Highway 80 toward the City of Vallejo, a largely blue collar community of 90,000 people about 25 miles north of Oakland. They were one of twenty-two two-officer teams tasked with locating the White brothers and the Camry. Each team had a designated geographical area to search, and they planned to cover the city street by street until they exhausted all their efforts. Mary knew Duke felt the same apprehension she did and voiced their shared concern.

"You know, if this expedition doesn't pan out, the Chief will probably give us a one-way ticket to patrol and dog watch Districts Four and Five. I almost wish we hadn't told Kelso about that registration slip. We're responsible for this recon battalion being sent to lay siege to Vallejo, and if we don't locate the White brothers or the Camry, our peers are going to give us a ration of shit for placing so much importance on one single slip of paper."

Duke grinned. "Since I have loads of seniority on your young butt, I'll take jive five. You can have District Four."

Mary gave him a puzzled look. "What is this thing you have with jive five?"

"Me and Bull cut our teeth out there when we were rookies. I guess it's like always having a bond with the place where you start your career. I know most cops don't like working knee-deep in the ghetto, with the endless family fights and burglary reports, where the TV being reported stolen has been stolen so many times that it's almost considered community property! But there's just something about hitting the streets *knowing* that a shooting, stabbing, or some other felony in progress will occur during your shift. Make sense?"

"Yeah, but only if you're a masochist," Mary replied. "My problem with jive five is that legitimate victims are so rare. Like the stolen TV you mentioned being considered community property. And most of the teens and young adults out there hate us. I once thought that being a black female officer would make me a role model, someone the kids would respect and emulate. But when I put that blue uniform on, all I represented was an authority figure, whose job was to keep people from smokin' their crack or stealing something that doesn't belong to them. And don't get me started on the women. Like when I'd investigate a domestic violence case and ask the woman what her relationship is to the man who hit her, and she'd answer, 'He ain't *nothin'* to me! He's just my baby's daddy!' I swear, Duke, if I've heard that once, I've heard it a hundred times!"

Duke took a tape recorder out of his carry-bag and pretended to turn it on. "Go 'head on, girl. You're on a roll!"

Mary frowned and playfully slapped his arm. "I should know better than to open up to you, Duke. There's our off-ramp ahead. Now, make yourself useful and check the map, so you can direct me to our assigned area."

~~~~

Rondell and Larry White rented a room in a seedy motel located in a rundown commercial area of Vallejo. It was an area where people minded their own business and perfect for their needs. Although Rondell didn't think the police sought the Camry, lately he began to have second thoughts about the car. He finally concluded that it would be a good idea to turn the Camry back into Save-A-Lot and have Nyisha replace it with another rental vehicle, and today was as good a day as any.

Rondell interrupted Larry watching a porno video. "Come on, blood. I'm gonna turn in the Camry and get another car. I'll drop you off to visit your little 'ho and then pick you up on the way back."

"All right," Larry said. "But I need a couple of Benjamins. I'm busted."

Rondell frowned as he reached in his wallet. "Shit, I'm gonna have to put you on a budget."

After winding through city streets, Rondell turned on to the Highway 80 on-ramp en route to Oakland. Up ahead, Rondell saw the flashing red and amber lights of an ambulance and two CHP cars, and he slowed down to a crawl in the backup. The traffic in the oncoming lanes also slowed down as the rubber-neckers turned their ghoulish attention to the injured being loaded into the ambulance. Rondell slapped the steering wheel in anger.

"Motherfucker! Every time we take this freeway there's an accident. Every time!"

Coming from the opposite direction, Mary and Duke got caught in the crush of cars locked into the traffic jam. Mary swiveled her head from side to side looking for an opening, when she suddenly slammed on her brakes for a vehicle stopped in front of them. The resulting crunch of their front bumper with the other vehicle's rear bumper was minor, but the other driver exited his car to inspect for damage. Now, Mary slapped *her* steering wheel in anger, for a city property collision would necessitate a lengthy report and delay them from their assignment. Both Mary and Duke left their vehicle to confer with the other driver.

"Doesn't appear to be any damage," the elderly male driver said. "If it's OK with you, I say we just forget about it and move on."

"I'm afraid we can't do that, sir," Mary said, as she showed him her badge and ID card. "Our department requires a collision report for liability reasons. So, we'll have to. . ."

Mary happened to glance to her left into oncoming traffic and looked directly into Rondell White's face. At first she stood rooted in place, too stunned to recover her composure and she continued to watch him as he inched past. She had no doubt it was him. But Rondell seemed so intent trying to get clear of the traffic jam that he did not notice Mary staring at him with her badge and ID card prominently displayed and a look of absolute shock on her face that would have shrieked at him that he was a wanted man.

"Duke!" Mary shouted.

Duke turned toward her and then shifted his gaze to where Mary fixed her eyes. The Camry passed by them now, but Duke got a glimpse of the vehicle's license plate and confirmed Mary's observation.

"It's them, Duke!"

Duke did not reply. He reached for his notebook, jotted down his and Mary's last names and serial numbers, and gave them to the other driver. "Sir, we have an emergency. Please contact the Oakland Police Department concerning this accident."

Mary threw herself behind the wheel and had their vehicle moving into the next lane, when Duke managed to launch himself inside and slam the door shut. Then Duke took the portable red light from the glove box and shined it to the rear, where the long lines of vehicles were backed up. Mary activated the vehicle's siren to a low growl and slowly turned into the other lane. The drivers grudgingly gave way when they saw the red light and heard the siren, and she finally made it to the off-ramp.

At the same time, Duke broadcast over the radio to other OPD units the direction the Camry headed, and he switched to the state's CLEMARS channel to alert CHP and Vallejo PD. He also requested a helicopter, but the dispatcher advised that none were available. Mary fought her way through traffic, crossed an overpass, and then entered Highway 80 in the same direction the Camry travelled. Mary jammed the accelerator into the floorboard and they shot past slower moving traffic.

"I'd say they were a couple of minutes ahead of us," Duke said. "Let's just hope they don't get off the freeway for some reason."

Several minutes passed and they had yet to spot the Camry.

"Duke, I think they got off the freeway."

"Doesn't matter now, Mary. We're committed. We just have to assume they're still on 80 and keep going."

OPD units overran the radio channel requesting updates on the Camry's location. Duke continually informed them that they were still on 80, but they had no visual yet on the Camry. They crossed the Carquinez Bridge, passed the cities of Pinole and

Richmond, and at last Duke conceded that the Camry probably left the freeway. Then Mary reached the top of a knoll and saw a dark green compact vehicle in the fast lane a couple of hundred meters ahead. She punched the accelerator and they gained on this vehicle. They went up an incline, and when they reached the crest, the vehicle was only a few car lengths ahead. Mary and Duke strained to make out the license number until both of them let out a simultaneous whoop.

"It's them!" Mary shouted.

"Got you now, assholes!" Duke added and then broadcast over the radio. "13A11, we have the Camry in sight westbound 80 number one lane just entering the Albany city limits. Advise all units *not* to activate their red lights until we're able to coordinate the stop."

Mary maintained separation from the Camry by several car lengths to avoid alarming the White brothers into a high speed chase. Mary took repeated glances in her rear view mirror to determine if other OPD units closed the gap. For the first time since the start of the investigation, she felt that they were in control of the situation and an arrest appeared imminent. All their long hours and hard work appeared ready to pay off.

~~~~

Rondell's anger still simmered over the accident that delayed them. But when he glanced at the speedometer and saw it hovering at 85, it occurred to him that he placed them at risk for a traffic stop, and he let his anger subside and slowed to 65. Then a quick look in the mirror immediately activated his police radar. An unmarked car with a male and female team followed directly behind them. Rondell smirked to himself. The police thought unmarked cars made them invisible, but Rondell could spot *any* kind of police car from a block away.

"Hey, blood," Rondell said. "Don't turn around or do any stupid shit, but we got a Five-0 behind us."

Larry jerked his head toward Rondell. "What you think?"

Rondell shrugged. "Don't know, but we'll play it low key for now."

~~~~

While Duke gave updates, Mary looked in her mirror and dismay registered on her face. A CHP unit, with its emergency lights blazing, rapidly closed the distance to their vehicle. This negligent action would certainly trigger a pursuit.

"What the hell's he doing?" Mary cried out, as the CHP black and white swerved around their unmarked car and pulled behind the Camry.

Rondell reacted instantaneously. The Camry swerved violently to the next lane and then shot across the other three lanes to the shoulder of the road, leaving the CHP cruiser and Mary and Duke trying to find a way to pick their way through heavy traffic. Duke broadcast the pursuit, and the freeway behind them lit up with red lights blinking on as the legion of following police vehicles joined in the chase.

Once they cleared the traffic jam, Rondell swerved again across all four lanes back to the fast lane and cranked up his speed to near top end. Rondell darted from lane to lane and Mary followed suit. More than once she thought a collision was unavoidable, but she managed to miss vehicles by inches. She maneuvered through gaps so small that Duke braced repeatedly for collisions that did not materialize. The Bay Bridge connector maze was next and the Camry bypassed the turn-off to the bridge and increased its speed as it blasted onto Highway 580.

"13A11," Duke broadcast. "We are still in pursuit but now eastbound on 580 in the number one lane."

The traffic thinned out and the Camry accelerated to a speed Mary could not match. Then she glanced in her mirror and a welcome sight came into focus. Another CHP unit charged past her and assumed the role as the primary pursuit vehicle. Rondell began the same evasion tactics to break free from his pursuers. He swerved from lane to lane and over to the shoulder of the road, but the CHP cruiser stayed with him. Then the Camry took an off-ramp, left the freeway, crossed an overpass, and took the one desperate move Rondell knew the police would not attempt to follow. He reentered the westbound 580 freeway traveling eastbound and became a wrong-way vehicle. As Mary and Duke watched in horror, the Camry *kamikaze* swerved right and left time after time in rapid succession to avoid oncoming vehicles.

Rondell pushed the Camry to its limit. As he swung the steering wheel to and fro to avoid head-on collisions, he grinned at the terrorized expressions on the other drivers' faces as they whizzed past. Larry gripped the sides of his seat so tightly that the color drained from his knuckles. He sat rigid and quiet as the onrushing cars flew by them with a whooshing sound or an occasional blaring horn. Then Rondell cut the wheel hard left, and they barreled down an on-ramp to the city streets and continued their flight on Golf Links Road. Mary countered this maneuver by also leaving the freeway, and she fell in behind the Camry as it roared by and again became the primary pursuit vehicle.

Golf Links Road's twisting, winding roadway had several blind curves, and the Camry spent as much time in the oncoming traffic lane as it did in its own lane. Mary held her breath on each curve and expected a head-on collision that did not occur. When Golf Links ended at 82nd Avenue, the Camry went through the intersection on two wheels, sideswiped a parked car, and then made a hard left turn to MacArthur Boulevard with Mary and Duke close behind. As the pursuit neared 98th Avenue, Mary looked in her mirror and concluded that every police car in Oakland joined in the pursuit. For several blocks the road formed a solid river of red lights flowing after them. The chase continued southbound on 98th Avenue, and the stampeding police cars thundered and wailed their way after the fleeing Camry.

Lieutenant Vic Kelso commanded this horde of motorized cavalry howling its way through the streets of East Oakland and he faced a quandary. As the titular head of this unorganized mob, it was his duty to enforce the pursuit policy as set forth in the department's General Orders, and the principal edict stipulated that only *two* vehicles would take part in a chase at any given time. Hell, LT Kelso agonized, there were at least *thirty* involved in this one and he was stuck in the middle! He attempted several times to gain control of this juggernaut force of marauders, but the cacophony of shrieking sirens and units all trying to use the radio at once drowned out his broadcasts time after time. He finally gave up and reconciled himself to go with the flow and hope no serious collisions occurred that he would have to explain later on.

After their survival as a wrong-way vehicle on Highway 580, Larry regained his ability to speak and besieged Rondell with a litany of inane questions and observations. "What we gonna do now, Rondell? Must be more than a hundred PO-PO's chasin' us! Where we goin'? You got a plan? Damn, blood, talk to me!"

Rondell flew through the 98th Avenue—E.14th Street intersection and then wove in and out of both the southbound and northbound lanes. The Camry strayed all over the road.

"How the fuck do I know what we're gonna do," Rondell yelled. "We'll just have to keep goin' until something happens that will give us a chance to get away from these motherfuckers."

As they neared the 98th Avenue-San Leandro Street intersection, the *something* that Rondell waited for *happened*. The railroad crossing arms for the Southern Pacific tracks were down, and both lanes in their direction were clogged solid with vehicles waiting for the train to pass. Rondell saw his chance, shot by the stopped lines of cars, and blasted through the crossing arms, sending shards of broken wood splintering in all directions. The oncoming train missed the Camry by less than a car length. The pursuing police vehicles coasted to a stop helpless to do anything but watch the hundred car freight train roll slowly by.

Once Rondell and Larry were free of their pursuers, they entered an industrial section close to the Oakland Coliseum. "I got an idea, blood," Rondell said. "Remember that old vacant steel factory on 85th Ave? An old homey of mine is a security guard there. If we toss him a few bucks, I'll bet he'll let us hide out in there until the PO-POs think we're gone and leave. Then we'll get rid of the Camry, hot-wire another ride, and split."

Larry nodded wearily. "Anything, man. Just get us the fuck out of here."

It only took $100.00 for Rondell to convince his old hoodlum friend, Jerry Beryl, to allow them to hide inside the huge vacant steel mill for the remainder of his shift. The enormous corrugated iron building met their needs perfectly as a temporary hideout while Rondell considered their next move.

25

Mary and Duke sat first in the long line of police vehicles and counted train cars as they passed. They had no recourse, and the train rolled by at a pedestrian pace so agonizingly slow that the train wheels' repetitive noise sounded like a metronome on valium. When the crossing arms' broken remnants at last lifted, the OPD task force went through the motions and searched the side streets, but they only conducted the perfunctory search in event the Camry broke down and the suspects had to abandon it. An unsuccessful hour later, LT Kelso ordered the task force to terminate the search and attend a debriefing at the police administration building.

"The day's been a disaster," Mary said. "A total fucking disaster."

They were on 85th Avenue en route to OPD, when Duke focused on the vacant DeSilva Steel Mill and thought how suitable it would serve as a hideout. But then he saw the security guard on duty and the thought vanished as quickly as it came. The suspects wouldn't be able to get the Camry inside without the guard knowing. But maybe he could salvage something out of his idea though.

"Mary, why don't we contact the security guard at the steel

mill? Maybe he saw something."

Mary's tired return look told him what she thought of his suggestion, but she turned into the mill's driveway and parked. While Mary remained in the vehicle, Duke contacted the guard. One look at Duke's face when he returned to their vehicle was all Mary needed to confirm that they had another failure to add to the day's long list. Mary was about to take the freeway on-ramp, when a pick-up truck behind them flashed its lights on and off, signaling for them to stop. Mary pulled over and resigned herself to the usual Q&A from a citizen seeking directions or making some trivial complaint.

"Hi," the man said. "I'm Morris Jennings. I own Jennings' Machine Shop on 85th Ave. I assume you're police officers?" When Mary and Duke nodded, Mr. Jennings continued. "I saw all the police activity earlier and wondered if it had something to do with the green Camry the guard let into DeSilva's."

Instantly, the day's disaster turned into the equivalent of Mary and Duke hitting the lottery, and after obtaining Mr. Jennings information, Mary and Duke made a quick U-turn and headed back to DeSilva's Steel Mill, where they confronted Jerry Beryl with his lie.

Jerry Beryl looked startled. "Who said I lied?"

"Mr. Beryl, a witness, saw you let the green Camry inside the mill property," Duke said. "Place your hands behind your back. You're being detained until we find out what's going on here."

After they secured Jerry Beryl in their vehicle, Mary and Duke took his keys and prepared to unlock the roll-up door.

~~~~

Rondell and Larry rested half asleep in the Camry, which they parked just inside the huge building, when they heard voices outside. Rondell crept to the wall, and through a small crack in the corrugated iron, he watched male and female plain-clothes officers handcuff Jerry Beryl and lock him in an un-marked police car. Larry joined him and looked through another crack. He turned to Rondell with terror in his eyes. Rondell scowled at Larry's panicked reaction and silently cursed his weakness. Then he led their retreat to the building's far recesses, where they waited in ambush for the search they knew would follow.

~~~~

Mary and Duke unlocked the massive door and rolled it open. The unoccupied Camry was parked just inside. They expressed shock to see the Camry materialize so suddenly, and Mary and Duke simply stared at the vehicle as if they feared it would vanish like a mirage. But after a few moments, they let their eyes roam the building's vast interior, and the structure's sheer size overwhelmed them.

"Shit," Duke said. "You could play a baseball game inside this sucker. That roof's got to be eighty or ninety feet high."

Mary sighed. "Searching this place will be like searching Carlsbad Caverns."

Two car doors slamming shut diverted their attention to the front gate.

"You two thinkin' of buyin' and renovatin' this ghetto fixer-upper?" Bull called out, as he and Becky walked toward them. "Saw your car and figured we'd see what you had goin' on." By the time Bull finished saying this, he and Becky were close enough to see the Camry inside, and Bull ceased his playful banter. "They in there?"

"Don't know," Mary replied. "Guess we'll find out soon enough."

After Duke briefed Becky and Bull about what happened, Becky drove their black and white inside the gate and transferred the guard to their "caged" car for added security. Then Becky started to broadcast on her transceiver their location and ask for additional units, when Mary reached over and placed her hand on top of Becky's radio to stop her. Becky gave Mary a confused look.

"I was just going to let the dispatcher know what we've got going. . ." Becky said.

Mary nodded. "I know." Then she scanned the other three faces. "It's just that maybe we ought to stop and think this out for a couple of minutes. Maybe we could come up with an alternative to the usual operational drill for barricaded suspects. Maybe we could be more *creative.*"

Bull furrowed his brow as he tried to decipher what Mary's vague remarks meant. Becky glanced at each face in rapid succession and began to understand Mary's veiled words for what they were.

Duke grimaced, ran a hand over his head, and turned away. His voice sounded strained. "Mary, we better be certain we all know what this means."

Mary looked at each of them and pleaded with her eyes. "We could take care of this ourselves. The four of us."

Bull finally understood. "Whoa now, Mary, whoa. . ."

Becky chimed in. "Just what are you saying, Mary? Spell it out."

Mary deliberated for a few seconds before she took a deep breath and spoke in a calm, deliberate voice. "Look, we know those two assholes are monsters. All the lives they've taken and ruined. They don't *deserve* a trial by a jury of their peers. They deserve justice and we can provide that justice. Right here. Right now. I am *not* saying we murder them. That's not what I'm saying at all. What I am suggesting is that we hunt them down, back them into a corner. . . and see what happens. Maybe they'll decide to fight it out. But if we seal this building down and bring in the entry team and a dog, then they'll probably surrender." She paused and then continued. "Or, if we take care of this now, we can be prosecutor, judge, jury, and executioner."

Mary backed off and watched them struggle with the import of what she proposed. She knew their decision had to be unanimous. One dissenter and it would be as if her proposal had never been raised in the first place. If they were going to do it, the verdict had to be all of theirs together or none at all.

Bull was the first to speak and chose his words carefully. "Just how far are we going to take this, Mary? There's a real fine line separating a lawful and unlawful shooting."

"I know what you're saying, Bull. But I'll repeat and emphasize what I said before. There *won't* be any murders. If we can't tempt or provoke them into a fight, then we'll just take them into custody and let the court try them."

Duke cleared his throat, "You know we're setting ourselves up for a lot of probing questions later on. A lot of obvious violations of departmental procedures. There's a laundry list of violations. But I'd like to make one point. I agree with Mary. These two murderers don't deserve their day in court. Just remember what they did to Rita. . ."

They were quiet for a few seconds until Becky brought them back to the decision they had to make. "So, just *how* are we going to explain our actions, Mary?"

Mary shook her head. "I don't know exactly. We can state that we thought the suspects were GOA, and we were doing a cursory search, when we blundered into them—but I don't know. It's something we'll have to work out later."

Becky laced her retort with sarcasm. "Work out later? Now that's a hell of a plan! Come on, Mary. We have to do better than that."

Mary smiled. "You're right, Becky. Absolutely right. There are a *few* gaps I can't account for. But one thing I do know and we can all agree on is how fickle and flawed the jury system can be. If these two assholes get their day in court, there's no guarantee what their final sentence will be." Mary paused again. "That's all I have to say."

The four of them regarded each other closely and the seconds dragged on. They all knew that unless they came to a decision quickly, their window of opportunity for action would close rapidly. They waited for someone to speak until the silence became uncomfortable. Bull broke the stalemate.

"I'm gonna side with Mary 'cause she's right. Those two assholes don't deserve to live, and I won't feel any pangs of conscience later on 'cause it'll be a fair fight. Besides, we'll be doin' this not only for Rita, but for Mike Torres too."

Duke did not hesitate. "I'm in."

For a few seconds the silence returned. Becky felt the discomfort of having the deciding vote. She felt like an outsider looking in. She shook her head disconsolately and looked away. When she turned back and sought eye contact, Bull and Mary dropped their gaze to the ground and Duke stared off into the distance. At last she spoke and her weary voice reflected how little enthusiasm she had for her decision.

"All right, against my better judgment I'm in too. Well, Sergeant Mary 'Don't Take No Shit' Sanders, AKA Ms. Wyatt Earp, lead the way to the OK Corral."

Mary smiled at Becky's sarcasm.

"What's first on the agenda?" Duke asked.

"We'll have to advise the dispatcher that we're off on an on-view," Mary said. "Bull, since it's your beat, why don't you put us out on a suspicious circumstances call, but state no further units are needed at this time."

Bull nodded. "Who's gonna stay with the guard and watch over the front entrance?"

Mary thought for a moment. "Becky, that'll be your job. Bull will keep you up to date on our situation on tactical channel four, and if things start to go sideways, you put out the 940-B over the main channel."

"Let's search by quadrants," Duke said. "We'll start on the west side of the building and go counterclockwise."

"Sounds good," Mary agreed. "OK, if there's nothing more, let's do it."

~~~~

The mill's interior resembled an immense cave. The only light filtered down through grimy windows at the tops of all four walls and skylights scattered across the roof. Enormous pieces of machinery blocked most of this hazy light, and dark, shadowy canyons crisscrossed throughout the building. A gigantic crane was poised high above the floor, and hulking drill presses, massive bending machines, and gargantuan pipe rollers rose from the floor like colossal slabs of granite. A dank, musty odor permeated the air and dust particles floated in the shards of light that managed to slice past the monolithic equipment. After staring in awe at the task before them, they began the search and quickly realized the magnitude of what they were attempting.

~~~~

Rondell and Larry did not have to wait long. The huge pipe they picked to conceal themselves behind covered a swath of floor in the second quadrant the hunters chose to search. As Rondell watched the three officers approach with guns drawn, beads of sweat coursed down his face, and his eyes darted back and forth like an animal watching predators on the prowl. He wiped away white specks of dried spittle at the corners of his mouth. He looked over at Larry and saw that his eyes were closed and his lips trembled. Rondell leaned close and whispered in Larry's ear.

"Larry, somethin's wrong, blood. Why ain't the PO-POs usin' a dog? And how come there's only four of them? Where's their back-up?" Rondell licked his lips. "Man, I don't like the looks of this shit. It don't make no sense."

~~~~

Becky watched her peers advance cautiously into the cavernous structure. Half bent over, they took slow deliberate steps, stopping periodically to assess the situation or change direction to avoid machinery that blocked their way. Becky held her pistol limply at her side and her hand trembled slightly, until she decided to holster the weapon. A few seconds later she thought better of her decision and removed the pistol and let it hang limp at her side again. Becky heard scurrying noises and glanced to her right, where a rat as big as a small dog crept warily across the floor. When the rat saw Becky, it stopped suddenly and its beady eyes focused on her as it attempted to evaluate the threat level she represented. Then the rat darted into a small crevice and disappeared. Becky felt a shiver of revulsion and then focused on her sister and brother officers, who crept through the mammoth steel mill hunting down two other species of vermin.

Mary occupied the middle position between Bull and Duke as they inched their way forward on line to search the first quadrant. She imbued each cautious step with feline grace, like a large cat stalking its prey. She held her Glock with both hands in a right-handed shooting posture, taking caution to index her trigger finger to prevent an accidental or premature discharge. Mary kept the weapon pointed directly in front of her, and whatever direction she turned, the weapon's muzzle turned and remained ready to fire. She glanced right and left to check Duke and Bull's position and then took another tentative step forward. Her heart hammered and her head throbbed.

Bull glanced to his right to insure he remained on line with Mary. If a firefight erupted, all three of them had to be on line to keep from inflicting friendly fire casualties on each other. Not too far in front of Mary, not too far behind. Sweat formed on his brow and he wiped the perspiration away with the back of his hand and flicked the drops to the floor. He moved as stealthily as his stocky, muscular body allowed, taking care not to expose himself any more than necessary. Gusts of wind outside the building shook the walls and ceiling, and he heard the corrugated iron creak, groan, and pop, as if the massive structure was a living creature to add an extra dose of drama to the tense scene. Bull glanced again in Mary's direction. Not too far ahead, not too far behind.

Duke picked his way through the detritus that littered the floor, glancing about repeatedly for any signs of impending danger. Stress creases etched their way into his forehead and cheeks, transposing numerous laugh lines into visible signs of apprehension. His gun-hand felt clammy and he transferred the pistol to his other hand and wiped the moisture on his pants. Duke stumbled noisily over an iron bar and almost lost his balance, causing Mary and Bull to instantly flatten themselves against the nearest cover. Mary frowned and shook her head, and Duke shrugged his shoulders apologetically.

So, they combed through the huge edifice, searching for two killers responsible for multiple murders. They crept from cover to cover, knowing full well that they could come under fire at any instant. But still they moved and methodically cleared section after section. Crouched over at the waist ready to spring for safety at the slightest threat. Hugging cold steel structures that protected them until their next move exposed them again. And as they moved, the shadows moved, and pieces of machinery played subtle tricks on their minds, taking human form and then dissolving as shafts of light revealed them to be inert metallic structures.

Then Mary heard a faint sound ahead. Not far off. An unusual sound. Unidentifiable. She paused and knelt behind a towering furnace for cover. Out of the corners of her eyes she saw Duke and Bull stop and crouch down. She cast Bull a questioning look, and he shook his head in a way that told her he heard the sound too. Mary concentrated and heard it again, louder this time but still unrecognizable. Then she heard a muffled, high-pitched moan. The barely audible moan slowly gained volume until it developed into an unmistakable whimper, and the whimper became a sob that finally burst forth in a soaring wail of despair.

Crying uncontrollably, Larry White rose, fired a random,

desperate shot in their direction that ricocheted harmlessly off the concrete floor, and then turned to flee the firefight that ensued. His single shot drew a furious fusillade of return fire that cut him down before he could take a step. His pistol flew up in the air, clattered to the concrete, and then slid across the floor until it came to rest a few feet away. Rondell fired wildly in their direction one shot after another without aiming. Within seconds his pistol was empty.

Mary made eye contact with Duke and Bull to insure they were all right. There were no movements or sounds coming from behind the pipe. Larry lay in a spreading pool of blood. Then Rondell slid his handgun across the floor and stood without saying a word. Mary rose to her feet and held her Glock at her side muzzle down. For a few moments she and Rondell stared at each other without moving. Rondell fixated on the pistol in her hand. He knew police officers played by the rules, but today's events suggested otherwise.

Mary's next action showed Rondell that the rules no longer applied. She walked slowly and deliberately forward and kicked Larry's pistol toward Rondell, and it scraped over the floor until it stopped a foot away from his feet.

Mary's calm voice broke the silence. "Pick it up, Rondell."

Rondell's face betrayed his fear. Mary saw his fear and smiled. His gangster cool was gone. In its place she saw the desperation of a cornered animal living out its last moments in abject terror. Rondell's eyes dropped down to the pistol on the floor.

"That's right, Rondell," Mary urged. "Go ahead and pick it up."

Bull's steady voice interrupted the face-off. "The line, Mary. Don't step over the line."

Mary didn't take her eyes off Rondell. "I won't, Bull. I'll give him his chance. But if he reaches for that pistol, he's shootable and he knows it. Don't you, Rondell? But you'll have more of a chance than you gave all the unarmed people you killed. Right, Rondell? More of a chance than the manager and dishwasher at the restaurant. Or the husband of the woman Larry raped. More than the helpless mother and her two daughters you murdered in the condominium garage. And one of our own, the unarmed OPD officer on the BART train. Helpless people. All of them. But I'm not helpless, am I? And that's why you won't pick up the pistol. Right, Rondell? What's the matter? Aren't you *man* enough to pick it up?"

For an instant Rondell's eyes burned with their former rage at Mary's emasculating insult, but then his anger dissolved and his fear returned.

Mary smiled again. "I thought so. Just like most ghetto gangsters, you're all talk and no walk. I've waited weeks to get you in this position, Rondell. Weeks. Dreamed of coming face to face with you. Felt the tension on the trigger of my pistol and then the release as I shot holes through your cowardly body. So, what do you do when my dream finally comes true? You punk out like the sniveling little bitch that you are. Don't worry, Rondell. You're safe until the State of California gets its act together and executes your punk ass. As for me? It wouldn't be worth the aggravation to kill you."

~~~~

With the firefight over and Larry White dead, the OPD informal assault team secured Rondell in Mary and Duke's vehicle, and the details of their actions that Mary said they would have to "work out later" took priority. The four co-conspirators huddled together to devise their game plan.

Duke spoke first. "Everybody all right?" He glanced around and made eye contact with all three of them. "We did what had to be done. We did it for Rita, Mike Torres, and the rest of the victims who couldn't do it for themselves."

Bull nodded. "We're OK, Duke. Let's get on with it. Mary?"

Mary thought for a few seconds. "Look, we'll claim expediency of the moment. The suspects were trying to escape and we had to take immediate action."

Duke grinned and couldn't help playing the devil's advocate. "What about us not notifying the dispatcher that we found the Camry and requesting additional units, Mary?"

Mary paused to think. "We'll say everything happened so quickly we didn't have time to broadcast over the radio until after the shooting stopped."

"Sounds weak," Duke said. "But if that's all we can come up with, I guess it'll have to do."

Becky gave Mary a hard look. "Jesus, Mary. . ."

Mary shrugged and continued. "Becky, go ahead and put out the shots fired broadcast, and a few seconds later, Bull will announce that the shooting's over and an ambulance and the fire department are needed code three for a suspect down at the scene. After the troops arrive, we'll just have to sound as convincing as we can."

Becky's broadcast brought the predictable sound of multiple sirens that broke the mid-day calm, and a few minutes later OPD units swarmed over the area and locked down the shooting scene. The evidence technician arrived and began her lengthy investigation. Officers conducted a canvass of the surrounding neighborhood searching for witnesses. Homicide investigators responded to reconstruct the shooting down to the minutest detail. The DA's office assigned personnel to the case, and the department allowed the officers involved in the shooting to consult with attorneys prior to giving formal statements.

OPD units transported Jerry Beryl and Rondell White to homicide for interrogation. As the transport officers drove them away, Mary flashed Rondell a broad smile and then puckered her lips and blew him an exaggerated air kiss. Rondell scowled and looked away. At homicide, Jerry admitted allowing the White brothers inside the steel mill, but he denied any knowledge about them being involved in prior criminal activity, and investigators released him from custody. The Public Defender's office assigned Rondell an attorney, but he declined to give a statement, nor did he give an account of Mary's goading him into picking up Larry's pistol. Duke summed up Rondell's refusal to report Mary's plan to engage him in a gunfight as a vain attempt to retain whatever he had left of his manhood. The last thing he wanted was for word to get around Santa Rita County Jail that he backed down from a woman.

~~~~

Captain Ernie Stanton joined a large number of command officers who responded to the shooting scene. Long before he received his promotion to captain, he served five years as a diligent homicide sergeant, who knew his way around an officer involved shooting scene. He had many of them on his investigative resume, and he immediately recognized when the four officers' accounts of the firefight didn't quite jibe with reality. The disturbing amount of tactical blunders they committed led him to believe there was more to this shooting than met the eye.

Captain Ernie focused on one officer in particular. Mary Sanders. He liked Mary. She was a spark plug, a dynamo of energy, a feisty investigator with the disposition of a Gila monster—once she latched onto a suspect, she never let go. But her nickname also spoke volumes about her emotional involvement in investigations. He concluded that whatever went on inside that steel mill, Mary's influence was probably the deciding factor. It didn't take him long to sketch out the scenario. The four of them went into the steel mill to kill the White brothers, and they violated barricaded suspect tactical procedures to insure there were no witnesses. Captain Ernie didn't have any problem with their intent. The White brothers were heinous killers who deserved to die anyway. But he retained enough of a veteran cop's ego to let Mary and the others know that he knew what *actually* happened. He waited until Mary was alone for a minute and then approached her with a smile.

"Great job today, Mary."

Mary returned the smile. "Thanks, Captain Ernie. Coming from you that's quite a compliment."

"Of course, I don't think the department will allow you or the rest of your crew to teach barricaded suspect tactics in the academy. You did violate quite a few procedures in your Iwo Jima assault today."

Mary tried to detect any hidden innuendos behind the Captain's words. "Well, we had to deal with the expediency of the moment, that kind of thing."

Captain Ernie laughed. "Yeah, but that expediency of the moment must have lasted quite a while. Probably took you three a couple of minutes to get that far into the building where the shooting took place. You couldn't get on the radio to advise what you had going on in all that time?"

Mary started to answer. "Well, you see. . ."

Captain Ernie cut her off. "Strange tactics. But what the hell, it all worked out in the end."

Mary didn't answer. Instead, she continued smiling but her eyes bored into his and made a statement more truthful than mere words could convey.

Captain Ernie started walking away but then turned around and stopped. "Too bad you weren't able to kill them both. It would have saved the taxpayers a ton of money that will now have to be spent on the trial. Oh, and I wouldn't be too concerned with any, ah, *contradictions* that may develop during the investigation." Captain Ernie stopped speaking for a moment to gauge her reaction. "I'm sure the contradictions will work themselves out. Take care, Mary."

Mary continued to watch Captain Ernie until he entered his car and drove away. Later, after they gave their formal statements at homicide, Mary informed Duke of her encounter with Captain Ernie.

"If he knows what happened, you think the rest know too?"

"I think they all know, Mary," Duke replied. "It wouldn't take a rocket scientist to figure it out. Not only that, but I'll bet they don't give a shit either. If they start probing our stories, the only thing they'd accomplish would be to open up a big can of worms that would compromise the investigation and serve no useful purpose. One White brother got what he deserved and the other will get his too." Duke stopped his lecture and grinned. "Looks like your brilliant plan, 'Something we'll have to work out later', did OK. Next, you'll be writing textbooks on unorthodox tactics for barricaded suspects. Your star is rising, Mary."

~ ~ ~ ~

Three weeks later, the OPD shooting board's investigation ruled the shooting justifiable. But rumors spread that some kind of cover-up occurred. There were whispers that the four involved officers intentionally violated tactical procedures to set up a situation that would lead to a shootout. The official finding did not address this insinuation or any other allusion to covert intentions. Instead, the four officers received the Medal of Merit for their actions, and the shootout at the DeSilva Steel Mill became another episode in OPD's legend and lore. To the participants themselves, however, the incident further embellished the sobriquet of one of their own: Mary "Don't Take No Shit" Sanders.

26

Narcotics officer Aaron Cook suffered from a full-blown case of acute paranoia. To avoid the constant nightmares that bombarded him while he slept, he took downers and alcohol to pass out at night. But even after he passed out, he thrashed in his sleep and eventually woke from these nightly episodes of sheer terror, trembling and bathed in sweat. Then in the morning he hit the crack pipe to recover from the lethargy caused by the depressants taken the night before. Aaron locked himself into a vicious cycle between tweaking and suffering the DT's, and the drug cycle, in turn, caused his paranoia to spiral out of control. All the while, the specter of years behind bars became the root cause behind his miserable condition. He couldn't stand the thought of being locked up. Every room he entered closed in on him. He left windows and doors open to ensure he had an escape route. His mind churned with schemes to avoid his fate, but for every convoluted plan he conjured up, reality revealed it as just another grandiose, fairytale plot. He finally admitted that he had only one course of action to save himself: become an informer and snitch off Sean and Hollywood.

~~~~

Lieutenant Hal Allen and Sergeant Rocky Rollins arrived early. They parked their unmarked car in the far upper parking lot of the Oakland City Zoo and waited for Aaron Cook's arrival.

"You think he wants to work out a deal?" Rocky asked.

"Yeah, probably." Hal replied. "Shit, one look at him and tweaker is the first word that comes to mind. Must be hittin' the pipe pretty hard to look as bad as he does. Too bad he's such an integral part of our investigation. If he wasn't, I'd get a urine test from him and suspend him immediately."

Aaron drove up and stopped next to their vehicle.

"What's up, Aaron?" Rocky asked.

Aaron shrugged in a manner that attempted to convey a casual response, but his face gave him away. Even from his position in the passenger seat, LT Allen saw Aaron's severely dilated pupils, and though the morning remained quite cool, a visible layer of sweat bathed his forehead. Aaron's cracked, burned lips, with dried white mucus lodged in the corners of his mouth, made LT Allen turn away in disgust.

Aaron saw the look in their eyes and dropped all pretenses of sobriety.

"Ah, Rocky, LT, I'm in a bad way here." He paused to assess their response, but they said nothing and waited for him to continue. "Look, I wanted to talk to you about something that's happened. Something I'm not proud of but something I want to own up to and make right."

Lieutenant Allen leaned toward the window. "Aaron, we're listening but we don't have all day. So, stop the bullshit and get to the point."

Aaron dropped his eyes. "Me. . .me and Sean been working a deal with Hollywood Hawkins."

Aaron stopped and thought that this jaw-dropping confession would elicit a shocked response from Rocky and the lieutenant, but when he saw to his dismay their calm reaction, he knew that they knew of his and Sean's traitorous association with Hollywood for quite some time. Instead of having the upper hand in further negotiations to reduce criminal charges brought against him, he now faced having to accept their terms carte blanche.

"OK, Aaron," Lieutenant Allen said matter-of-factly. "What

can you give us that we don't already know?"

Aaron stared at them dully with crushed resignation, and he unraveled the story with no thought of holding anything back as a bargaining chip to wheedle any leniency. When he finished, he solved all the mysteries surrounding OPD's search warrant failures on Hollywood Hawkins.

"All right," LT Allen said. "We'll call you a taxi for your ride home, so you don't DUI and total that City of Oakland vehicle. You're off for the rest of the day. We're not promising you anything, but if you cooperate, I think we'll be able to reduce the eventual charges filed against you. And one more thing. Lay off that fucking pipe!"

~~~~

"I need to talk to you, LT," Aaron said over the phone.

"Important?" Lieutenant Allen answered.

"Big time important."

"All right, we'll meet you at the zoo in half an hour."

When Rocky and Lieutenant Allen arrived, Aaron waited for them. Over the past two weeks Aaron cleaned up dramatically, and it showed in the way he carried himself.

"Hollywood just got a big shipment of coke in last night," Aaron said.

"How *big* is big?" Rocky asked.

"Informant says 200 kilos or more."

Rocky whistled. "That's big. The informant reliable?"

"Yeah, you know him," Aaron replied. "Leroy Chilton. I've used him a few times. No problem."

"How's Leroy know about all this?" Lieutenant Allen asked.

"Leroy says he was there when they unloaded the dope from a van in Hollywood's garage, and one of the duffel bags snapped open and a few kilos fell out on the floor. He figured from the number of duffel bags they unloaded there must have been over 200 kilos."

Rocky frowned. "So, why's Leroy doin' us this *good deed* by snitching Hollywood off to us?"

"Leroy says Hollywood fucked him over for some big money not too long ago, so he's got a hard on for him now."

Rocky nodded. "Any way of getting corroboration on the

coke?"

Aaron shrugged. "Just Leroy. But I've used him three times and each time resulted in a conviction."

The LT shook his head. "The scenario is kinda iffy, but we might have enough for a search warrant."

"One more thing," Aaron added.

Lieutenant Allen raised his eyebrows. "What?"

Aaron cracked a vengeful smile. "Leroy says Sean Morris was there front row center, when the dope fell out of the duffle bag."

Shocked looks crossed Lieutenant Allen and Rocky's faces that questioned why Sean would expose his connection to Hollywood and become an active member of a narcotic trafficking organization, rather than remain a clandestine, behind the scenes informer.

Aaron explained Sean's changing role. "Leroy says Hollywood is bringing Sean into the operational part of business. Sean convinced Hollywood that because he's a police officer, he can mule dope with considerably less chance of attracting attention. Of course, Sean wants a *lot* more money for his efforts."

"Well," LT Allen said. "We've just been handed the key to unlock the treasure chest that holds criminal indictments for Hollywood Hawkins and Sean Morris. The investigation's timetable just advanced significantly."

~~~~

Late that afternoon Lieutenant Allen had the search warrant in hand, and he coordinated plans to serve the warrant the next day. Finally, Lieutenant Allen informed the rest of the narcotics squad about the ongoing Morris/Cook investigation.

"Those *pinche cabrones!*" Jose Lima said.

Harold Osgood shook his head in dismay. "All this time those two were just playing us along. . ."

Bill McGuire didn't say a word, but he clenched his teeth so tight that his jaw muscles knotted up on both sides of his face.

"We'll take Sean into custody tomorrow morning," Lieutenant Allen said. "We're holding Aaron in protective custody until the warrants are served."

~~~~

Sean arrived at work the next morning in a dark mood. The day before, the LT informed him that Aaron called in sick, and his attempts to locate him proved futile. He first thought Aaron tweaked out somewhere but with every failed attempt to contact him, Sean's concern grew until he seethed with anger and vowed to take the *appropriate* action once he found him. Then another troubling thought occurred to him. He recalled Aaron's constant harping that OPD would inevitably discover their association with Hollywood. What if Aaron rolled over and cooperated with the task force and turned on him and Hollywood? Now, a new sense of urgency drove him to find Aaron and deal with him as soon as possible.

Sean's mind remained a tinderbox of anxiety, when he stopped off at the cafeteria for a cup of coffee before heading to the office. Tex-Mex and Jose Lima stood in line ahead of him, laughing at a shared joke. When Jose glanced back and saw Sean, he nudged Tex-Mex and whispered something that caused the Texan to turn and give Sean a sneering look. Jose duplicated the look.

Tex-Mex nodded at Sean. "What's up, bro?"

Sean tossed the two of them a head nod and grin, but their slightly arrogant greeting put him on edge. He continued to watch them for further suspicious cues, but then just as suddenly the distrustful feeling left him and he laughed at himself for his growing paranoia. Hell, he was getting as bad as Aaron!

When Sean entered the office and settled in at his desk, the other narcotics officers plowed through paperwork to start another long day. He reviewed the surveillance project left over from the day before, but he didn't really concentrate on the project. He still focused his attention on Aaron and what he would do when Aaron finally surfaced. He planned his response to whatever bullshit reason Aaron gave for his disappearance, when he had a vague notion that something changed in the office. The sounds of rustling paper, desk drawers opening and closing, and voices ceased. Utter silence prevailed. It took a second or two for this change to register, but then he raised his head and saw that the other five narcotics officers surrounded him on all sides. Sean knew it was over at once. He did not say a word.

He avoided their faces and stared straight ahead. Firm hands gripped his arms and he felt one of the narcotics officers remove his pistol from its holster. Then they lifted him to his feet, twisted his hands behind his back, and handcuffs clicked into place. Lieutenant Allen stepped forward and waved an arrest warrant in front of Sean's face.

"You're under arrest, Sean, for obstruction of justice and other charges. You have the right to remain silent. . ."

While the lieutenant droned on, Sean stared down at his desk. When Lieutenant Allen finished and asked him the obligatory question if he understood his rights, Sean perfunctorily nodded and at last raised his eyes and scanned the other narcotic officers' faces. Tex-Mex and Jose brandished bitter, contemptuous smiles, replicas of their smiles Sean saw in the cafeteria. Harold Osgood's look reflected his trauma for trusting someone only to have that person violate that trust and turn traitor. Rocky's face flushed crimson with hatred for a man who disgraced and dishonored his fellow squad members. Sean felt Bill McGuire's intense expression of loathing as a palpable, physical sensation. Lieutenant Allen's sad, weary look showed immense relief that such an embarrassing episode in OPD's history finally ended. Sean dropped his eyes under their withering stares. As they led him away for further interrogation, Sean at last spoke the only words he would utter until his preliminary court hearing.

"Where's Aaron?" Sean asked.

Lieutenant Allen faced him. "What's your interest in Aaron?" When Sean merely shrugged, the LT continued with a slight smile. "I told you yesterday, Sean. Aaron called in sick."

~~~~

Immediately after Sean's arrest, the narcotics office swirled with activity. The Feds, DEA, and officers from other agencies involved with the task force congregated there and in OPD's transportation yard to organize serving the search warrant on Hollywood Hawkins. Dressed in civilian clothes, with a marked penchant for biker or drug culture styles, the task force group looked more like a mob of deviant misfits than an elite law enforcement contingent about to bring down a major drug trafficker. Because of this potential for recognition problems, narcs always included uniformed officers to accompany them on their raids to prevent the bad guys from thinking that a rival drug cartel was about to rip them off, and to assure average citizens that a horde of Huns were not sacking and pillaging their neighborhood. And based on Officer Bull Brewster's prior *cordial* encounters with Mr. Hollywood Hawkins Esquire, the LT chose him to lead the assault on Hollywood's mansion. Becky accompanied him as his cover officer for a reenactment of the Carney Park showdown.

The long line of marked and unmarked police vehicles left OPD and snaked through city streets into the Oakland hills. Within minutes they surrounded Hollywood's mansion. Then Bull and Tex-Mex used a heavy, steel, handheld ramming device, nicknamed the "key," to smash in the front perimeter gate, and the task force swarmed onto the grounds like a medieval army laying siege to a castle. While most of the officers covered the mansion's rear and sides, Bull and Becky joined Lieutenant Allen and others at the front door. The LT made the announcement required by law that they had a search warrant and commanded that the door be opened. When the door failed to open, Bull and Tex-Mex again used the key to smash open the door and the task force rushed inside.

Hollywood and a few of his henchmen approached the front door, when it gave way with a booming crash. Hollywood's face reflected shock and confusion. While Bull, Becky, and other officers handcuffed and guarded Hollywood and his lackeys, the remainder of the task force fanned out to conduct the search. Hollywood wore a red sequined smoking jacket with matching pajamas, and his ensemble caused Bull to have an inspired vision of his photograph gracing the front page of tomorrow's newspaper dressed in his foppish finery. He decided to phone Harry Radcliff, the *Oakland Tribune* police beat reporter, and have him present with a camera when they transported Hollywood to jail. A smoking jacket? In jail? The other inmates would laugh themselves silly, and Bull knew that laughter was the most devastating punishment a man like Hollywood Hawkins would ever endure.

Less than thirty minutes later, the task force officers piled four duffle bags containing 225 kilos of high grade cocaine on the floor in front of the drug kingpin. Each time they dumped another duffle bag on the floor, Bull and Becky took great pleasure writing down on pieces of paper the increasing number of years Hollywood would be sentenced to prison and showing them to him. The first duffle bag rated ten years, and Bull held the paper over his head like a judge at a gymnastics meet. Hollywood tried to ignore Bull's antics, but eventually he exploded in anger just as he had at Carney Park.

"Fuck you, Brewster! And fuck that little cunt cop next to you!"

Hollywood's tirade brought Lieutenant Allen into the room to see what the hell was going on. Becky turned around in circles holding the last card with forty years printed on it, and the other task force members applauded and whistled enthusiastically. Then Becky changed tactics and assumed the role of a maid in old Victorian England. Taking her cue from Hollywood's outlandish casual attire, she curtsied in front of him and asked in a perfect parody of a British accent.

"Will your Lordship have a spot of tea before your dreadful incarceration in the Oakland City Jail?"

The LT joined the other task force members as they roared their approval, while Hollywood scowled in response. But then the LT motioned Becky and Bull over to him.

"All right, you two have had your fun," the LT said. "Now, let's try to remember that we're law enforcement professionals, not comedians. OK?"

"All right, LT," Bull replied. "We were just fuckin' with him a little."

Bull's smile broadened as the amount of evidence piled up on the floor. Numerous firearms, some altered to fire full automatic and others reported stolen, added further criminal charges to Hollywood's growing list. The task force found more than a half million dollars in cash in several bags and stacked them next to the dope.

When the time came to transport Hollywood and the other suspects to jail, Bull's phone call to Harry Radcliff at the *Tribune* paid big dividends. Harry snapped some great Kodak moments of officers loading Hollywood into the wagon in his silk outfit, and the caption under the paper's front page photograph the next day caused readers all over the Bay Area to share a laugh at Hollywood's expense: "Alleged Drug Czar's Avant-garde Fashion

Statement To Replace Traditional Inmate Overalls?" And as the wagon and task force caravan made their way down the long driveway out to the street, numerous nearby residents weary of Hollywood's long-standing criminal enterprise stood in front of their homes and applauded as the victorious police conquerors passed in review. It was a time of great joy, and Becky and Bull celebrated by flashing absolutely huge grins that grew exponentially with every mile they drew closer to the OPD Hilton.

27

The White brothers' and Hollywood Hawkins' demise and the two OPD Benedict Arnolds' infamous fall from grace had little impact on OPD's daily routine. Burglaries occurred, husbands and wives fought, drivers crashed their vehicles, kids ran away from home, and officers responded to these and a myriad other crises. They handled one call, moved on to another, and then repeated the cycle. Police work resembled an assembly line of human problems. The calls for services never stopped. It went on 24/7, never took a day off, and seemed to have a built-in momentum all its own.

Bull Brewster linked his life to this law enforcement conveyor belt. He literally lived for police work. To don a blue uniform, pin on a badge, strap on a gun, and hit the streets in a black and white was the high point of his day. He almost never called in sick. He spent his off-duty time hanging out at the Hit 'N Run bullshitting about police work over a drink or ten. He played softball and went fishing with other cops. In essence, he belonged to an exclusive club and wearing a badge was the only requirement to join. Some people had hobbies. Others belonged to churches. Bull worshipped police work.

Then Bull's priorities changed. Becky entered his world and

a transformation occurred. Instead of his nightly rendezvous with Tex-Mex or some other free spirit at the Hit 'N Run or some other local watering hole, he coupled up with her and spent time doing "domestic stuff" he never would have considered before. Simple dinners at her condo, taking her Jack Russell Terrier, Scampy, for rambling walks in the park, or just spending a quiet night watching TV became favorite pastimes. Bull's addiction to police work started to wane.

~~~~

A sunny Sunday morning dawned in mid-October, and Eve caught up with Becky and Bull as they checked out their vehicles in transportation in preparation to hit the street.

"We still on for tonight?" Eve asked. "Tex-Mex is picking up the chicken, ribs, and links, and he'll have the barbeque fired up and ready to go by the time we get off work."

"Just tell the Texan to make certain those brewskis are ice-cold," Bull said.

"And make the barbeque sauce tangy and hot," Becky added.

"Done deal," Eve said.

"2L31?" the dispatcher called. "There's a DOA on your beat."

Bull gave Becky and Eve a sour look. "Hope it's not a stinker."

"Cook up some coffee grounds," Becky advised. "Lots of coffee grounds!"

~~~~

High in the North Oakland hills the eucalyptus trees waved briskly in a stiff breeze. The temperature hovered in the low eighties, and except for the wind, the air had a balmy feel that made it a perfect Indian summer day. But the air remained dry. Very little rain fell for months, and posted warnings placed the fire hazard critically high. Just the day before OFD personnel responded to fight a wild fire that erupted near the hills' apex. OFD personnel declared the fire officially extinguished and the firefighters left the scene. But as Sunday's winds continued to increase, the barely perceptible smoldering remnants ignited again, and the fire was reborn.

~~~~

Bull finally cleared the DOA a little after 10:00 A.M. A red light violator caught his attention and he conducted a traffic stop to issue a citation. A computer check revealed the driver had a felony warrant for his arrest. Since there was no wagon available, Bull drove the warrant suspect to the jail himself. Bull didn't mind the prisoner transport. The trip in gave him an opportunity to bullshit with the desk officer, Jim Spencer. A crusty old-timer who had more years on OPD than anyone else on the department, Jim shared an avid interest for trout fishing with Bull. Over the years, they journeyed to the mountains many times in search of lunker Rainbows lurking in remote streams and lakes. After booking the prisoner, Bull found Jim on the phone dealing with an irate citizen.

"Sir," Jim said, "you're talking to the desk officer at the Oakland Police Department. I don't have anything to do with the Oakland Fire Department. I'm a police officer, not a firefighter."

Bull sat down in a nearby swivel chair and rocked back and forth as he listened to the salty desk officer try to mollify a taxpayer who did not want to be mollified. Bull watched Jim's face redden in anger as he exhausted his verbal communication skills and began expressing himself more and more vehemently. Thinking that he would help Jim calm down, Bull made a series of contorted facial expressions to brighten Jim's increasingly hostile attitude. He placed his thumb on his nose and wagged his fingers in the classic "kiss my ass" hand signal. He stuck two pencils in his nostrils and rolled his eyes back to imitate a dead walrus. And he placed his middle finger in his mouth to simulate oral copulation and moaned in ecstasy. Jim shook his head and smiled at Bull's antics and then turned away to keep from laughing and upsetting the enraged citizen even more. But instead of relenting, Bull opened a desk drawer and bombarded Jim with paper clips, forcing the harried desk officer to hold up his free arm to block the steady barrage of office artillery raining down on his head. Bull also made whistling sounds like bombs falling and then explosive sounds when his missiles hit their target. Jim finally hung up the phone and turned on his tormentor with a savage smile.

"You fucking asshole, Brewster!"

"Now, now, Jimmy boy," Bull replied and wagged his finger at him. "Just remember some of the shit you've done to me. So, what was that all about?"

"Ah, some guy's pissed off because the fire OFD supposedly put out yesterday started up again today. I told him to file a complaint with the fire department, but he claimed they wouldn't talk to him, so he wants the police to do something about it. Nobody's ever satisfied."

The phone rang again. "Oakland Police, Officer Spencer speaking."

Bull let Jim alone this time. While the phone conversation droned on, Bull looked at his watch and thought about getting Becky on the tactical channel to ask her when she wanted to have lunch. Then he let his imagination run wild and considered phoning Tex-Mex at home and pose as a salesman for some new sex product. He knew the Texan experimented with anything that allegedly increased his virility and stamina, and he could probably fool him for a minute or two. He was about to reach for the phone, when Jim finished this second call and turned to him with a perplexed look.

"That was Captain Ernie. He wants all units on special assignment at Jack London Square to report to the north end immediately. He says the hill fire is really gaining strength and we're gonna need all available units. Must be some fire."

The phone rang again. Bull sensed that he wouldn't be talking trout fishing with Jim anytime soon, so he lobbed one last paper clip at the desk officer and left for the ride back to the district. The fire piqued Bull's curiosity. Instead of taking the short route back to his beat, he elected to go the long way, which gave him a full view of the hills where the fire raged. He was on the 980 connector to Hwy 580, when the huge plume of black smoke loomed into view.

The cloud's sheer size startled him. It covered an enormous area that stretched from the Berkeley border to well beyond Highway 24. Sirens sounded everywhere and Bull switched radio channels to the west and north end's Frequency Two to listen in on what was going on with the fire. A sense of rampant urgency charged the radio transmissions. The dispatcher frantically queried units to respond to rescue people trapped by the fire on Charing Cross Road just north of Highway 24, but all units told the dispatcher they were Code 6, or some distance away. Even though the fire occurred in District Two and well out of his jurisdiction, Bull abandoned his return to District Five, activated his lights and siren, and shot upwards toward the location where the people were last reported.

"2L31," Bull broadcast. "I'm on 24 now and responding."

"2L31 is close and responding," the dispatcher repeated. "Units to assist?"

A flurry of radio traffic erupted as other units volunteered. Bull took an off-ramp and wove his way through a maze of streets obscured by a pall of thick smoke. It was like trying to negotiate his way through a black fog bank. It had been years since he last worked the north end, and he tried to jog his memory to take the most time-saving route. The winding streets combined with the smoke disoriented him. His response slowed to a near crawl, and he struggled to stay on the road to keep from plunging down the steep hillsides.

A gust of wind cleared the smoke for a few seconds and gave him a chance to get his bearings. A glance at a street sign confirmed he was on Charing Cross Road. Then the dense black curtain closed in again. Bull inched along, running over unseen objects in the street and hoping he would not encounter anything that blocked his path. Up ahead, he concentrated on a patch of blue sky that opened wider until he burst through the smoke into the clear. He assessed the situation and realized his precarious position. Towering sheets of flame surrounded him to his front and both sides. Houses exploded into mushrooming balls of fire as the blazing wall of fire swept over them. Heat from the galloping inferno increased dramatically.

Then he saw them. A knot of people shuffling down the road toward him. A man held two small children in his arms and a woman cradled an infant. They turned partially sideways to shield the children from blasts of oven-like wind. Bull reached them in seconds. He stopped his car, threw open the doors, and ushered them inside. The two older children were hysterical, the infant wailed, and the parents wheezed and gasped for breath. Bull started driving in the direction the family came from, but the man grabbed his arm to attract his attention.

"No, no!" the man shouted over the firestorm's roar. "Tree down! Road blocked! Turn around!"

Bull glanced in his mirror. The coal black smoke boiled in violent swirls to their rear. He turned around and they reentered the darkness. Smoke seeped into the car even though he had the windows tightly closed. Bull's eyes watered and he continually blinked and rubbed them to clear his vision. Again he crept along, guiding his vehicle through the blackness, hoping that the road would remain clear. He recalled the bus fire and how he almost gave up hope that he would get those children and himself out of that blazing furnace. But he succeeded then against overwhelming odds, and now he would get this family out of this conflagration too.

The decreased visibility made their descent agonizingly slow. A few yards forward. Back up to avoid an obstacle. Drive over another. Now the firestorm's roar became so fierce that it sounded like an enraged beast, and the red and orange glow closed in on all sides. The heat made it difficult to breathe. They gasped and strangled on super-heated air. Bull crawled forward until his vehicle ground to a halt. The inky blackness cleared slightly, and Bull saw that a large fallen tree blocked the road. Bull gunned the engine to push the tree out of the way, but the car's tires spun on the asphalt. Then he tried backing up and ramming the tree, but it would not budge. The red and orange glow turned to a solid sheet of scarlet that advanced in leaps and bounds. They had no alternative now and Bull stopped and flung the doors open for the family to get out. He took one of the children and shouted to make himself heard over the thunderous roar.

"Climb over the tree and stay on the road!"

He waited while the man and woman scrambled forward and then he followed. Smoke filled his lungs. Heat seared his throat. He stumbled blindly. The eight year old girl he carried stopped crying and went limp in his arms. But he kept moving forward. He had no idea what happened to the man, woman, and the other two children. There was no way to know without stopping and groping around in the dark. But Bull knew that if he stopped for even a few moments it would mean certain death. He could not help the rest of the family. He would only be able to save this little girl. He kept moving.

He felt for the pavement under his boots. One careless step might cause him to veer off the road and they would plunge down the steep hillside. But his caution slowed him down. He floundered now. His legs buckled. He shifted the child over his shoulder and staggered on. Then he felt the first hint of losing consciousness. A light-headed sensation that laid siege to his senses. A profound feeling of fatigue that he could not shake. He fought it off and kept his legs churning. One step. Then another. All those years of pumping iron in the gym came back to him. Leg squats that made his legs as strong as tree trunks. A few more steps. And a few more after those. One foot in front of the other. He reached deep within himself to gut it out.

But then there were no steps left. No more reserves of strength to draw from. He was drowning. Drowning in a thick, viscous mist of scalding smoke. His legs gave out and he dropped to one knee. His chest heaved, he rose, and managed another few steps. Then he crumpled to both knees and instinctively knew it was over. And once again he became obsessed with time. Not enough time. Time finally ran out. His life's grains of used up time vanished into eternity. The fire's roar sounded like a freight train bearing down on them. At least the child remained unconscious, he thought, as the wall of heat engulfed them and he wrapped his massive arms around her to shield her from the end.

Over the next few hours, the radio dispatcher repeated the call over and over.

"2L31, come in."

Again. "2l31, Officer Brewster, please acknowledge."

And again. "Officer Bull Brewster, 2L31, please answer."

Countless times. "2L31."

And then the dispatcher stopped calling.

Tex-Mex joined the thousands who attended the funeral. Law enforcement agencies from all over the state sent their delegations of mourners. Even Las Vegas PD provided a sizeable contingent led by Sergeant Heston and a good portion of the Lucky Seven Bar & Grill crowd. Tex-Mex participated in numerous police funerals over the years, and they were virtually all the same.

Bagpipes played. Speakers eulogized. A line of police vehicles, all with their emergency lights activated, stretched for miles on the roadway leading to the church. These huge turnouts demonstrated the bond of solidarity that existed in the law enforcement community. They were times for tallying up the survivors and instilling in them a firm resolve to close ranks and soldier on. Most important, police funerals illustrated the sacrifices officers made in the line of duty. And Bull made the ultimate sacrifice.

~~~~

After the funeral services, badges from numerous PD's gathered at the Hit 'N Run, the secular shrine where Bull served as such a faithful apostle. It was a traditional Irish wake that focused on informal eulogies shared by those who knew him best. They roamed from table to table, shaking hands and dispensing hugs. They dredged up old stories from the past and retold them with animated gusto. They debated the veracity of these long dormant quasi-mythical accounts of Bull's extraordinary feats, and since the statute of limitations no longer applied, they exhumed and brazenly extolled the many tales of departmental intrigue and minor malfeasance.

One salty veteran held court at a nearby table. "Did you hear about the time Bull responded to a burglary in progress and found citizens holding a suspect in custody? It seemed that the owner of the store he broke into opened fire with his trusty twelve gauge, and the burglar jumped through a plate glass window to escape. So, there he was, lying on the sidewalk shot full of holes and cut to ribbons from the glass, when Bull rolled up on the scene. A large crowd formed and Bull had his usual flair for the dramatic working. In an inspired moment, Bull pointed at the suspect and shouted out in his best oratorical voice for the entire crowd to hear, 'You see! Crime does not pay!' He had the crowd in stitches over that one."

The table roared its approval. Then another raconteur took the stage.

"Remember Captain Deerbon? The day he retired Day Watch held a ceremonial inspection, and the captain went down the inspection line, shaking hands and wishing everyone farewell. It was a formal event. The captain dressed up in his tunic and tie.

The tech took photos. The whole nine yards. When the captain reached Bull, he saw that instead of having his long baton in his O-ring, he had this enormous dildo. Captain Deerbon pulled out the dildo and was about to make some comment, when Bull took a replica .40 caliber water pistol from his holster and started squirting water on the captain's shoes. Now, the captain tried to be a good sport and just smiled, shook his head, and went on the next man in line. But Bull wasn't through yet. He took a battery operated toy police car, put it on the floor, and the toy car wove in and out among officers' shoes, its little red light blinking and its tinny siren wailing. Captain Deerbon had enough, and he threw up his hands in disgust and went back into the line-up room!"

The Bull Brewster stories piled up one on top of another. There was no end to them. Outrageous. Cutting edge. But the storytellers recounted them with an affectionate tone that left no doubt that his peers held him in high esteem and regarded him as one of a kind who would never be replaced. A doleful feeling of melancholy also permeated this celebration of his life, but it was a fitting sendoff that Bull would have heartily endorsed without reservation.

The usual suspects were present and accounted for. Bull's inner circle of confidants occupied a table in the center of the bar. Duke, his wife Brenda, Mary, Rocky, Becky, Eve, Tex-Mex, Captain Ernie, and Chief Carter anchored this quorum firmly in place. At first, this elite cadre felt somewhat intimidated by the Chief's presence, but as the afternoon wore on, they grew ever more astonished at some of the shady derelictions of duty the Chief 'fessed up to from his days of sowing wild capers as a young officer. And more than a few of these instances of conduct unbecoming an officer he committed in consort with a certain Officer Bull Brewster. The stories continued and the Chief roared with delight at the Pinto Bean Caper and the Days Inn Battle of The Ex's.

But *the* tall tale of the evening needed no verification, for visual evidence existed to convince even the most jaded skeptic of the tale's authenticity. When Tex-Mex, Eve, and Becky trotted out a citizen's video tape of the Great Las Vegas Corvette Chase and Bull's momentous tackle of the purse-snatcher caught by the casino's security camera, the entire bar shook from floor to ceiling with tremors of laughter as they watched Bull and his side-kicks in action. Bull's ferocious tackle brought the assemblage to a standing ovation. They showed it over and over again, and still the audience could not get enough. But when Eve announced that they were only going to replay the video one more time, the gales of laughter slowly subsided and then faded away alto-gether. As the video rolled a last time through Bull's scenes, there was not a dry eye in the bar. Even the saltiest veterans used the backs of their hands or napkins to wipe the moisture away.

Gradually, the Hit 'N Run emptied until only a few strag-glers remained. And with each person who left, the bar became a little quieter. A little more subdued. Soon Captain Ernie and Chief Carter took their leave and only Bull's diehard posse stood their ground and refused to retreat. It was their duty to preserve his memory. Duke looked from person to person and groped for something to say. Something meaningful and not a mere plati-tude. But what else was there to say? He and Bull went through so much together. During the war, they lived from one moment to the next not knowing if it would be their last. They cheated the Grim Reaper. For a while. But the Reaper finally caught up with one half of his quarry on an Oakland hillside. Duke still had difficulty trying to cope with survivor's guilt. Maybe if he had been with Bull in that firestorm, then they would have somehow made it out of there together just as they did in The 'Nam. Maybe. But words? How do you convey with mere words the sum of a man's life to those who grieve for him. Words proved so in-adequate.

Duke glanced over at Becky and saw the tears form in the corners of her eyes. He reached over and gently pulled her to him, and she laid her head on his shoulder. Brenda reached around Duke's shoulder and stroked Becky's hair. No one spoke and they stayed that way until the bartender flicked the lights on and off to signal the bar's closing. Then they filed out into the night.

The seven of them stood there unwilling to take the next step, wanting the moment to linger. Tex-Mex looked up and fo-cused his attention on a street light directly above them. The street light evoked memories of times past, when he and Bull closed down many a watering hole and felt impelled to aggressively mark their territory by laying waste to the city's property. A mischievous, leering grin formed beneath his Pancho Villa mustache. Mary followed his line of sight, saw the grin, and immediately knew what it meant.

"Tex-Mex," she said. "Don't do it."

The others looked back and forth from Mary to the Texan and back again. Then they tilted their heads skyward and fixated on the target. The single gunshot echoed through the industrial neighborhood, the street light blinked out, and bits of glass tinkled when they hit the pavement.

"That was the last one, Bull," Tex-Mex vowed. "It was for you. The last one was for you."

EPILOGUE

EARLY DECEMBER, 1994

The horse's hooves made a rhythmic clacking sound as they struck the pavement. With its head down and straining at its load, the horse exhaled puffs of steam from its nostrils and wispy clouds of vapor floated off its hide in the chilly winter morning air. Hitched to the horse was a wagon and inside the wagon lay an ornate coffin adorned with garlands of flowers heaped together in a haphazard mound. Holding the horse's reins on the wagon's lone seat, a man dressed in an antique tuxedo and top hat guided the hearse along its path to the coffin's final resting place. He joined the horse, wagon and coffin in a bizarre tribute to the corpse soon to be buried.

A line of limousines and luxury vehicles, stretching two blocks long, followed the horse-drawn hearse. Roll Royces, Mercedes Benzs, BMWs, and Jaguars formed the caravan. The *mourners* flouted funeral tradition, and their taste in clothing mirrored their choice of vehicles. Ostentatious attire replaced traditional black funeral apparel. Women in gaudy colored dresses and pants suits and men in flamboyant white tuxedos served as the fashion statements of the day. The funeral procession rocked with laughter and a festive atmosphere, and in the limo's rear seats passengers sipped from flutes of champagne, as the motorcade followed the horse-drawn hearse through the streets of Oakland.

People on the street stopped and gawked as the strange cortege passed by. Bystanders stood two and three deep straining to get a better view. They questioned one another concerning the identity of the deceased. A politician, perhaps. Or a famous sports figure. Maybe, an entertainer. But certainly a celebrity of some renown. Then rumors spread among the ranks of onlookers that the deceased once ruled Oakland's lucrative narcotics trade as the city's most powerful drug lord. Their reactions varied. Some showed outright disgust that a common criminal would receive such an extravagant, lavish funeral. Others felt unabashed admiration for the funeral organizer's extolment of the thug life that the deceased represented.

The funeral's organizers felt no such ambivalence. They meant to make the drug czar's funeral one that the city would never forget, and they intended to thumb their noses at the criminal justice system which convicted and incarcerated him. By arranging the exorbitant funeral, they flaunted their wealth and demonstrated that the narcotics trade would continue to flourish, and a long line of ruthless gangsters eagerly awaited the opportunity to assume the reins of power.

Their dead czar was Hollywood Hawkins. Only a few months after a jury found him guilty and sentenced him to life in prison, a fellow inmate murdered him in an argument over a minor debt he failed to repay. What Hollywood would have once considered "chump change" became the catalyst that cost him his life.

Tex-Mex Garcia and Rocky Rollins sat in an unmarked car watching the procession file slowly past. They were assigned along with other OPD units to monitor the funeral to insure no violence erupted during the long route to the cemetery. In addition to the trail of luxury cars following the hearse, an informal retinue of wannabe gangsters joined the procession bringing up the rear, and with every mile the number of these vehicles increased significantly.

"Requiem for a dope dealer," Tex-Mex mused.

Rocky shot the Texan a surprised look. "Didn't know you were so cerebral, Tex-Mex."

Tex-Mex grinned. "I have my moments." He paused and gazed at the traffic that extended for blocks down E. 14th Street. "Look at all those assholes following the main procession. I'll bet each one of them dreams of becoming the next Hollywood Hawkins. One head honcho dies and a hundred more are waiting in the wings to take his place. And it'll never stop."

"It means job security for us, Tex-Mex," Rocky said. "All we gotta do is stay on the OPD treadmill long enough to retire and then move to some island paradise and forget that this shit ever happened. Right, bro?"

Tex-Mex laid his head back on the headrest. "I guess. But it's like we're jousting with windmills, like Don Quixote and his sidekick Sancho Panza."

Rocky's look went from surprised to incredulous. "All these years and I thought you were illiterate. What's next? You gonna start quoting Willie Shakespeare?"

Tex-Mex grinned again but didn't answer. He studied the horse's slow, deliberate gait and concentrated on the rhythmic cadence of its hooves. As the seconds passed, the sound grew more faint and then faded away completely. What remained were the incessant police calls emanating from their radio. Calls that never stopped. Several distant gunshots broke the morning stillness, and a minute or two later he listened in and caught the change in inflection of the dispatcher's voice as she put out a hot assignment.

"Any unit for a 245 shooting in the 7000 block of Favor?"

Units answered up for the assignment and Tex-Mex shook his head and stared out the window in the direction where the shooting occurred, only a few blocks away from their location. Another pending homicide. Another future funeral. Another statistic for the count and the amount. And another day closer to retirement. Tex-Mex never thought he'd see the day when he would look forward to pulling the pin, but with Bull gone, police work lost a lot of its allure and retirement no longer seemed like the end of the world as it once did. He recalled his and Bull's many zany escapades and smiled ruefully. For every one of their capers that broke one of OPD's sacred rules and regulations, there followed the disciplinary suspensions that the department levied against them. They did their crimes and they did their times. But Tex-Mex never thought of them as suspensions. Instead, he regarded them as their many sunny sojourns spent on faraway sandy shores, quaffing ice-cold brews and treasuring their leisurely days on the beach.